One Italian Summer

A Novel

Rebecca Serle

ATRIA PAPERBACK

New York Amsterdam/Antwerp London
Toronto Sydney/Melbourne New Delhi

ATRIA
PAPERBACK

An Imprint of Simon & Schuster, LLC
1230 Avenue of the Americas
New York, NY 10020

This Atria Paperback edition October 2025

ATRIA PAPERBACK and colophon are trademarks of Simon & Schuster, LLC

Interior design by Yvonne Taylor

Manufactured in China

1 3 5 7 9 10 8 6 4 2

Library of Congress Control Number: 2021035522

ISBN 978-1-6682-0377-4

Also by Rebecca Serle

Expiration Dates

In Five Years

The Dinner List

Young Adult

Truly Madly Famously

Famous in Love

The Edge of Falling

When You Were Mine

Praise for

One Italian Summer

"An unconventional love story that embraces people's flaws and selfishness as part of what makes them human."

—*Kirkus Reviews*

"Poignant and ultimately uplifting. The mouthwatering descriptions of Katy's food and the lush Italian coast bring a strong, atmospheric sense of place. Recommend to fans of Helen Fisher's *Faye, Faraway* and those who enjoy being transported to other countries through fiction."

—*Booklist*

"Going down as easy as a limoncello on a hot summer's day, this daydream of a story affirms what it means to love and be loved. An enchanting book for the last cold days of winter, but also suggest it to readers come summer."

—*Library Journal*

"A touching story . . . The mother-daughter bond is made palpable through Katy's grief and desire for connection."

—*Publishers Weekly*

"Rebecca Serle is known for her powerful stories that tug at the heartstrings—and her latest is just as unforgettable."

—*Woman's World*

"In these cynical times full of snark and memes, it's nice to surrender to magic every now and then. Plus, the wanderlust that the book conjures is worth it as is . . . A story about love, loss, and that point in adulthood where we learn our parents are human, too, and not always perfect."

—Associated Press

"[A] moving novel."

—*PopSugar*

For my mother,
the queen of my heart.
Long may she reign.

I just feel like I need more time . . . I really just feel ambushed, you know? I mean, I thought I had so much more . . . time. I thought I had all summer to impart my wisdom about work and life and your future, and I just feel like I had something to tell you. Oh! On the bus, make sure you choose a good seat, you know, because people are creatures of habit, and the seat you pick in the beginning could be your seat for the rest of the year, you know?

Get a window seat, honey, 'cause there's so much to see.

—LORELAI GILMORE

Chapter One

I've never smoked, but it's the last day of my mother's shiva, so here we are. I have the cigarette between my teeth, standing on the back patio, looking at what was, just two months ago, a pristine white sectional, now weatherworn. My mother kept everything clean. She kept everything.

Carol's rules to live by:

- Never throw away a good pair of jeans.
- Always have fresh lemons on hand.
- Bread keeps for a week in the fridge and two months in the freezer.
- OxiClean will take out any stain.
- Be careful of bleach.
- Linen is better than cotton in the summer.
- Plant herbs, not flowers.
- Don't be afraid of paint. A bold color can transform a room.
- Always arrive on time to a restaurant and five minutes late to a house.
- Never smoke.

I should say, I haven't actually lit it.

✦

Carol Almea Silver was a pillar of the community, beloved by everyone she encountered. In the past week, we have opened our doors to sales associates and manicurists, the women from her temple, waiters from Craig's, nurses from Cedars-Sinai. Two bank tellers from the City National branch on Roxbury. "She used to bring us baked goods," they said. "She was always ready with a phone number." There are couples from the Brentwood Country Club. Irene Newton, who had a standing lunch with my mother at Il Pastaio every Thursday. Even the bartender from the Hotel Bel-Air, where Carol used to go for an ice-cold martini. Everyone has a story.

My mother was the first person you called for a recipe (a cup of onions, garlic, don't forget the pinch of sugar) and the last one you called at night when you just couldn't sleep (a cup of hot water with lemon, lavender oil, magnesium pills). She knew the exact ratio of olive oil to garlic in any recipe, and she could whip up dinner from three pantry items, easy. She had all the answers. I, on the other hand, have none of them, and now I no longer have her.

"Hi," I hear Eric say from inside. "Where is everyone?"

Eric is my husband, and he is our last guest here today. He shouldn't be. He should have been with us the entire time, in the hard, low chairs, stuck between noodle casseroles and the ringing phone and the endless lipstick kisses of neighbors and women who call themselves aunties, but instead he is here in the entryway to what is now my father's house, waiting to be received.

I close my eyes. Maybe if I cannot see him, he will stop looking for me. Maybe I will fold into this ostentatious May day, the sun shining like a woman talking loudly on a cell phone at lunch. Who invited you here?

I tuck the cigarette into the pocket of my jeans.

I cannot yet conceive of a world without her, what that will look like, who I am in her absence. I am incapable of understanding that she will not pick me up for lunch on Tuesdays, parking without a permit on the curb by my house and running inside with a bag full of something—groceries, skin-care products, a new sweater she bought at Off 5th. I cannot comprehend that if I call her phone, it will just ring and ring—that there is no longer anyone on the other end who will say, "Katy, honey. Just a second. My hands are wet." I do not imagine ever coming to terms with the loss of her body—her warm, welcoming body. The place I always felt at home. My mother, you see, is the great love of my life. She is the great love of my life, and I have lost her.

"Eric, come on in. You were standing out there?"

I hear my father's voice from inside, welcoming Eric in. Eric, my husband who lives in our house, twelve and a half minutes away, in Culver City. Who has taken a leave of absence from Disney, where he is a film executive, to be with me during this trying time. Whom I've dated since I was twenty-two, eight years ago. Who takes out the garbage and knows how to boil pasta and never leaves the toilet seat up. Whose favorite show is *Modern Family* and who cried during every episode of *Parenthood*. Whom just last night, I told in our kitchen—the kitchen my mother helped me design—that I did not know if I could be married to him anymore.

If your mother is the love of your life, what does that make your husband?

"Hey," Eric says when he sees me. He steps outside, squints.

He half waves. I turn around. On the glass patio table, there is a spread of slowly curling cheese. I am wearing dark jeans and a wool sweater, even though it is warm outside, because inside the house it is freezing. My mother liked to keep a house cold. My father only knows the way it's been.

"Hi," I say.

He holds the door open for me, and I step past him inside.

Despite the temperature, the house is still as welcoming as ever. My mother was an interior designer, well respected for her homey aesthetic. Our house was her showpiece. Oversize furniture, floral prints, and rich-patterned textures. Ralph Lauren meets Laura Ashley meets a very nice pair of Tod's loafers and a crisp white button-down. She loved textiles—wood, linen, the feel of good stitching.

There was always food in the fridge, wine in the side door, and fresh-cut flowers on the table.

Eric and I have been trying to plant an herb garden for the past three years.

I smile at Eric. I try to arrange my mouth in a way I should remember but that feels entirely impossible now. I do not know who I am anymore. I have no idea how to do any of this without her.

"Katy, you're grieving," he said to me last night. "You're in crisis; you can't decide this now. People don't get divorces in the middle of a war. Let's give it some time."

What he did not know is that I had. I had given it months. Ever since my mother got sick, I'd been thinking about the reality of being married to Eric. My decision to leave Eric had less to do with my mother's death and more to do with the remembrance of death in general. Which is to say I began to ask myself if this was the marriage I wanted to die in, if this was the marriage I wanted to see me through this, my mother's illness, and what would, impossibly, remain after.

We didn't have kids yet—we were still kids ourselves, weren't we?

Eric and I met when we were both twenty-two, seniors at UC Santa Barbara. He was an East Coast liberal, intent on going into politics or journalism. I was a Los Angeles native, deeply attached to my parents and the palm trees, and felt that two hours away was the farthest I could possibly go from home.

We had a class together—Cinema 101, a prereq we were both late in taking. He sat next to me on the first day of the spring semester—this tall, goofy kid. He smiled, we started talking, and by the end of class he'd stuck a pen through one of my ringlets. My hair was long and curly then; I hadn't yet started straightening it into submission.

He pulled his pen back, and the curl went with it.

"Bouncy," he said. He was blushing. He hadn't done it because he was confident; he had done it because he didn't know what else to do. And the uncomfortableness of this, the ridiculousness of his, a total stranger's, pen through my hair, made me laugh.

He asked me to get a coffee. We walked to the commons and sat together for two hours. He told me about his family back home in Boston, his younger sister, his mother, who was a college professor at Tufts. I liked the way he saw them, the women in his family. I liked the way he spoke about them—like they mattered.

He didn't kiss me until a week later, but once we started dating, that was it. No breaks, no torrid fights, no long-distance. None of the usual hallmarks of young love. After graduation, he got a job at the *Chronicle* in New York, and

I moved with him. We set up shop in a tiny one-bedroom in Greenpoint, Brooklyn. I worked as a freelance copywriter for anyone who would have me, mostly fashion blogs whose hosts were grateful for help with language. This was 2015, the city had rebounded from financial ruin, and Instagram had just become ubiquitous.

We spent two years in New York before moving back to Los Angeles. We got an apartment in Brentwood, down the street from my parents' house. We got married, we bought a starter home, farther away in Culver City. We built a life that perhaps we were too young to live.

"I was already thirty when I met your father," my mother told me when we first moved back. "You have so much time. Sometimes I wish you'd take it." But I loved Eric—we all did. And I had always felt more comfortable in the presence of adults than young people, had felt since the time I was ten years old that I was one. And I wanted all of the trappings that would signal to others that I was one, too. It felt right to start young. And I couldn't help the timeline. I couldn't help it right up until last night, when I suddenly could.

"I brought over the mail," Eric says. My mother is dead. What could any piece of paper possibly say that would be worth reading?

"You hungry?"

It takes me a moment to realize that my father has asked this of Eric, and another second to understand that the answer is yes, actually, Eric is nodding his head yes, and a third, still, to realize neither knows how to prepare a meal. My mother cooked for my father, for all of us—she was great at it. She'd make elaborate breakfasts: goat cheese frittatas with scooped-out bagels. Fruit salad and cappuccinos. When my father retired five years ago, they'd begun to eat outside, setting up on the veranda for hours. My mother loved the *New York Times* on a Sunday, and an iced coffee in the afternoon. My father loved what she did.

Chuck, my dad, worshipped Carol. He thought she hung the moon and painted the stars in the sky. But the deep secret, although it couldn't have been one to him, is that I was her great love. She loved my father, certainly. I believe there wasn't a man on earth she would have traded him for, but there was no relationship above ours. I was her one, just like she was mine.

I believe my love with my mother was truer, purer, than what she had with my father. If you'd have asked her *Who do you belong to*, the answer would have been *Katy*.

"You're my everything," she'd tell me. "You're my whole world."

"There are some leftovers in the fridge," I hear myself saying.

I think about dishing lettuce onto plates, heating the chicken, crisping the rice the way I know my dad likes.

My father is gone, already in pursuit of the La Scala chopped salads that are no doubt soggy in their containers. I can't remember who brought them over, or when, just that they're there.

Eric is still standing in the doorway.

"I thought maybe we could talk," he says to me.

I left last night and drove here. I let myself in like I had thousands of times, with my own key. I tiptoed up the stairs. It was nearly midnight, and I poked my head into my parents' bedroom, expecting to see my father fast asleep, but he wasn't in there. I looked in the guest room and didn't find him there, either. I went down the stairs into the family room. There he was, asleep on the couch, their wedding photo in a frame on the floor.

I covered him. He didn't stir. And then I went upstairs and slept in my parents' bed, on the side that was hers.

In the morning I came downstairs to find my dad making coffee. I didn't mention the couch, and he didn't ask me why I was up there, or where I had slept, either. We're forgiving each other these oddities, what we're doing to survive.

"Katy," Eric says when I don't respond. "You have to talk to me."

But I don't trust myself to speak. Everything feels so tenuous that I'm afraid if I even say her name, all that would come out would be a scream.

"Do you want to eat?" I ask.

"Are you coming home?" There is an edge to his voice, and I realize, not for the first time in the past few months, how unused to discomfort we both are. We do not know how to live a life that the bottom has fallen out of. These were not the promises of our families, our upbringings, our marriage. We made promises in a world lit with light. We do not know how to keep them in the darkness.

"If you just communicate with me, I can help," Eric says. "But you have to talk to me."

"I have to," I repeat.

"Yes," Eric says.

"Why?" I realize how petulant this sounds, but I am feeling childish.

"Because I'm your husband," he says. "Hey, it's me. That's what I'm here for. That's the point. I can help."

I am overcome with a sudden, familiar anger and the boldface, pulsating words: *Unfortunately, you can't.*

For thirty years I have been tied to the best person alive, the best mother, the best friend, the best wife—*the best one.* The best one was mine, and now she's gone. The string that tethered us has been snipped, and I am overcome with how little I have left, how second-best every single other thing is.

I nod, because I cannot think what else to do. Eric hands me a stack of envelopes.

"You should look at the one on top," he says.

I glance down. It's marked *United Airlines.* I feel my fingers curl.

"Thanks."

"Do you want me to leave?" Eric asks. "I can go pick up sandwiches or something . . ."

I look at him standing in his oxford shirt and khaki shorts. He shifts his body weight from one foot to the other. His brown hair hangs too long in the back; his sideburns, too. He needs a haircut. He has on his glasses. *Dorky handsome*, my mother said when she met him.

"No," I say. "It's fine."

He calls my parents by their first names. He takes his shoes off at the door and puts his feet, in socks, up on the coffee table. He helps himself to the refrigerator and puts more soap in the dispenser when it's empty. This is his home, too.

"I'm going to go lie down," I say.

I turn to leave, and Eric reaches out and takes my free hand. I feel his fingertips, cold, press into my palm. They seem to be Morse coding the one word *Please.*

"Later," I say. "Okay?"

He lets me go.

I walk up the stairs. I travel down the wood-paneled hallway, past the room that used to be mine, the one that my mother and

I redecorated during my second year of college, and then again when I was twenty-seven. It has striped wallpaper and white bedding and a closet full of sweatshirts and sundresses. All of my skin-care products sit, expired, in the medicine cabinet.

"You're fully stocked here," my mother would say. She loved that I could sleep over if it got late, and I didn't even have to pack a toothbrush.

I stop at the entrance to her room.

How long does it take for someone's smell to fade? When she was here, at the end. When the hospice nurses came and went like apparitions, the room smelled like illness, like a hospital, like plastic and vegetable broth and soured dairy. But now, all trace of sickness gone, her scent has come back, like a spring bloom. It lingers in the blankets, the carpet, the curtains. When I open the doors to her closet, it's almost as if she were crouched inside.

I flick the light switch on and sit down among her dresses and blazers, jeans ironed, folded, and hung. I breathe her in. And then I turn my attention back to the envelopes in my hand. I let them slip down to the floor until I'm just holding the one on top. I slide my pinkie in the seam and wiggle it open. It gives easily.

Inside, as I expect, are two plane tickets. Carol Almea Silver was not a woman who handed her phone to the gate agent to scan. She was a woman who demanded a proper ticket for a proper trip.

Positano. June 5. Six days from now. The mother-daughter trip we had talked about for years, made manifest.

Italy had always been special to my mother. She went to the Amalfi Coast the summer before she met my father. She loved to describe Positano, a tiny seaside town, as "pure heaven."

God's country. She loved the clothes and the food and the light. "And the gelato is a meal itself," she said.

Eric and I considered going for our honeymoon—taking the train down from Rome and hitting Capri—but we were young and saving for a house, and the whole thing felt too extravagant. We ended up finding a cheap flight to Hawaii and spending three nights at the Grand Wailea Maui.

I look at the tickets.

My mother had always talked about going back to Positano. First with my father, but then as time went on she began to suggest the two of us go together. She was adamant about it—she wanted to show me this place that had always lingered in her memory. This special mecca that she played in right before she became a woman and a wife and then a mother.

"It's the most spectacular place in the world," she'd tell me. "When I was there, we'd sleep until noon and then take the boat out onto the water. There was this great little restaurant, Chez Black, in the marina. We'd eat pasta and clams in the sand. I remember like it was yesterday."

So we decided to go. First as a fantasy, then as a loose, down-the-road plan, and then, when she got sick, as a light at the end of the tunnel. "When I'm better" became "when we go to Positano."

We booked the tickets. She ordered summer sweaters in creams and whites. Sun hats with big, wide brims. We planned and pretended right up until the end. Up until the week before she died we were still talking about the Italian sun. And now the trip is here, and she is not.

I edge my back so it's flat against the side of her closet. A coat rubs up against my shoulder. I think about my husband

and father downstairs. My mother was always better with them. She encouraged Eric to take the job at Disney, to ask for a raise, to buy the car he really wanted, to invest in the good suit. "The money will come," she'd always say. "You'll never regret the experience."

My mother supported my father through the opening of his first clothing store. She believed that he could create his own label, and believed they could manufacture the product themselves. She was quality control. She could tell how good a spool of thread was just by looking at it, and she made sure every garment my dad had was up to her standards. She also worked as his desk girl, answering the phones and taking the orders. She hired and trained everyone who ever worked in their business, teaching them about an invisible stich, the difference between pleating and ruching. She planned the birthday parties and the baptisms of their employees and their children. She always baked on Fridays.

Carol knew how to show up.

And now here I am, hiding in her closet in her absence. How did I not inherit any of her capability? The only person who would know how to handle her death is gone.

I feel the paper crinkle between my fingers. I am gripping it.

I couldn't. There's no way. I have a job. And a grieving father. And a husband.

From downstairs I hear a clattering of pans. The loud sounds of unfamiliarity with appliances, cabinets, the choreography of the kitchen.

We are missing our center.

What I know: She is not in this house, where she died. She is not downstairs, in the kitchen she loved. She is not in the family room, folding the blankets and rehanging the wedding photos.

She is not in the garden, gloves on, clipping the tomato vines. She is not in this closet that still smells like her.

She is not here, and therefore, I cannot be here, either.

Flight 363.

I want to see what she saw, what she loved before she loved me. I want to see where it was she always wanted to return, this magical place that showed up so strongly in her memories.

I curl my knees to my chest. I sink my head down into them. I feel the outline of something in my back pocket. I pull it out, and the cigarette, now warm and mangled, disintegrates in my hands.

Please, please, I say aloud, waiting for her, for this closet full of her clothes, to tell me what to do next.

Chapter Two

"Are you sure you don't want me to take you?" Eric asks.

I'm standing in the entryway to our house, the one I have no idea if I'll be returning to, with my suitcases at the door like an attentive child.

Eric is wearing a salmon-colored polo T-shirt and jeans, and his hair is still too long on the sides. I haven't said anything about it, and neither has he. I wonder if he notices, if he realizes he needs a cut, too. I've made all those appointments for him. Suddenly his inability to get his hair cut feels hostile, an intentioned attack.

"No, Uber's on the way." I hold up my phone. "See, three minutes."

Eric smiles, but it's small, sad. "Okay."

When I told Eric I wanted to go to Italy, to take the mother-daughter trip alone, he told me it was a great idea. He thought I needed a break—I'd been caring for my mother around the clock. Months earlier I'd taken a leave of absence from my job as an in-house copywriter for an ad agency in Santa Monica. I'd left when she first came home for treatment, and I didn't know when I'd go back. Not that anyone had asked. At this point I'm not even sure the job will still be waiting for me.

"This will be good for you," Eric said. "You'll come back feeling so much better."

We sat at our kitchen counter, a box of pizza between us. I hadn't bothered to take out plates or utensils. All that was next to the box was a pile of napkins. We had given up caring.

"This is not a vacation," I said.

I resented the idea that what was standing in the way of a new outlook on life was a few sun-soaked weeks on the Italian coast.

"That's not what I said."

I could see his frustration and his want to control it, too. I felt a bolt of compassion for him.

"I know."

"We still haven't talked about us."

"I know," I said again.

I had come home a few days earlier. We slept in the same bed and made coffee in the morning and did laundry and put away plates. Eric went back to his job, and I made lists of people to reach out to—thank-you notes that had to be written, phone calls that needed to be returned, my father's dry cleaner.

It only resembled our old routine. We were skirting around one another like strangers in a restaurant, pausing to acknowledge if we bumped into each other.

"You came home. Does that mean you're staying?"

In college, before a big test, Eric would bring over a sandwich from this deli called Three Pickles. It had Swiss cheese and arugula and raspberry jam, and it was delicious. He had taken me there on one of our first dates, and insisted on ordering for me. We took the sandwiches outside, found a curb, and unwrapped them. Mine looked like melted, colored wax, but the tang of the Swiss with the peppery greens and tart raspberry was sublime.

"You can trust me," Eric had said then.

I knew he was right.

I trusted him on our move to New York, on the purchase of our first home. I trusted him through my mother's treatment, even. The plans the four of us made, where her care would be best, the medications, the trials.

But now. Now how could I trust anyone? We had all betrayed her.

"I'm not sure," I said. "I genuinely don't know if I can be married to you anymore."

Eric exhaled like I'd socked him in the stomach. I had. It was unkind and harsh, and I shouldn't have said it like that. But he was asking me an impossible question. He was asking about a future I could no longer fathom.

"That's brutal," he said.

Eric plopped a piece of pizza on a napkin. It was a ridiculous thing to do now. To eat. To *begin* eating.

"I know. I'm sorry."

My apology pivoted him. "We can get through this together," he said. "You know we can. We have been through everything together, Katy."

I picked up a slice. It seemed like a foreign object. I wasn't sure whether to eat it or take it outside and plant it.

The problem, of course, is that we hadn't really been through everything together, because we hadn't been through anything before. Not until now. Our life had unfolded with the ease of an open road. There were no forks, no bumps, just a long stretch into the sunset. We were, in many ways, the same people who had met at twenty-two years old. What was different was where we lived but not how. What had we even learned in the past eight years? What skills had we acquired to get us through this?

"This is too big," I said.

"I'm just asking to be a part of it." He looked at me with big, round brown eyes.

Before Eric and I got engaged, he asked my parents for permission. I wasn't there, of course, but Eric reports that he went to their house one evening after work. My parents were in the kitchen, making dinner. Nothing would have been unusual about this. Eric and I dropped by my parents'—separately and together—often. On this particular evening he asked if he could talk to them in the living room.

We had just moved to the house in Culver City. I was twenty-five, and we'd been together for three years, two of them spent in New York, far away from my folks. We were home now, and ready to build a life together, beside them.

"I love your daughter," Eric said once they were settled. "I think I can make her happy. And I love you both, too. I love being a part of your family. I want to ask Katy to marry me."

My father was thrilled. He loved Eric. Eric had a way of fitting into our family that still allowed my father to be the boss. If you asked either of them, the structure didn't need to change.

It was my mother who was quiet.

"Carol," my father had said. "What do you think?"

My mother looked at Eric. "Are you two ready for this?"

In addition to her kindness and hospitality, my mother had a frankness that made her respected and a little bit feared. She could tell it like it was, and she did.

"I know I love her," Eric said.

"Love is beautiful," my mother told him. "And I know how true that is. But you're both so young. Don't you want to live a little more before you settle down? There's so much to do and so much time to be married."

"I want to live my life with her," Eric had said. "I know we have a lot to experience, and I want us to experience it together."

My mother had smiled. "Well," she had said. "Then congratulations are in order."

Looking at Eric across the table, the pizza between us, I thought that maybe her initial hesitation had been right. That we should have lived more. That we did not really understand the vows we'd taken. *For better or for worse.* Because now here we are, experiencing all that life has to deal out, and it has broken us. It's broken me.

"I'm going to go to Italy," I said to him. "I'm going to go on that trip. And I think while I'm gone we should take some space."

"Well, you'll be in Italy," he said. "So space seems inevitable." He tried for a smile.

"No, like a break," I said.

I knew in that moment we were both thinking about the *Friends* episode, the ridiculous, impossible idea that a break was somehow a hovering, and not a speeding car out of town. It almost made me laugh. What would it take to take his hand, turn on the TV, and snuggle down together? To pretend that what was happening wasn't.

"Are you thinking about a separation?"

I felt cold. I felt it down into my bones. "Maybe," I said. "I don't know what to call it, Eric."

He turned stoic. It was a look I'd never seen from him before. "If that's what you want," he said.

"I don't know what I want right now except to not be here. You, of course, are free to make your own choices, too."

"What does that mean?"

"It means whatever you want it to mean. It means I can't be responsible for you right now."

"You're not responsible for me; you're married to me."

I stared at him, and he stared back. I got up and put the dishes in the dishwasher and then went upstairs. Eric came to bed an hour later. I wasn't asleep but the lights were off, and I was pretending, matching my breathing to the rhythm of a light snore. He crept in, and I felt his body next to mine. He didn't reach for me; I didn't expect him to. I felt the weight of the space between us, how vast and tense eight inches could be.

And now the Uber is here.

My phone flashes with a number I don't know. It's the driver. I pick up.

"I'll be right out," I tell him.

Eric inhales and then exhales.

"I'll call you from the airport," I say.

"Here, let me help you."

The driver doesn't get out. Eric takes my suitcases out to the car. He puts them into the open trunk.

They are filled with dresses and shoes and hats my mother and I picked out together. Every time I'd pack for a trip, she'd come over, even if was just a weekend away. She knew how to fit ten outfits into a carry-on—"The trick is to roll, Katy"—and how to make a pair of jeans last all week. She was the queen of accessories—a silk belt as a headscarf, a chunky necklace to take a white shirt from day to night.

Once Eric is done, we stand facing each other. It's an unseasonably cool June day in LA. I'm wearing jeans, a T-shirt, and a hooded sweatshirt. I have a voluminous cashmere scarf in my bag, because my mother taught me to always travel with one. "You can curl up against any windowsill," she'd say.

"So, have a safe trip, then," he tells me. Eric has never been good at pretending. I am better. The heaviness of our conversation hangs between us. It causes the immediacy of what's before us—a split, divorce?—to be in direct opposition to the obvious: that we might already be strangers. That we are standing on opposite sides now. I think, briefly: of course people get divorced in wars. When everything has been obliterated, how do you carry on with doing laundry?

I see the pain in Eric's face, and I know he wants me to reassure him. He wants me to tell him that I love him, that we'll figure this out. That I'm his. He wants me to say *your wife will be right back*. Your life will be right back.

But I can't do that. Because I do not know where she or it went.

"Yeah, thank you."

He moves to hug me, and reflexively I pinch back. People must have hugged me, these weeks. All of those visitors must have put their arms around me. Buried their faces into my neck. But I cannot remember it. It feels like I haven't been touched in months.

"Jesus, Katy, are you kidding?" Eric puts his hands on his face. He rubs the skin of his temples. "I fucking loved her, too, you know."

He puts his head in his hands. He has cried this week. He cried at her memorial service and on the first day of her shiva. He cried both when his mother and sister arrived, paying their condolences to our family, and when they left. He cried when he hugged my father, and my parents' best friends, Hank and

Sarah. I do not know how to feel about his grief. I know it is real, grounded in his own connection to her, and yet it feels indulgent. It feels like he's letting something out to dance that should be locked away. I wish he'd stop.

His bottom lip quivers, trying to hold it in, but he can't. It's bigger than him, this emotion, and it breaks over him now.

I put my hand on his shoulder, but I do not feel the thing inside me I should. I do not feel protective of him, sorry for him. I do not feel compassion, and it does not stir my own grief. I am too afraid. If I let myself see his pain, what will that say about mine? Since she died, I have not cried. I can't meet it, not with a plane to catch.

"I have to go," I tell him. "I'm sorry, Eric."

Eric says I never call him *Eric* unless I'm upset with him. It was never "Eric, come cuddle me." It was "Eric, it's trash day." Or "Eric, the dishwasher is full." But I'm not sure that's true. I had a million nicknames for him. *Baby* and *bunny* and *hotsauce.* But *Eric* was my favorite term of endearment. I loved naming him. I loved the specificity of his name. Just the one. Eric.

I'm not a romantic, and I do not think I'm a particularly sentimental person—I'm Carol's daughter, a woman who understood the importance of a neutral palette and temperament. But Eric is. He has piles of receipts, movie tickets, the stubs from concerts. We store them in shoeboxes in the garage. He is a man who cries watching *Finding Forrester*, and reading the Modern Love column in the *New York Times.*

I remove my hand. He rubs his palm across his face. He exhales. He takes a solid breath then, in and out.

"I have to go," I say one last time.

He nods. He says nothing.

And just like that, I get in the car. I feel a sensation close to relief, but heavier, thicker.

"LAX," I say, even though the driver already knows, of course. He has an app, he's already charting the course.

"Twenty-three minutes," he tells me. "What a beautiful day, and no traffic!"

He smiles at me in the rearview.

He doesn't know, I think as we drive away. He doesn't know that here, in the backseat, there are no beautiful days anymore.

Chapter Three

Positano is not an easy place to get to. First you have to fly into Rome, and then you must make your way from the Rome airport to the Rome train station, at which point you board a train to Naples. From Naples, you need to find a ride down the coast to Positano. I land in Rome thirteen hours after leaving LA surprisingly refreshed. I'm not a good flier, never have been. And this is the longest trip I've ever taken, not to mention the only one I've ever taken alone. But I'm strangely calm on the flight. I even sleep.

The train station is a quick taxi away, and the ride to Naples is a beautiful hour and a half through the Italian countryside. I've always loved a train. When Eric and I lived in New York, we'd sometimes take the train to Boston to see his family. I loved the theater of it—how you could look outside and see what season it was, right there on display. Leaves in red and burnt orange in the fall, snow on the ground in December, ushering in the holidays like a red Sharpie on a printed calendar.

The Italian countryside is just like you'd imagine it: green hills, small homes, the tan of farms mixed with the bright aqua blue of the sky.

By the time I arrive at the Naples train station—and spot a man from the Hotel Poseidon holding a sign marked *Katy Silver*—I'm smiling.

I am not in Erewhon, picking out the week's groceries, wanting to call her and say they have a two-for-one on olive oil, and does she want some. I am not at the bottom of Fryman Canyon, staring out at the trail, waiting for her to join me on our weekend hike. I'm not at Pressed Juicery, waiting for her to walk down San Vicente in her wide-brimmed hat and buy us both a Greens 3. I am not in my home; I am not in hers. I am somewhere new, where I have to be nimble, alert, present. It forces me into the moment in a way I haven't been in a year, maybe even ever. When my mom was sick, it was all about the future—the worry of what was coming, what might happen. Here there is not space for thought, just action.

We chose Hotel Poseidon because it was very close to where my mother had stayed many years ago and also a hotel she remembered fondly. "They had the kindest staff," she said. "Really good people." The hotel was old—everything, my mother used to say, is old in Italy. But it was charming and beautiful and warm. It had so much character and life, my mother said. And the terrace was to die for, somehow constantly bathed in sunlight.

I hand my bag over to the chauffeur named Renaldo—the hotel was nice enough to send someone to collect me from the train station—and climb in the back of the sedan. The car is a Mercedes, as plenty of run-of-the-mill taxis are in Europe, but it still feels indulgent. A Honda Civic dropped me off at LAX.

"Buongiorno, Katy," Renaldo says. He's a stout man, no

more than fifty, with a contained smile and what I imagine is a patient temperament. "Welcome to Naples."

The drive out of Naples is picturesque—apartment buildings with women hanging clothes on the line, small terra-cotta houses, the wild tangle of greenery—but when we get to the coast, the real delight begins to set in. The Amalfi Coast is not so much splayed out before us as beckoning us closer. Hints of clear blue sea, houses built into the hillside.

"It's absolutely beautiful," I say.

"Wait," Renaldo tells me. "You wait."

When we finally come into Positano, I see what he means. From high up on the winding road, you can see the entirety of the town. Colorful hotels and houses sit chiseled into the rocks as if they were painted there. The entire town is built around the cove of the sea. It looks like an amphitheater, enjoying the performance of the ocean. Blue, sparkling, spectacular water.

"Bellissima, no?" Renaldo says. "Good for photo."

I grip the side of the car and roll down the window.

The air is hot and thick, and as we wind down—closer and closer to town—I begin to hear the sounds of cicadas. They sing out, the delights of summer in full swing.

We picked June for the trip because it was still a little ahead of tourist season. Once July hits, it's a madhouse, my mother said. Best to go in June when things were a little less touristy, a little less crowded. She wanted to be able to stroll the streets without being jostled by influencers.

I was sent lists of dinner reservations to make and places to visit from friends. Boats to rent for day trips to Capri, beach clubs along the ocean requiring water taxi service. Restaurants high up in the hills with no menus and endless courses of farm-fresh food. I sent them all to my mother, and she planned the entire thing. In my hands is our itinerary, marked down to the minute. I tuck it into my bag.

As we descend I'm met with the stirrings of small-town summer life. Older women stand on stoops, chatting. There are men and women on Vespas, the sounds of late-afternoon activity. A smattering of tourists along the tiny sidewalk have their phones out, snapping pictures. It's summer in Italy, and even though it's nearing five o'clock, it is still bright and sunny. The sun is high in the sky, and the Tyrrhenian Sea sparkles. White boats sit out on the water in rows, like flower beds. It is beauty beyond measure—the sun seeming to touch everything at once. I exhale and exhale and exhale.

"Ah, here we are," Renaldo says.

We pull up to the Hotel Poseidon, which is, like the rest of the town, nestled into the hillside. The entrance is all white, with a green carpeted staircase. Brightly colored flowers sit in potted plants by the entrance.

I open the car door and am immediately greeted by the heat—but it feels welcoming. Warm in its embrace, not at all oppressive.

Renaldo takes my suitcases out of the trunk and climbs the steps with them. I take out the money I exchanged at the airport—one of Carol's rules was to never exchange money at the airport, she said the exchange rate was terrible, but I was desperate—and hand him some crisp bills.

"Grazie," I say.

"Enjoy our Positano," he tells me. "It is a very special place."

I climb the steps to the entrance and then am greeted by a blast of cool air from the open lobby. To the left, a spiral staircase leads up to a second level. The welcome desk is to the right. And behind it is a woman who appears to be in her fifties. She has long, dark hair that swings down her back. Next to her is a young man who speaks in clear, enunciated Italian.

"Ovviamente abbiamo un ristorante! È il migliore!"

I wave at the woman, and she smiles a warm and welcoming smile back.

"Buonasera, signora. How can I help you?"

She's beautiful, this woman.

"Hello. Checking in. It's under Silver."

Something knocks on my sternum, cold and hard.

"Yes." The woman's face softens into compassion. There is a tenderness behind her eyes. "It's just you with us this week, sì?"

I nod. "Just me."

"Welcome," she says, placing her hand on her heart. Her face radiates a smile. "Positano is a wonderful place to be alone, and Hotel Poseidon is a wonderful place to make friends."

She gives me the keys to room 33. I climb the stairs to the landing level, then take the small elevator to the third floor. I have to close the doors before the machine will move. It takes nearly five minutes to go up the two flights, and I commit to taking the stairs for the duration of my time here. That was another one of Carol Silver's rules—never take the elevator if you can take the stairs, and you'll never have to work out a day in your life. When I was living in New York, this was definitely true, but it doesn't quite work as well in Los Angeles.

My room is at the end of the hall. There is a small lending library just outside, stocked with books. I use the key and turn the doorknob.

Inside, the room is sparse and filled with light. There are two twin beds, made up with white sheets and small quilts, that sit across from two matching dressers. On one side of the room is a closet, and on the other is a set of French doors that are flung open, welcoming in the afternoon sun. I walk to them and then step out onto the terrace.

While the room is small, the terrace is nearly sprawling. It looks out over the entire town. The panoramic views span from the hillside down through the hotels and homes and shops to the sea. Right underneath me to the left is the swimming pool. A couple is in the water, hanging off the side, glasses of wine on the ledge. I hear the splashing, the clink of glassware, and laughter.

I am here, I think. It is really Italy below me. I am not watching a movie in my parents' den or on the couch at Culver. This is not a soundtrack or a photograph. It is real life. Most places in the world I have never touched, never met. But I am here now. It is something. It is a start.

I inhale the fresh air, this place that seems to be dripping in summer. There is so much beauty here; she was right.

I go back inside. I shower. I unpack everything right away, my mother's daughter, and then I wander out onto the terrace again. I sit down on a lounger and tuck my feet underneath me. All around me Italy swells. I feel the air thick with heat and food and memory.

"*I made it*," I say, but only I can hear.

Chapter Four

The city bells chime seven. It is evening in Positano. I remember my mother talking about the Church of Santa Maria Assunta, and the ringing bells that alert the town of the hour. They sound far-off, distant, dreamy, a far cry from the "Beacon" alarm setting on my iPhone.

I go to the closet and find the dresses I brought. I choose a short white ruffled dress and slip into a pair of gold flip-flops. My hair is dry from the shower and hangs in frizzy ringlets down my back. In my normal life, I blow it dry and begin the long process of straightening it, but in the past few weeks I've done little more than wash it twice a week. For a long time, it hung limp, unsure what to do without direction. But now the curl is starting to come back, reawakening to its original form.

I rub some tinted moisturizer into my skin, swipe blush across my cheeks. I apply lip gloss, grab my room key, and head downstairs.

I arrive on the second level, like the woman at reception instructed, and am met with the pool and a terraced restaurant.

My mother told me about the terrace. The way it hangs over the whole town, like it's suspended.

Couples sit in white chairs covered with red upholstery overlooking the scenery, and waiters in white collared shirts carry trays of bright Aperol spritzes and small ceramic dishes filled with snacks—plump green olives, hand-baked potato chips, salty cashews.

A young man approaches me. He wears black pants and a white shirt with *Il Tridente,* the hotel restaurant's name, stitched in red lettering.

"Buonasera, signora," he says. "Can I help you?"

I realize I left my itinerary upstairs. I have no idea if we had reservations for tonight here, or somewhere else, even, but I haven't eaten since a panini at the train station, maybe seven hours ago.

"Is it possible to have dinner here?" I ask.

He smiles. "Of course," he says. "Anything is possible. We are at your service."

"Grazie," I say. It sounds harsh and so American. "Thank you."

He gestures for me to follow him out onto the terrace. "Right this way."

Half of the terrace is the pool and lounge chairs, with a row of small tables for drinks and food, but to the right is a covered area, dripping in vines and flowers, with lanterns strung overhead like lights. There are white metal tables covered with white-and-red-checkered cloth, and waiters in slim ties weave in and out of the glass doors.

"For you," he says. "The best table we have to offer."

He leads me over to a two-top on the edge of the terrace, right up against the wrought iron fence. The view is breathtaking. A front-row seat to a sun that seems as if it will never set. All around the light is golden and liquid and heavy, like it's just beginning on its second glass of wine.

"This is beautiful," I say. "I've never seen a place like this before." Every corner is just begging to be photographed. I think about the camera I have tucked away upstairs. Tomorrow.

He smiles. "I am so glad you are happy, Ms. Silver. We are here to help."

He leaves, and another young waiter appears with a menu, a bottle of still water, and a basket of bread.

I unfold the white napkin and pull out a slice, still warm from the oven. I spill some olive oil into an oval plate, hand-painted with blue fish, and dip. The bread is delicious, the olive oil tangy. I eat two more slices immediately.

"Something to eat and drink?"

The waiter is back, hands tucked by his sides.

"What do you recommend?" I ask. I haven't even opened the menu.

At home we don't cook; we mostly order in or go to my parents' house. Eric likes Italian food, but the vaguest remnants satisfy him. We get pizza from Pecorino, or even sometimes Fresh Brothers. Chinese takeout from Wokshop, salads from CPK. Once a week, I pick up a roast chicken from the market—Bristol Farms or Whole Foods—and some bags of broccoli and carrots. I have always felt a little bad for Eric that I did not inherit my mother's skill in the kitchen, but he always says he's just as happy with a sandwich as he'd be with a steak.

It strikes me that I'm not sure I've ever been out to eat alone. I cannot recall sitting down at a table, opening up a napkin, being poured a glass of wine, and picking up a fork without some level of conversation.

He smiles. "Tomato salad and the homemade ravioli. Simple. Perfect. You want wine, too, no?"

"Yes." Definitely, yes.

"Excellent, signora. You will be very happy."

He leaves, taking the menu with him, and I sit back into my chair. I think about my mother here, all those many years ago. Looking out over this same view. Young and carefree, with no idea what the future held for her or how things would turn out. I find myself wishing that I had a blank slate. That I hadn't already entangled myself so deeply—marriage, a house, a life that is not movable, at least not without destruction.

"Ms. Silver."

I hear a voice behind me. It's the woman from the front desk. She stands, her hands held in front of her. She's wearing a crisp white button-down and a pair of jeans.

"Hi, good evening," I say.

"Yes, good evening. You look well. Positano is already good for you."

I look down at my dress. "Oh, thank you."

"Are you settling in?"

I nod. "Yes, it's gorgeous here, thank you."

She smiles. "Good. My name is Monica. I realize we did not get to properly meet downstairs. This is my hotel. Anything you need, you ask us, okay? We are your family here."

"Okay," I say. "I really appreciate it."

"You have a boat ride for tomorrow. To Da Adolfo beach club, and a reservation for lunch. It is early in the season, so it will not be a problem if you want to schedule it for a different time. Perhaps you can rest here and explore the town a bit tomorrow."

She smiles that warm, open smile. I look out over the remaining pool loungers.

"That would be great," I say. "Thank you. That sounds better."

"Perfetto," she says. "Tony told me you are having the ricotta ravioli tonight. Excellent choice. I always put a little lemon in to brighten it up. I hope you enjoy."

I laugh. It surprises me, it has been that long. "He chose for me."

"One should always let waiters choose food, and builders choose wood," she says. "Something my father used to say."

She begins to back away, and I stop her. "Monica," I say. "Thank you."

She smiles. "You are most welcome." She surveys the terrace. "It's a beautiful night." She turns her attention back to me. "Tomorrow I'm going to Roma on business for a few days, but anything you need, my staff will take care of. We hope you enjoy your stay, Ms. Silver. We are so very glad you have come to us here."

She leaves.

Come to us here.

When my mother tells the story of when I was born, she says it was a freezing cold winter night. They were, at the time, living in an apartment in Silver Lake, not far from Sunset Boulevard. The apartment was more like a tree house, according to my mother. It had a steep flight of stairs and an oak tree that ran straight through the living room.

It had been her place, which my father had moved into right after they got married. I couldn't imagine my mother on the other side of the 405, let alone in Silver Lake—an artsy, bohemian community even now, today. She's a Westsider through and through—classic. But they brought me home from the hospital to that place, wrapped in a white wool blanket. My mom said that it was the only time in Los Angeles she'd ever seen it snow.

She'd labored for twenty-six hours at Cedars-Sinai hospital before I arrived. "All hair," she told me.

"You looked like a baby ape," my father would add.

"That's how we knew you were ours," my mother said.

Come to us here.

I no longer belong to my mother. I do not belong to my father, who no longer belongs to himself—shuffling around the house that was theirs, piecing together the schedule—on what days does Susanna come and clean? I do not belong to my husband, whom I've told I may no longer want to be my husband at all. I do not know where home is anymore. I do not know how to find my center without her, because that's what she was. I was Carol Silver's daughter. Now I am simply a stranger.

The tomatoes come out. Tony sets them down proudly.

"Buon appetito," he says. "Enjoy."

I pick up my fork, spear a tomato, and taste the most heavenly, sweetest, ripest, saltiest thing I've ever encountered. I swallow them, glorious and geranium red, along with my grief.

I devour the plate, along with another basket of bread. Then the ravioli arrives—creamy and light, ricotta clouds. Delicious. I add the lemon, as instructed.

It feels like I haven't eaten in months—perhaps I haven't. The microwavable meals, untouched, thrown away still encased in plastic. The bags of stale chips, the mealy apples. Those were food, maybe, but not sustenance. The life force in this meal, in every bite, is like another ingredient. I can feel it nourishing me.

The bells chime once more, indicating a new hour has passed. As if on cue, the yellows and oranges of the sky begin to give way to lavenders and pinks and baby blues. The light moves from drunken, heady, and golden to delicate, fleeting. The ships on the shore bob along, a chorus to the sinking sun. It's magnificent. I wish she could see it. She should have seen it.

A few tables over, a couple asks Tony to take their photo. They both lean across the table, framed by the overhead vines. I think about Eric, thousands of miles away.

If he were here, he'd go right up to their table. He'd offer to take a few more shots, if they wanted that. Then he'd inquire as to where they were from. In ten minutes' time, he'd be asking them to join us, and then we'd be spending the rest of this holiday on a double date. Eric talks to everyone—the checkout clerk at Ralphs, the lady in line in front of him at the movie theater, the vendors at the farmers market. He knows the detailed family tree of our postman, George, and most people who come within a ten-foot radius of him on a Tuesday. It drives me nuts, because it means we're never alone. Also, I hate small talk. I'm not good at it. Eric is a professional. I like to disappear in my day, be anonymous. Eric would wear a T-shirt that had FREE TO HEAR ABOUT YOUR EAR DOCTOR APPOINTMENT FOR THE NEXT FOUR AND A HALF HOURS in bold lettering.

I told Eric I'd never go on a cruise with him because by the second day there would be nowhere to hide. I've often wondered why he can't just keep to himself. Why he's always insisting on interjecting into everyone's day, making himself known, taking up space with inane conversation.

The couple thanks Tony and goes back to their meal. I realize suddenly that if I stay down here any longer, I will run the risk of falling asleep at the table.

I go upstairs, pulled by the food and wine and night air. I take my cell phone out onto the balcony and call Eric. The phone rings three times, and then his familiar voicemail picks up: *Hi, it's Eric. Leave me a message, shoot me a text, and I'll get right back to you. Thanks, bye.*

"I made it," I tell him. "I'm here."

My voice hovers as I wonder if there is more to say, if I should try and describe this place, if I should give him some guidance, some direction, something to plant in my absence. But I do not know what that would be. I hang up before the exhale.

I put my phone along with my jewelry in the safe.

When I sleep, I dream of her—here with me, vibrant and alive.

Chapter Five

The ringing of the bells begins early, and it is this that, despite the jet lag, pulls me out of bed and onto the terrace, to greet the day.

Morning in Positano is reminiscent of the evening, but even lovelier. The marina is swathed in blue light—the day hasn't fully broken open yet. A hint of a chill still hangs in the air, ready to be blown away by the first speck of sun.

I stand on the terrace in my striped poplin pajamas emblazoned with *KS*. We all have the monogrammed set—me, Eric, my mom, and my dad. They were for a holiday card we did two years ago. I remember my mother delivered them to our house. Eric's are blue; mine are yellow; hers and my father's are red. A family of primary colors.

"Carol, these won't fit," Eric said, holding them up. They looked a little truncated, and Eric is not a short guy.

"They'll be perfect," she said. "It's one picture." She smiled at him, which meant: *Try them on.*

"Now?" he asked her.

"Why not?"

Eric did a half eye roll, half laugh and went into the powder room. "Oh, for Pete's sake, Eric! It's not like it's anything I haven't seen before!" I remember my mother calling after him playfully. It was true, she'd seen him in various stages of undress—when he got his appendix out, every holiday in a bathing suit, Saturdays at their pool.

"We'll take the photos Saturday," she said to me while he changed. "I want to get them done early this year."

It was October. A bright, lingering summer day.

I should have known then that something was wrong. I should have known when she called the following week, after the pictures, to ask if Eric and I could come for dinner. I should have known when she said, over our pumpkin soup, "I have some news."

The pajamas fit, incidentally. She was right.

I change, into a plain pink cotton sundress and sandals and a wide-brimmed hat. I tuck sunscreen and a wallet into my small Clare V. cross-body bag and leave the room. When I open the door, there is a man standing a foot away from me.

I scream and jump back. He yelps.

"Ay!"

"Sorry," he says. "Sorry."

His hands are held up in surrender, and in one he is holding *A Moveable Feast*. I realize he has been browsing the small lending library outside my door. A nook of books, tucked into the side wall. I usually bring two to three books with me on a trip, and even if they don't get read, I leave them behind. I have paperbacks I've picked up along the way, too. *The Girl in the Flammable Skirt* from an Airbnb in Joshua Tree, *Lulu Meets God and Doubts Him* from the Fontainebleau in Miami. This is the first trip I can remember that I didn't pack a single novel. Ironic, as there's no one else to keep me company.

"Just making a trade," he says. "Crichton for Hemingway. Not a fair one, but not meant to do bodily harm, either."

He takes a copy of *Jurassic Park* off the shelf and shows it to me.

"No thanks," I say. "I already saw the movie."

He cocks his head at me and smiles. "Never heard of it."

"Funny."

He's American, with a confident stance and a sky-blue linen button-down he's paired with brightly colored board shorts. The whole thing practically screams Cape Cod clambake.

"Are you trying to browse?" He gestures to the shelf.

"Oh, no, thanks. I'm just going to . . ." I point to the hallway down to the stairs.

"Right, yes." He slips Hemingway under his arm. "See ya around."

I leave him at the books and walk downstairs.

Breakfast is on the same terrace as dinner, and the sun is lighting the town on fire. The chairs have been swapped out—what were red last night are now bright florals this morning. The water below us sparkles like it's made of actual crystals.

"Buongiorno!"

Tony is not there, but a stout man with a wide smile is. He comes up to me and greets me by grabbing onto my forearms. "Ms. Silver," he says. "Welcome!"

He smiles and gestures to the same table I had for dinner.

"Be our guest," he says.

"Has Monica left?" I ask.

He looks around. "She is somewhere, probably. I will tell her. I am Marco. I'm glad you have met."

I sit and am brought a silver carafe filled with coffee. It

comes out steaming and strong—nearly black—and I pour a touch of cream into it and watch it transform.

Breakfast is a buffet set up inside. There are platters of fresh fruits fanned out like rainbows—melons and kiwis and bright yellow pineapple. There are breads, muffins, cinnamon rolls, and croissants next to ramekins of butter dusted with sea salt. There are eggs, sausage, and cheeses—Parmesan and blue, Halloumi and a soft chèvre.

I put a buttery roll, a chunk of juicy grapes, and some pear on a plate and take it outside. When I emerge back out onto the terrace, the man from upstairs is sitting at a table two feet away from mine.

He waves.

"Hello," he says. "You again. How's the spread this morning?"

I tilt my plate toward him in answer.

"I've been here a week," he says. "I think I've put on ten pounds of pure zeppole."

He's in very good shape, so I take his self-deprecation to be hyperbole.

I look to the seat across from him. It's empty. But who comes to Positano alone? Who but me.

"It looks great," I say. "The spread, I mean."

He laughs. "Your plate looks like a warm-up."

I look down at it. The sliced pear is already wilting. I think about last night's ravioli. "I think you're right."

He stands, tossing his napkin down on his chair.

"Follow me," he says.

I put my plate down and pivot back inside. He hands me a fresh one from a stack. They're warm. I press my palms into the underside.

"Okay, you got fruit, that's good," he says. "But you skipped the watermelon. It's the best they have."

He piles some juicy, bright pink slices on my plate.

"Now the cheese. Skip the soft ones, but a small slice of Parmesan in the morning is a delicacy. Trust me."

He uses silver tongs and slips a grainy piece onto my plate. Then puts another.

"For good measure," he says.

"Next we skip the eggs and head to secure a cornetto. If we come at eight-thirty, these are gone."

By the window there is a tray of Italian croissants. He lifts two onto my plate.

"Trust me," he says when I begin to object. "They put a hint of lemon in them. You will want another."

"I am beginning to see what you mean with the ten pounds," I say.

"It's Italy," he tells me. "Pleasure is the cornerstone of the program."

He holds his arm out in front of him, and I lead the way onto the balcony.

When we get back, we each stop in front of our respective tables, but neither one of us sits.

"This seems silly," he says. "Would you like to join me?"

"Is someone else coming down?" I look up toward the stairwell, a ceremonious gesture.

"Nope," he says. He sits, rotating his plate in front of him. "It's just me. I'm here for work."

"Not a bad gig."

He looks up at me, and I notice how symmetrical his face is. One eyebrow doesn't even lift higher than the other. Everything in equal and perfect order.

I sit.

"How about you?" he asks. He pours me coffee from the pot. "What brings you to Positano?"

When we first decided we wanted to go, for real, it was almost three years ago, nine months before she got sick. My mother wasn't someone who put things off, but even though she spoke often about Italy, about wanting to return, the idea was not made manifest until then.

There was always a reason not to. It was far, true. She didn't want to leave my father for that long. The cost was prohibitive to do it the way she'd want to. But I could also always tell how she felt about this place. The reverence with which she spoke about it.

It was Eric who told me I should buy the plane tickets and surprise her for her sixtieth birthday.

"Just do it," he said. "She'll love it, and she won't say no."

I printed out the receipt and slipped it onto the table the next Friday night at my parents' house.

"What is this?" my mother said, picking it up.

"Read it," Eric said. He was grinning. He took my hand under the table.

She looked from the paper back up to me. "Katy. I don't understand."

"We're going," I told her. "You and me. For your sixtieth. We're going to Italy."

Her eyes got wide, and then she did something I rarely saw my mother do. I can count on one hand the number of times, in all thirty years I spent with her, that I remember seeing my mother cry. But that night at the kitchen table she looked over the paper, and she wept.

Eric looked alarmed, but my eyes welled with tears, too. I

knew this meant something to her—to go, to show me who she was before I came along—and I felt a fierce pull of love for her, for all the women she had been before me, all the women I never got to know.

"Are you happy?" I asked, even though I knew.

"Darling," she said. She looked up. Her eyes were wet and open. She touched her fingertips to my face. "I couldn't have dreamed it better."

The man across the table stares at me. His question hangs between us: *What brings you to Positano?*

"A small vacation," I say. "I was supposed to come with a friend, but she couldn't make it."

I realize, when I say this, that I do not have my wedding and engagement rings on. I took them off yesterday when I arrived—my fingers swollen from the travel and humidity. They are in the safe with the rest of my jewelry and cell phone. I have not opened it since.

"Her loss," he says. "My gain."

It is not flirtatious, at least not entirely. It's more just a statement of fact. He uses a knife to cut a watermelon slice diagonally and then spears it with a fork. Some sticky juice runs down the side of his plate and pools in the center.

"So good," he says, mouth full. "You need to get in on this."

I do the same. He's right: it's perfect. Cold and crisp and sweet.

"What job requires you to eat breakfast on a balcony in Positano?" I ask him. "Travel writer?"

"I work for a hotel chain," he says.

"Ah," I say. "Which one?"

He doesn't immediately answer.

"Do you want me to guess?" I ask.

He squints. "I would love that, actually. But you'll never get it."

"Hyatt."

He shakes his head.

"St. Regis."

"Nope."

"Hilton."

"Well, now I'm just offended."

"I give up," I say.

"The Dorchester," he says. "I'm on the team in charge of new acquisitions."

I spring forward, surprising us both. "The Bel-Air, right? It's one of my favorite places in Los Angeles." I smile, a little embarrassed. "That's where I live."

"The Beverly Hills," he says. "But yes."

"You live in LA, too?" I say. "That's a coincidence."

He shakes his head. "Officially Chicago. But I'm there often for work. Can't beat the weather."

"Can't you?" I gesture outward, toward the emerging day.

"Point taken, but only for the prime season."

"You've been here a week?"

He nods. "Scouting some locations, more or less. It's just special here, special to me. Positano took a hit a few years back, but this town doesn't change much. It's been popular for a long time, and I feel like I've been coming for almost that long myself. I imagine it will only continue, so now my company wants to invest. Own a little piece of paradise, so to speak."

"Your company, the Dorchester Group."

"Indeed." He waves his hand in front of his face like he's clearing away a bug.

"So," he says. "Lonely traveler. What's your name? I don't even know."

"Katy," I say.

"Katy what?"

"Katy Silver."

"Adam Westbrooke," he says. He holds out his hand. I take it. "It's nice to meet you."

"You too."

We eat in silence for a few moments, punctuated by the activity of the morning. Couples come down to eat; the street below us becomes active with cars and bicycles. The bells ring out: it's 9 a.m.

Adam stretches. "That's my cue," he says. "I should probably head out."

"Busy day?"

"I have a few meetings," he says. "But if you're free later, would you like to meet for a drink?"

I think about my wedding band tucked upstairs. Is this a date? Or just two fellow travelers enjoying each other's company? We just met. We're in a foreign country. I'm alone.

"Yes."

"Great," he says. "I'll meet you downstairs here at eight."

"Sounds good."

"Have a great day, Katy," he says. He pushes back his chair and stands. His hair is blond, then red. It changes color in the sun.

He leans down close and plants a kiss on either cheek. I smell his smell—cologne, sweat, the scent of the sea. I don't feel even the hint of stubble.

"See you later."

When he's gone, I think about what I want to do today. The

itinerary is tucked upstairs, but I still want to visit my mother's favorite places. Now that I don't have a schedule, I can, as Monica said yesterday, explore. There was a restaurant she always talked about in town. Chez Black, right on the water. We were supposed to go tomorrow night. But today I want to explore as she did when she was first here.

Just then Marco appears, right at my chair.

"You left this," he says, holding out my room key and gesturing to the other table.

"Oh, yes, sorry. Thank you."

"And I see you've met Adam."

"Upstairs," I say, tucking the key into my bag. "He was borrowing a book from the little library and introduced himself."

Marco shakes his head. "He'd borrow this whole place if he could."

"What do you mean?"

Marco rolls his eyes. "This young guy here." He gestures to Adam's empty seat. "He's trying to buy my hotel."

Chapter Six

"Adam, he comes here every year. This year he comes and he has this stack of papers." Marco holds his hands like an accordion in front of him. "And he tells me, proposal. He wants to buy Poseidon."

I'm struck by two emotions. The first is anger at Adam at trying to Americanize this Italian gem. The second is bewilderment that Marco is sharing this information with me so readily, and easily. We just met an hour ago.

"I'm assuming you are not interested?" I ask.

Marco laughs. "This hotel has been in our family for many years! Never. Poseidon is like my child."

"You should tell him to back off, then," I say. I think about Adam's smile at breakfast. His easy confidence. His charm. They annoy me now.

Marco shrugs. "He knows; he does not care. It is no matter, though. There is very little we must do that will not be done in time."

I nod, although that is a blatant lie. If we had caught my mother's cancer earlier, if we had *done something* about it, she wouldn't be dead. She'd be here right now, with me, listening to Marco with a compassionate ear. She'd have the best advice for him, too.

I push back my chair.

"I have not upset you, Ms. Silver?"

"No, of course not," I say. And then in a moment, a flash, a millisecond, I find myself crying. I cried up until my mother's death, daily, hourly, even. Everything set me off. Touching the coffee maker before the sun came up, the elaborate one I had wanted but wouldn't buy for myself, so she'd given it to us for our wedding. The gardenia soap in the shower we bought on a trip to Santa Barbara years ago, and which I now keep a steady supply of. The drawer of plastic forks from delivery and take-out meals, because she could never bear to throw away plastic. Everything was a reminder of what I was losing, of what was slipping away.

But after her death it was like something in me shut off. I was numb. Frozen. I couldn't cry. Not when the hospice nurse declared her gone, not at her funeral, not when I heard my father, a stoic man, wailing in the kitchen below us. I didn't know what was wrong with me. I was worried, maybe, that she had taken my heart with her.

Marco does not look surprised or uncomfortable. Instead, he puts a large, warm hand on my shoulder.

"It is hard," he says.

I wipe my eyes. "What?"

"You have lost the one you were meant to come with, no?"

I think about my mother, radiant and alive, in a visor, white pants, and a loose open linen shirt, straw bag over her shoulder, laughing. I haven't thought about her this way, so vibrant, in so long. The image nearly startles me.

I nod.

Marco smiles small. He tilts his head to the side. "Positano is a good place to let life return to you."

I swallow. "I don't know," I say.

Marco's face brightens. "In time," he says. "In time, you will discover. And in the meantime, enjoy."

He releases me and looks out over the balcony. The sun is now fully up. Things are light and clear.

"Have a lovely day, Ms. Silver. I suggest a walk to town. Take in the beach and have a lovely lunch at Chez Black."

I'm startled by his suggestion. It's the one place I've known by name for years.

"The caprese is excellent, and you can watch all the people go by," he continues.

"Do I need a reservation?"

"For lunch? No. Just walk in and say you're a guest of Hotel Poseidon. They will take care of you."

"Thank you, Marco."

"Pleasure. You need anything else, you ask. No hesitating."

He leaves, and I head downstairs. I spot a young woman at the front desk. She's stunning: dark hair, olive skin, probably in her mid-twenties. She has a beautiful turquoise pendant around her neck, held together by a leather chain.

She is helping a couple in their sixties plan a day trip.

"Is a small boat better for seasickness or a ferry?" the man asks.

The woman at the desk gives me a small wave, and I wave back.

I walk outside and am met with cheerful noise. A store across the street sells produce outside. Lemons sit next to plump tomatoes. Two young women spill out, speaking fast and furious Italian. They swig from sweating lemonade glasses.

I put my hat on and start following the sidewalk downward. Tiny Italian cars and Vespas pass, but the road isn't super busy. When I get a few paces down, I spot a cluster of clothing boutiques. Dresses hand painted with oranges. White linen and lace cover-ups. I finger an ocean-blue slip dress with spaghetti straps and tiered hem.

I keep walking. Viale Pasitea is the main and only road that leads down to the ocean, unless you take the steps. In and around shops and pensiones, hotels and markets, there are staircases leading up into the hills of Positano and down to the sea. Hundreds and hundreds of stairs.

The dome in the center of town belongs to the church, where the bells ring out. Right now they are silent, but as I pass by the square where the Church of Santa Maria Assunta stands I see the ocean. It's down one short flight of stairs and then a pathway filled with shops. When I get down, there is a clothing stand, then the restaurant, splayed out right in front of the sand.

I move quickly toward it, my heart rate accelerating. It is early, but there are still some customers sitting and smoking. Turquoise chairs are tucked under white-clothed tables. A seashell sign contains the words *Chez Black*.

"Buongiorno, signora," a waiter says. He can't be more than seventeen, with bright green eyes and pockmarked skin. "Can I help you?"

"Just looking," I say. I can feel my heart in my lungs, the surge of anxiety and excitement, the possibility, the *hope*.

"Perfetto." He gestures his arm toward the inside of the restaurant. I scan the tables. I don't know what I'm hoping to find—some relic she left behind thirty years ago, her name scrawled into the wall, or a message telling me what to do next?

But the restaurant is near empty, the patrons undisturbed. She is not here, of course. Why would she be? She is dead.

I hear the familiar siren of oncoming dread. The sound of a roaring engine before a tsunami. The past forty-eight hours have been a reprieve of this grief, the intensity of her absence. But now I feel it curling back—about to crescendo and sweep me under.

"Excuse me," I say.

"You eat, miss?"

I shake my head. "No, I'm sorry. I'm so sorry."

I leave, take up my sandals in my hand, and pace down to the ocean. Some families are already at the small beach, on towels, playing in the sand. Charter boats bob close to the dock where people huddle, waiting for the next ship to Capri, Ravello, the beach club for the day. A woman on the dock trips, and a man catches her. They embrace, their lips meeting. The roaring in my chest gets louder and louder.

At the water's edge, I sink down. I don't have a towel, so I sit in the damp sand. I want to call Eric. I miss my mother. I suddenly feel utterly and completely foolish for coming here. What did I expect to happen? Did I think I'd find her, sitting at a table at Chez Black about to order lunch?

I realize what a long way from home I am, how many planes and trains and cars it will take to get back. I've never even been on a weekend away by myself, and now I'm alone on the other side of the world.

I miss her I miss her I miss her.

I miss her warmth and her guidance and the sound of her voice. I miss her telling me it was really all going to be okay and believing it, because she was at the wheel. I miss her hugs and her laughter and her lipstick, Clinique Black Honey. I miss the way she could plan a party in under an hour. I miss having the answers, because I had her.

I look out over the horizon, the sun high overhead. The wide expanse of sea. It seems impossible she is nowhere. It seems impossible, but it's true.

I swallow down an unsteady breath and stand. I cannot be here for two weeks. I cannot even be here for two days. I hadn't considered the fact that I've never been alone in my life, not really. I didn't think about how I went from my parents' house to a dorm room to an apartment with Eric. I do not know how to do this.

I'll go home. I'll tell Eric I made a mistake, that this is hard and I'm sorry. I'll make amends, and life will go on.

I climb the stairs back up to the church. I take the road back up to the hotel, past the shops. A woman calls out: "Buongiorno, signora!" I do not turn. I am already gone.

Outside the hotel, a young man arrives for his shift. He parks his Vespa out front as he chats with a woman across the street, the one who must own the small grocery. They speak quickly, and I do not understand them.

I take the four stairs up to the lobby, and when I step inside, there she is. She is talking to a man behind the desk. She is wearing a dress from one of the shops in town—green with yellow lemons, revealing her slim and tan shoulders. Her sunglasses are perched high atop her head, holding her long auburn hair in place. She waves her arms around. A small package sits on the welcome desk in front of her.

"No, no, the hotel always mails for me. I have done it before. Many times. I promise."

"To post?"

"To post, yes." She looks relieved. I have not exhaled. "Yes, to post! And here, for payment." She slides a bill across the table.

"Perfetto, grazie," the man at the desk says.

I am trying to get a good look at her, to confirm what it is I already know to be true, when she turns. And when she does, the wind is knocked out of me. Because I'd know her anywhere. I'd know her in Brentwood and I'd know her in Positano. I'd know her at sixty and sixteen and thirty, as she stands in front of me today.

Impossibly, the woman at the desk is my mother.

"Mom," I whisper, and then the world goes black.

Chapter Seven

When I come to, I am lying on the cold marble of the lobby floor, and my mother—or the thirty-year-old version of her—is holding me.

I open my eyes and quickly close them again because I'm right, she's here, and this feels so good, being in her arms, I don't want to lose a single second of it. She smells like her and sounds like her, and I want to live here, in this moment, forever.

But I can't, because in an instant she's gently shaking me, and I force my eyes open again.

"Hey, are you okay? You just fainted," she says. She peers at me. I have a flash of her ten years from now—bent over me with a thermometer during a particularly bad bout of the flu.

The man from the desk is crouched next to us, too. "Is hot, is hot," he says. He fans himself as if demonstrating, then me.

"Water," my mother commands, and he scurries off. "We'll get you something to drink, just a second."

She studies me, and I study her back.

Her skin is smooth, young, and tan—subjected to a sun that has not done its damage yet. She looks exactly as she did in the old photos, the ones dotting the shelves of my parents' television room. Her hair is down—long and straight, nothing like my curly mane. Her eyes are liquid green.

"You're here," I say.

Her eyebrows knit together. "You're going to be all right," she says. "I think Joseph is right—you just had some heat-stroke." She looks over her shoulder, toward the direction he disappeared in. "Do you know your name? Where you are?"

I laugh, because it's absurd. My mother asking me for my name. *It's me*, I want to say. *It's me, your daughter.* But I can tell from the way she's looking at me that she's never seen me before in her life. Of course she hasn't.

"Katy," I say.

She smiles; it's almost sympathetic. "That's a very nice name. I'm Carol."

I scramble to my feet, and she stands up, too. "Easy, now," she says as Joseph appears with the water.

"Thank you." She takes the bottle from Joseph and twists the top off before handing it to me. She looks on encouragingly. "Go on," she says. "You're probably dehydrated."

I drink. I take four large gulps and then replace the cap.

She looks satisfied. "There you go. Do you feel better now?"

How can I possibly answer that? My dead mother is standing in front of me at a seaside hotel on the coast of Italy. Do I feel better? I feel insane. I feel ecstatic. I feel like something might be seriously wrong with me.

"What are you doing here?" I ask her.

She laughs. "Right place, right time, I suppose," she says. "Joseph was helping me with a package. I rent a little pensione not far up the road. It's just a room, really."

I feel a smile spread over my face, too, mirroring her own.

It's so simple and wonderful and obvious. A room of her own. *I rented this little pensione up the street from Hotel Poseidon. We slept until noon and drank rosé on the water.*

I've found my mother in her summer of freedom. I've found her in the time before me or my father. I've found her in the summer of Chez Black, days on the beach and long nights spent talking under the stars. Here she is. Here she actually is. Young and unencumbered and so very much alive.

I got her back, I think. *Come to me.*

"Are you sure you're all right?"

"Yes," I say. And then, empowered by her, here, in front of me now, I plow forward: "I'm sorry, you're right, it must be the heat. I just got in and I'm not used to it. Probably dehydrated from the trip yesterday, too."

"You just arrived!" she says. "How wonderful. From where? There aren't many Americans now, seeing as it's still early in the season. I've been here for a few weeks, and I feel like I already live here. It's a small town."

She talks with her hands, just like always. Animated and energetic.

"It's perfect," I say, watching her.

She's beautiful, I realize suddenly. Not that I didn't always know my mother was pretty; I did. She had impeccable style, and her hair was always in place, and her features were sharp and striking. But here, now, she glows. Her face is radiant, not a stitch of makeup, the light shining through her sun-kissed skin. Her legs are strong and lean, wearing just the slightest dusting of a bronzed tan.

"California," I tell her. "Los Angeles."

Her eyes get wide. "Me too!" She throws her hands up and then lets them settle on top of her head. "What are the odds?"

Zero. One hundred percent.

"I've been in LA about five years now, and I love it. I came from Boston, can you believe it? It's freezing there just about all the time. Who are you here with?" She glances up the stairs and squints, as if she can intuit the answer.

"I'm alone," I tell her.

She smiles wide. "Me too."

Joseph looks back and forth between us. "Okay, miss?"

"I think so," I say. "Thank you so much."

"I should get going," my mother says. She flips her watch over.

I grope forward. She cannot leave. I cannot let her leave.

"No!" I say. "You can't go."

She looks curiously at me, and I recover.

"I mean, we should have lunch."

Her face relaxes. "I'm going to Da Adolfo today. You can join if you'd like. The boat leaves at one or one-thirty."

"Sorry, one or one-thirty?"

Carol laughs. "It's Italy," she says. "Sometimes it's one, sometimes it's one-thirty, sometimes it's not at all." She holds her hands out like a Roman scale. "You just show up and hope for the best!"

She gives Joseph a little bow. "Thank you, truly." To me: "I'll meet you at the dock at one, then, yes?"

I nod. "Yes. I'll be there."

And then she leans in close to me. I breathe in the heady smell of her. My mother. She kisses me, once on each cheek. "Ciao, Katy."

It's when she pulls back that I realize I'm still clutching her arm.

She places her hand over mine. "You'll be fine," she says.

"Just water and a little prosecco, maybe. Have a coffee and lie down. All the beverages!" Another rule of Carol's: you can never drink enough water.

She turns, waves, and walks through the doors, disappearing down the steps and into the street below.

When she's gone, so is Joseph, and Marco comes strolling inside. I rush up to him.

"Marco," I say. "Did you just see a woman leaving here? She had lemons on her dress. Her hair was brown and long and straight. She's beautiful. Please tell me you just saw her."

Marco lifts his hands. "Half the women in Positano have lemons on their dresses," he says. "And they are all beautiful." He winks at me.

"What time does the boat for Da Adolfo leave?" I ask him.

Just then the young woman appears behind the desk.

"This is Nika," Marco says. "She is family. She works here with me. Nika, say hello to Ms. Silver."

"We met earlier," I say. "Briefly, at the desk."

"Of course," Marco says. "That is right. Nika, she is everywhere."

"Hi," I say.

Nika blushes. "Hello," she says. "Buongiorno."

"Ms. Silver would like to go to Da Adolfo today."

"Oh," I say. "No, I don't need a reservation. Just wondering what time the boat leaves."

"One," Nika says.

"Or one-thirty." Marco holds his hands up and gently shakes his head back and forth, like, *Italy.*

Chapter Eight

I get to the dock at 12:45. I do not want to risk anything. I most definitely do not want to risk missing her. I'm now wearing a fringe-trimmed caftan cover-up over a bathing suit. My mother and I bought it on a trip to the Westfield Century City Mall. It was supposed to be for a weekend Eric and I were taking to Palm Springs for the wedding of his colleague. We ended up getting the flu and skipping the trip, and I've never worn it before. Today I paired it with waterproof sandals and my trusty, wide-brimmed sun hat.

It occurred to me, while I was getting ready, that perhaps I hit my head harder than I thought. That maybe I was in some kind of fever dream—could my mother really be here? But I saw her before I fell, and the recent memory is too real to be an imagined fiction. I have no other explanation besides the impossible.

The clock sneaks to 1:00, and I look around with anticipation. A family with two young children walks up to the dock, but they've booked a private water taxi. As they climb inside, one of the children, a boy probably four years old, starts yelling, "Il fait chaud! J'ai faim!"

One o'clock gives way to 1:15, and I take a seat on the ledge of the dock. The sun overhead is high and beats down hard. I take some sunscreen out of my bag and reapply it on my arms, shoulders, the back of my neck.

One-thirty. I stand. An expectant bubbling in my stomach settles into a knot. No boat, no Mom. I shake my head. Stupid, foolish, that I thought she'd show. Maybe, even, that I thought she was here at all. How could I have let her out of my sight?

And then in the distance I see a boat bobbling on the horizon. A red wooden fish is fixed to the top with *Da Adolfo* printed on it.

"Da Adolfo!"

In a split second, two things happen. The first is that someone grabs my arm, hard. The second is that my sandal gets caught in the wooden slats of the dock. I wobble, swinging my arms to steady myself, but it's no use. I'm right at the ledge, and before I can blink, I fall back-first into the water. It's not until I hit the surface that I realize whoever grabbed my arm has toppled in with me.

I come up, splashing and gasping, to see my mother, next to me, bobbing to the surface.

"Katy!" she says. She flicks some hair out of her face. "We have to stop meeting like this!"

She smiles at me, and I burst out laughing. I tread water, overcome with a relief so strong it's comical. I can't remember the last time I laughed, and I let it take me over now. I float up onto my back, still hiccuping in hysterics.

"Out of water!" the driver calls. The boat hasn't yet reached us but is beginning to slow down. I see that it's small, a tiny speedboat, and I can make out the driver now that he's close enough. He looks young, early twenties, maybe.

"Oy, Carol!"

A man on the dock waves, swings his legs over the edge of the dock, and reaches down his hand. Carol gestures for me to be helped first. I swim over and reach out my hand to meet his, and he grabs on. It feels like my arm is being pulled out of its socket, but once I've gotten a little height, I plant my free hand on the dock, and with every ounce of strength in my five-foot-four body, I hoist myself onto the dock. I lie there, breathing hard.

My mother's rescue is much simpler. She uses one foot on the side of the dock for leverage and then swings her body over. It definitely helps that she's taller.

We stand back on solid ground, looking at each other, the remnants of laughter still bubbling through our bodies.

Our rescue hero steps forward, and my mother makes introductions.

"Katy, this is Remo. Remo, Katy," she says, still out of breath.

"Hi, Remo," I say. "Nice to meet you."

Remo slips his arm around my mother. My stomach tightens.

"Ciao, Katy."

My mother wasn't one to talk about the details of her past, romantically speaking. She was a woman with well-drawn lines around her life. She lived in color about so much—her sense of beauty, design, her love of community—but her romantic past always seemed off-limits. She'd say things to me like "That was another lifetime, Katy. Who could remember?"

I called her and told her when I met Eric, then when I realized I first loved him, but we didn't talk about sex the way some daughters and mothers do. I didn't ask her questions—about her own experience—or share the details of mine. There was nothing outside the walls of our relationship, really, but sex felt like it was right on the perimeter. And we just didn't cross the line.

When she told me about this summer in Positano, she would say it had been magical, transformational, and full of good food and wine, but she never talked about another person.

Yet here Remo is.

The driver calls out to us. "Da Adolfo!"

"Antonio, *aspetti,* we're *coming*," my mother says.

She goes over to the boat, and the driver, Antonio, presumably, holds out his hand for her. She gets in, then me, then Remo. I'm soaking wet, the cotton of my caftan clinging to me like a second skin.

She is still in her lemon dress, and as soon as we're seated she pulls it up and over her head, revealing a black one-piece with pinpoint polka dots underneath. She leans her head back and closes her eyes, soaking up the sun. I shudder to think of Carol Silver, sans sun hat, letting the rays into her skin like they're welcome.

"I like your bathing suit," I say. It feels stupid to compliment her like this, but I want her to open her eyes, to engage with me.

"Take off your dress and you'll dry faster," she tells me, eyes still closed. "That thing looks like a wet blanket on you."

She didn't like it when we bought it, either. "You look like a grandmother, but I know it's the style now."

The boat begins to peel away. Remo and Antonio speak in harsh staccato at the wheel over the increasing sound of the water.

I exhale. Then I peel up the hem and yank it up and off. My sun hat flies against the back of my head, kept in place by the string around my neck. I'm wearing a pink-and-yellow bikini, tied on the side. The wind picks up as we get moving, and she yelps, pulling her hair back.

"Antonio!" she yells. "Take it easy! Katy hasn't been on a death ride before."

"This is a place for lunch, right?" I yell to her.

"You'll love it!" she says to me. "It's a restaurant in this little cove. They have the best seafood!"

How do you know all of this? I want to ask. *Who is Remo? How long will you stay?* But the boat is moving fast now, and all my words are caught up in the wind and tossed out to sea before they can be heard.

I take out my camera, an old Leica, the one Eric bought for me after our honeymoon. He told me the photos on my iPhone were grainy. Back then, he was right. I haven't taken a photo in forever—it's something I used to love, another thing that has been lost to the Time Before.

I take the lens cover off, and I aim the camera at her. The boat jostles me around, the water kicking up and dusting us as we move. She stretches her legs out on the seat and tosses her head back, her lips parted. I snap the picture. I feel a tug of something so deep down inside me, so hidden, I wonder if it belongs to me at all.

This is my mother. My glorious, dazzling mother. Here, now, in all her glory. Unencumbered, I think, by anything that comes after.

Chapter Nine

My parents had a good marriage. Was it great? I think maybe, probably, even, but I'm not sure I can be the judge. I only know that when it came to my family, it often felt like my father was an outsider, the one observing the natural rhythm of my mother and me. I knew they loved each other. I saw it in how much time they chose to spend together, the gifts my father would bring home to my mother—flowers, clothing, the special-occasion necklace she had seen and loved but would never buy. I saw it in the way my mother made his favorite meal every Friday night, did all of his shopping, and, for thirty years of marriage, cut his hair. I saw it in the way he looked at her.

What I wasn't sure of, what I did not know, was if they were soul mates, if they even believed in them. I did not know if my father lit my mother up on the inside. I did not know if they had the kind of marriage that made you say: *I just knew.*

Chuck and Carol were set up through mutual friends. She was a young gallerina from the East Coast, and my father was an up-and-coming clothing designer, born and bred in LA.

They bonded over a shared love of *Casablanca*, guacamole, and Patti Smith.

"He used to play me records until three o'clock in the morning," my mother would say.

Did she recognize him when she saw him? Was it love at first sight? Or was it the quiet recognition of the possibility of a good life?

The boat slows, and Antonio hops out, wading through the water to pull us to what can barely be described as a pier. It's really just a wood plank that leads up to the shore of what surely is the world's tiniest beach, if you can even call it that. Women in bikinis and men in swim trunks lounge atop rocks and in green-and-white-striped canvas chairs wedged into the rocky-sand beach. Behind them are two restaurants—an all-white building and the blue of Da Adolfo.

Remo hops onto the dock and offers his hand to my mother, who nods to me. "Katy first."

The boat wobbles violently, but I'm still wet from our prior encounter, so what's the worst that could happen?

I take Remo's hand and make it to the pier. She follows. And then the three of us make our way to shore.

"Come back when you come back!" my mother calls to Antonio. Her hand is holding her hair back like a clip.

There is an ease, a casualness to her that I've never seen. Or if I have, I don't remember it. *Come back when you come back?* Who is this woman?

Remo gets us a table close to the sea, and we sit. A basket of bread and some olive oil is already waiting for us. The oil comes in a little blue-and-red ceramic dish outlined with white fish. Black flies land periodically on the table, but the wind keeps them away, for the most part. The ocean crashes on the rocks next to us, and two couples lounge in beach chairs by the edge. Otherwise, it's empty.

"You are lucky to be here now," Remo says. "Another three weeks, and Positano is infested."

"Tourists," Carol clarifies. "Not bugs."

"Same, same," Remo says, smiling.

They sit on one end of the table, and me the other. I study my mother. Again and again and again. The living, breathing beauty of her now. So current, so present, practically overflowing, that I feel if I squeezed her, I'd be able to capture the runoff.

"Remo, do you live in Positano?" I ask.

I take a moment to really look at him. He's handsome, there's no doubt about that. He looks a little like a Roman god. Tanned torso, locks of curly brown hair, and crystal-blue eyes.

"I live in Naples, but in the summer I come to Positano because in the summer, that is where the money is."

"Remo works at Buca di Bacco," she says.

"The hotel?" I remember reading about it during our research for the trip.

"Hotel e ristorante," Remo says. "I am a cameriere, ah, waiter." Remo smiles.

"It's a very respected profession in Italy," she says. "It's a shame America doesn't really have the same tradition."

My parents only go to two restaurants regularly, and they're both in Beverly Hills: Craig's and Porta Via. They get the same four entrées. My father is a creature of habit. Rarely and occasionally my mother will get him to try something outside his comfort zone—Eveleigh in West Hollywood, Perch downtown.

The waiter appears, and Remo shakes his hand warmly. "Buongiorno, signore."

"Buongiorno," Carol says. She takes a long swig of water and wrings out her hair onto the sandy floor.

Remo begins ordering swiftly in Italian. I look to Carol.

"Everything will be delicious," she says. "Don't worry. Remo brought me here last week, and it is best to just go with it."

I've never heard my mother use the phrase *just go with it*, not once.

"Are you guys . . ." I start, but Carol answers before I can finish.

"Friends, yes?" she says. "He's taken me under his wing and shown me Positano from a local's perspective." She leans across the table conspiratorially. "But he is very handsome."

I look to Remo. He is still immersed in conversation. "Um, yes."

"So what brings you to Positano, Katy?" my mother asks. "Besides the obvious."

"And what's that?"

"Italy," she says, winking at me.

A bottle of rosé and glasses show up, and Remo pours for us, turning back to the table, to the conversation.

"It's a beautiful place, no?" Remo says.

I nod. I'm not sure what to say. *My mother died and I don't know what to do with my life anymore, so I left my husband and came here to Italy.*

Oh yeah and by the way, you're her.

"I needed a break," I say, truthfully. My mother smiles; Remo refills his water glass.

"Well, I'll drink to your break," she says.

We clink, and the liquid goes down crisp and sweet and smooth.

I flash on the last normal lunch I had with my mother. It was a warm December day, and we had just done some shopping at the Grove in West Hollywood. She wanted to try a new place and sit outside with me, so we settled on a vegan Mexican restaurant called Gracias Madre on Melrose. They have an outdoor patio and exceptional guacamole.

"Should we have a glass of wine?" she asked when we sat down.

My mother wasn't a daytime drinker. She'd have half a glass of wine if we were pouring, nothing if we weren't. I'd seen her order a martini at a late lunch once in my life, at a New York bar after a Broadway production of *Jersey Boys*.

I wanted to ask if she was sure. She was two months into the cancer, into treatment. We hadn't yet moved onto the dire stuff, though. It was a concoction of pills that sometimes left her exhausted but hadn't changed her face or her hair. You wouldn't know anything was wrong to look at her.

"Yes," I said. "Let's do it."

We got two glasses of Sancerre, and the waiter poured at the table. She tasted.

"Delicious," she said.

I remember she was wearing a short-sleeved orange cashmere sweater and brown plaid trousers. She had on brown loafers and a handkerchief tied around her Longchamp shopper.

"Do you think we should go back for the skirt from J.Crew?" she asked me.

It was velvet and short, with a sparkle at the hem. Cute but overpriced, we had ultimately decided. And the fabric wasn't as good as she wanted it to be—fast fashion never was. And it made her furious that nothing was ever lined. I was surprised she brought it back up now. My mother didn't have second thoughts too often.

"I think it's fine," I said.

She smiled. "It would be pretty with a black T-shirt."

"I have enough skirts."

"Still," she said. "I think we should get it."

I remember she downed her glass of wine quickly. And I remember thinking that even though we had been granted this day, this time—shopping, lunch, midday wine—so buoyant and joyful—the actual evidence of her sickness was the indulgence itself.

But sitting here with her now—thirty years earlier, on the other side of the world—watching her drink chilled rosé like it's water—I think that maybe there were parts of her I never made an effort to see. Parts of her that just wanted to drink outside in the sunshine on a Wednesday. And go back for skirts, just because.

Lunch is good, but Il Tridente at Hotel Poseidon is better. There is grilled Halloumi on a bed of lettuce, calamari, caprese, and lots of wine.

"Remo took me to Capri last weekend," my mother says. "It's overrated, in my opinion. Positano is far more beautiful. More authentic, too. It feels far more connected to the Italian culture here than it does there."

Remo shakes his head. "Capri is nice on the water. On the land, less."

My parents and I took a trip to London when I was twelve years old. We stayed near Westminster, saw a production of *Wicked*, and rode the London Eye. That's as close to a European vacation as I've ever gotten.

"It is a hard place to get to, and a hard place to leave, but a very easy place to stay," my mother says. "I came for the first time with my parents when I was a little girl, and I never forgot it."

I'm not sure I knew about that trip. There's so much I never asked. And there is so much I want to know, now.

"Where else have you been here?"

"I went to Ravello, which was heaven. And Naples, which I didn't care for. That's where Remo is from. Rome is wonderful, obviously."

"I've never been to Italy before," I say.

"Well," my mother says, reaching across the table for my hand, "you've picked a perfect time to be here."

Remo tells us about the beauty of Ravello, one town over, and asks if I've been to Capri—I tell him I just got here.

"There is plenty of time," Carol says. "Italy is about taking it slow."

When we finally stand, I feel a little light-headed.

We push back our chairs and make our way outside to the rocks. There is a lounge chair open, and my mother throws her bag down, and I do the same. Then she lifts her dress up and over her head. I'm struck by the motion—so carefree, so thought-less. I think about my mother in Palm Springs, in Malibu. Her one-piece always offset by a well-placed sarong, her arms covered from the sun in a light linen shirt. She had a great body, always did. But there was a modesty to her that is not apparent here. When did it arrive? When did she decide that her body was something she should pay so much attention to? That it shouldn't be admired?

She always loved the water, though. She loved to swim. She'd do laps in the pool every morning, her L.L.Bean hat like a ball floating on the surface.

I follow her, and then we're padding into the ocean. I duck under the water, and when I come up, she's floating on her back, eyes closed. I want to photograph her, capture this moment, but instead I copy her. We stay that way, just floating, until Antonio's boat appears at the dock.

We board, soaked, and are transported back to the port of Positano. By the time we get there the sun is sinking lower in the sky. The boat docks, and Remo helps us off. We thank Antonio, and he tips his hat before pulling away.

"Thank you," I say to my mother. "I had a really great day. The best I've had in a while."

"Thank *you*," she says. "It's lovely to make a new friend."

I realize I haven't even asked her how long she is staying. "Will you be here tomorrow?" I say. I can feel the freneticism growing inside. The sudden desperation to hold on to her after a day of leisure.

She smiles. "Of course. I'm taking you to La Tagliata. It's this incredible restaurant high up in the hills. You won't believe it. The bus leaves at four from your hotel, so I can meet you there."

"Where will you go now?" I ask.

"I have to drop Remo off and then pick up a few things at the market. The woman who owns the flat I'm renting is in tonight."

I'm met with images of my mother cooking, laughing, sharing a meal with another woman. I feel a wave of jealousy come over me.

"But I'll see you tomorrow, yes?" She peers at me. And for the briefest, tiniest slivers of time, I think that maybe she recognizes me, too. Maybe something in her is reaching through time and space to deliver her the information she needs to know. That she belongs to me. That we are each other's. Only us. But then Remo taps her shoulder, and the moment is broken.

I nod.

"Good. Tomorrow," she says. She turns to leave, and I am suddenly—standing on the pier, the water moving below us and the wine coursing through my veins—met with the intense need to hug her. I feel it viscerally.

So I do.

I lean forward and capture her in my arms. She smells like salt water and wine and *her.*

"Thank you for today," I say, and release her. Tomorrow.

Chapter Ten

I wake up to a soft rapping at my door.

"One moment," I say, the haze and pressure of a hangover setting in. I look at the clock: it's after 8 p.m. I came back from lunch, just thinking I'd lie down, and now I've been cold asleep for over three hours.

I grab a glass water bottle on the dresser and chug it as I open the door. On the other side is Nika, dressed in a white shirt and high-waisted jeans, hair down. She has a little blush on her cheeks. She looks lovely.

"Hi," I say.

"Hello," she says. "Good evening. You're all right?"

I look down at my crinkled cover-up and feel my face. Despite the sun hat, it feels tight and hot—sunburned, no doubt, from today. I don't think I reapplied sunscreen once after the dock, and the restaurant was almost entirely uncovered.

"Yes," I say. "Too much wine at lunch. Are you . . ."

"Oh!" she says. She rolls her eyes at herself. "The gentleman downstairs was concerned. I told him I would come to check on you. See to it that you are okay."

Adam. Shit.

"Tell him I'll be right down," I say. "And I'm so sorry. Thank you."

Nika nods. "I will."

"Hey, Nika," I say, remembering. "Marco told me Adam is trying to buy the hotel?"

Nika laughs. "Marco thinks everyone is always trying to take this place from him. It is not as desirable as he thinks."

"Really?"

Nika shrugs. "Well, I think it's desirable, of course. I love it. It has been my family's life for many years. I don't know about Adam. Maybe he is trying. But we could use help."

"I'll be right down," I tell her. "Thank you for coming to get me."

"I'll let Mr. Westbrooke know," she says with a smile, then closes the door behind her.

I get in the shower.

It takes me twelve and a half minutes to rinse off, put on a floral summer dress, run a brush through my hair, and put on the most minimum makeup within reach. Blush, lip gloss, a fast swipe of mascara.

When I get downstairs, Adam is seated at the same table he was at breakfast.

"She lives," he says, standing. He's dressed in tan linen pants and a white linen shirt. He has a mala bracelet on, made out of wooden beads. The kind you see at yoga studios all over LA. His blond hair flops down over his forehead. He looks . . . good.

"I'm so sorry," I say. "I had too much wine at lunch and fell asleep. I never day drink."

He grins at me. His teeth, I notice, are very white. "Italy," he says. "What are you going to do?"

Adam gestures to the chair across from him, and I sit.

"You skipped cocktail hour," he says. "But I thought we could have dinner."

Seated now, I feel the familiar sensation in my stomach, like an engine starting. Lunch was ages ago.

"Yes, please," I say. "I'm starving."

Adam opens his menu. "What do you like?" he asks me.

It's such a simple question. Unordinary. But I find myself unable to answer it. I am so used to the pleasure of habit. Do I even like the chopped salad at La Scala? The hazelnut creamer, the color white? Is familiarity a taste? Or just an accustomed tolerance?

"The tomato salad and ravioli are delicious," I say.

Adam smiles. "Oh, I know. But in my opinion, nothing beats their primavera. And there is a salt fish here that is—" He brings his pinched fingers to his lips in a chef's kiss.

"I'll leave it to you, then."

"Why don't we get both," he says. "I'll share if you will."

The way he says it, like he's daring me, makes something inside me turn over.

"Wine?" he says.

I close one eye.

"Oh. Right. Lunch. We'll take it easy."

He orders a glass of Barolo for himself, and I get an iced tea. It takes a little while to explain to our waiter—the same gentleman who served us at breakfast, I learn his name is Carlo—what is involved in an iced tea. What ends up coming out is a pot of black tea and a cup of ice. Fair enough.

"So, Katy," Adam says. "Tell me what your deal is."

"My deal?"

"Your deal."

"I heard you're trying to buy this place," I blurt out. I sit back, rubbing a hand over my face. "I'm sorry; it's none of my business. But Marco seemed kind of upset this morning. And also, I think you lied to me?"

Adam laughs. "I think *omitted* is probably a better verb."

"Lie by omission, then."

Adam holds his hands palms faced upward in surrender. "Fair enough. It's just that people get understandably prickly when they think you're trying to mess with a local and storied establishment. Also, we just met."

"So why are you?"

Adam takes a sip of wine. "I work for a hotel company. That part was true, obviously. I told you they want a piece of property in Positano, also true. I just neglected to mention that this is the piece of property they would like."

"But Marco doesn't want to sell."

Adam shrugs. "They were hit hard recently. I'm not sure they have the money to stay open the way they want to right now. They're struggling. Their margins are close. Remember, Positano only sees tourism four, five months a year, tops."

"This hotel has been in their family for a hundred years." I don't know if that's true, actually, but it *feels* true.

"More like forty, but yes." Adam leans his elbows onto the table. His body hovers closer to me. "Do we really have to talk about this?"

I feel my entire body flush. Right down to my toes.

This is the moment. This is the moment when I say, *Hey, just for the record, I'm married. I mean I don't know HOW married I am, currently, whether this is a break or the beginning of a full-blown divorce or what, exactly, is going on with me and Eric, but there are rings upstairs that up until twenty-four hours ago sat on my finger for five years.*

But I don't. Instead, I say, simply, "No."

Adam sits back. "Good."

The fish comes and it's whole—head, tail, everything—and entirely encapsulated in a giant salt crust. Carlo proudly displays it on a clean white serving dish.

"Gorgeous," Adam says. "Bravo."

Carlo sets up a deboning station a few paces over and starts knocking away the salt crust. It comes off in big, satisfying chunks.

I think about what Eric would do if he were here. Eric is the pickiest eater on the planet. He likes chicken and pasta and broccoli. My mother used to say he never evolved his palate, that he ate like a six-year-old child. She was right, and I think, now, that the reason this experience is so extraordinary is that California Pizza Kitchen was on regular rotation in our household. The only time we ate well was when my mother cooked.

Carlo brings the plates over; the filleted whitefish sits beside sautéed vegetables and roasted baby fingerling potatoes. My stomach rumbles in anticipation.

"This looks incredible," I say.

"Enjoy," Carlo says.

He leaves, and I pick up my fork, lifting off a flaky bite.

"I swear," I say, "I think this hotel has my favorite restaurant in the world?"

Adam looks at me. "It's up there," he says. "But this just tells me you have not been nearly enough places."

I think about Eric and our yearly trip to Palm Springs, about our five-year anniversary in Miami.

"You're not wrong," I say.

"Have you been to Europe before?"

"Yes," I say. It's true, technically. London counts, right?

We sink into the meal. The fish is perfectly buttery; the vegetables are drenched in olive oil; the pasta is al dente. I finally cave and end up ordering a glass of wine.

Adam was raised in Florida but now lives in Chicago. He loves Italy, but not as much as he loves France—France actually has better tomatoes and cheese, he tells me. Provence has the best produce in the world. His mother was born in Paris and spent her childhood there. He speaks fluent French.

He likes hiking, dogs, and air travel. He doesn't love being in the same place too long.

He's single.

He offers the information up in the form of an ex-girlfriend he went to Tokyo with a few months back. It's subtle, but effective.

"It was a terrible trip, but I guess I can't blame the city for our breakup; it was a long time coming."

"I'm sorry," I say.

"I'm not," he says. "Who knows where I'd be now. One thing different, everything different."

I fiddle with my wineglass, swallowing the remainder.

"Are you a dessert person?" Adam asks me.

I have a sweet tooth; I always have. I get it from my father. My mother never cared for sugar, and neither does Eric. "Give me a bag of pretzels over a bar of chocolate any day," my mother used to say.

"Yes," I say. "Definitely."

"They have this berry torte that's seasonal. I'm not sure it's on the menu this year, but I think we can get Carlo to deliver us one."

Sure enough, the berry torte idea is welcomed with enthusiasm, and then minutes later a delicate berry and cream concoction is delivered to our table.

"Ladies first," Adam says, sliding it over to me.

I take a spoonful. It's predictably divine.

"Ohmygod."

He takes a bite, too. "I know."

"I think this is the best thing I've ever tasted. I'm not kidding."

Adam sits back and looks at me. Really looks at me. I feel his gaze on me like it's a hand.

"You haven't told me if there is anyone at home," he says. He picks up an espresso cup that Carlo brought out with the dessert.

I swallow and down some water. I nod.

Adam raises his eyebrows. "So that's a yes."

"Yes, it's a yes."

"I can't say I'm surprised."

"What does that mean?"

He stares at me. His gaze seems to soften, lift. Like before where his palm was, now it's just his fingertips. "You seem like the kind of woman who likes to belong to someone."

I feel his words physically. They strike me right in the sternum.

"I was supposed to be on this trip with my mother," I tell him. "She always loved Positano. She was here . . ." My voice trails off as I think about Carol, just today, seawater spraying off her on the boat, her mouth half-open, her eyes closed.

"What happened?" Adam says gently.

"She died," I say. "And then everything that I knew went with her. My marriage . . ." Adam reacts but doesn't say anything. "I don't really know who I am anymore."

"And you came here to find out?"

I nod. "Maybe."

Adam considers this. "What's he like?"

"Who?"

"Your husband."

"Oh," I say. "We've been together since college. He's, I don't know, he's Eric."

Adam inhales. "You know what I think your problem is?"

I clear my throat. I'm not sure whether to be impressed or pissed off. "Seriously?"

He looks at me like *Come on*.

"Fair, fine. What's my problem?"

"You don't feel like you have any agency over your life."

"You've known me for two hours."

"We had breakfast, lest you forget. And you were late to dinner. Let's call it thirteen."

I wave him on.

"You act like you don't know how you got here, like you just woke up and looked around and thought, *Huh*—but I have news for you. Even inaction is a choice."

I just sit there, staring at him. It's a strange thing, to have a stranger tell you off and then be right.

"Is that all?"

"Yeah, you're cute, too."

I feel that blush again. My toes tingle. "That's a problem?"

He leans forward. So close I can smell the sweet berries and espresso on his breath. "For me? Definitely."

Chapter Eleven

I wake up early again. The sun is just barely cresting the horizon; it's not even 6 a.m. I take some tea out onto the patio, overlooking the sea, the whole town bathed in that same hazy blue light.

I parted ways with Adam at the elevator last night. He's on floor two—a suite, he said, with a great view. I laughed. Everywhere has a great view in this place.

Right now, this morning, all I can think about is her. I'm anxious to see her tonight, anxious to know if she'll show up, anxious to discover whether yesterday was all a lucid dream, just a little too real around the edges. I feel the caffeine hit my system, but instead of making me jittery, it seems to make me more alert, like I've just put on glasses. And I know, in the way only certainty can present, that it really was her, that she's here. That somehow I have stumbled into some kind of magic reality where we get to be together. That time here does not only move slower but in fact doubles back on itself.

It doesn't even seem that unbelievable. The crazier thing, the far more baffling, is that she is gone.

I go back inside and set my mug down. I go to pull some ChapStick out of my carry-on when I see our original itinerary for the trip, the one I stuffed down in the bag just a day ago. I take the crinkled paper out. There are restaurants on there—Chez Black, of course, the lemon tree restaurant in Capri. And then written on this morning's agenda is *hike up to the path of the gods.*

I remember my mom telling me about this. How when she was here she'd take the steps all the way up to the top of Positano, to where there is a path that links Bomerano and Nocelle, the towns above.

I pull out my tennis shoes, a pair of shorts, and a sports bra. I've never been super athletic, but I've always enjoyed exercise. I started playing soccer in elementary school and didn't stop until junior year of high school, when I tore my meniscus. In college I discovered swimming, and when we lived in New York, bike rides along the Hudson kept me sane. For the most part these days, I go to the gym or the Pure Barre studio around the corner from our house.

I grab my baseball hat, douse myself in sunscreen, and slip downstairs.

It's just Marco at the desk this morning, looking perky for such an early hour.

"Buongiorno!" he tells me.

"Good morning, Marco," I say.

"You off for the walk?" He moves his arms by his sides like he's skiing.

"I was going to do the steps up to the Path of the Gods," I say.

Marco reacts, sweeping the back of his hand against his forehead.

"So many stairs!" he says, like I've just suggested the impossible. "Up and up and up!"

"Is the start or entrance close?" I ask.

He points out the door to the right, and I get a glimpse of the street—still sleepy at this hour.

"You find the stairs, you go." He points his finger straight to the ceiling. "You keep going and then you get there."

"Thank you!" I wave, but Marco stops me.

"Wait!" he calls.

He returns with a bottle of water stamped with the hotel's insignia. "The Positano sun is strong," he says.

I thank him and leave. A few paces up there is a clothing store with all types of elegant linens hung in the window—tablecloths and napkins and lace-trimmed handkerchiefs—and a shop next to it with a granita machine. I see the bright yellow lemonade churning and churning. And then there, to the left of the store, is the first flight of stairs. I take them up. Stone steps, one after the next, after the next. Up, up, up. They wind to the side of small hotels and houses. I peek in the windows at the stirrings of life. After sixty seconds, I'm out of breath.

I can't remember the last time I went on a walk, let alone a run or to the gym. I am out of shape, out of practice, unfamiliar with pushing my body this hard. My legs have stood still this last year. They have stood still while my heart and gut and soul ran in circles, screaming, hysterical, but I notice that moving my body, now, seems to have the opposite effect. While I am sweating, gasping, my insides are quiet. All I can think about right now is the next step.

Marco is right: the stairs are steep and seemingly endless. But after about ten minutes of heart-pumping cardio, I reach a landing. Out of the immediacy of Positano, the town becomes more residential. Nonne begin to sit outside, chatting with neighbors over morning coffees before their households awaken. I wave to a woman sweeping her stoop. She waves back.

I'm struck by the timelessness of Italy. It is not the first time I've had this thought—that the Italy I'm returning to, now, is not all that different from the one my mother first fell in love with thirty years ago. The country has been around for thousands of years. Unlike America, progress is rated differently. It happens slower. Houses are limewashed in the same color palette used for a hundred years; institutions prevail. Churches and icons have been here for centuries, not just decades. The same dishes return year after year.

After another five minutes of climbing, I'm thoroughly drenched. I unscrew the cap off the bottle Marco gave me and drink appreciatively. I survey my surroundings.

I've reached the end of the stairs, and from here there's a dirt-and-stone path that disappears into much more natural surroundings. This must be the mouth of the Path of the Gods. From a quick summary on our itinerary, I learned that the Path of the Gods gets its name from a legend. Apparently, the gods used the path to come down to the sea and save Ulysses from the Sirens that enticed him with their singing. For centuries, it was the only way between the towns of the Amalfi Coast. It is well traveled and well loved.

The view up here is breathtaking, reminiscent of the one leading into town. The boats on the water, once entirely sketchable, are now tiny white dots on the sea. Here you can see the sweeping wash of blue and the hotels and houses of Positano like watercolor droplets. We are high above it all.

I take a seat on a little stone step. My legs are quaking underneath me, and the sun is now fully birthed, coming into the world today raging and singing light. I no longer feel even the slight remnants of the fog of a hangover. No wonder everyone can drink wine so freely here.

I think about this path. How many people have come and gone along this trail. How many stories, how many steps.

I think about my mother here, all those years ago. I think about her here now. Her long auburn hair, her wide smile, her sundress and sneakers, the gleam of sweat off her suntanned brow. The same person, and yet someone else entirely.

"There you are!" she says, panting. "I practically had to chase you up here!"

She's real again, in the flesh. All the dewy youth of someone awakening to a new day of nothing but salt water and wine.

I scramble to my feet. "You came here to find me?" I say breathlessly and with so much relief.

She sticks her hands on her hips and leans down, winded. "You passed by my balcony this morning. I waved but you didn't see me, so I tossed on my sneakers and came up. You owe me a massage, probably."

I look at her lean torso, her strong legs. "Don't you do this path every day?" I ask her.

She looks at me like I'm nuts. "Are you kidding? I've never been up there. That's like twelve thousand stairs." She straightens up, surveying the view. "But I have to say, I am so glad I followed you. This is pretty spectacular."

I go to stand next to her. I think about a postcard from this place. It probably looked the same a hundred years ago. I hope that will be true a hundred years from now, too.

"Back home in LA we have this hike off Mulholland called TreePeople," she says. "Have you been?"

I shake my head.

"I like to go sometimes. I'll bring a sketchbook up. It's a great place to draw. I haven't been in too long, though. This just reminded me."

"I like photography," I say. "I used to bring a camera with me to Fryman Canyon. That's the hike my . . . That's the hike I like to do."

"I'll bet you're a great photographer."

"Really?"

She nods. "I can tell you have very good taste. With the exception of that dress from yesterday, of course."

She smiles; it makes me laugh.

We stand up there, side by side, not speaking.

"Carol," I say. The word sounds both foreign and familiar. "I have to tell you something."

She turns to me, and I see the sweat running down her face. Her green eyes flashing in the sun.

I want to tell her that she's my mother. I want to ask her to dig deep, to see if she can access some other time and place. I want to know if she can peer into the future and see her child swaddled against her chest. I want to know if she can see the two of us in contrasting floral dresses running down the beach in Malibu, me at her heels. I want to know if she can see herself, in our kitchen, plucking my fingers out of the cookie dough. Does she know? How could she possibly not remember?

But of course she doesn't. Here she's just a woman out for a summer adventure, and I'm the other American tourist with whom she happened to cross paths.

"Yes?" she says, still looking at me.

"I'm not sure I liked Da Adolfo," I spit out.

Carol laughs. She squints her face together and shakes her

head. "Then I have to tell *you* something," she says. "I'm not sure I do, either. But you can't really beat the scenery."

"The food was not so amazing," I say.

"The standards are high here," she says. "Especially if you're staying at Poseidon."

"Where do you go back home?" I ask her. "I mean, in LA. Where do you like to eat?"

She smiles. "I cook a lot," she says. "I have this very cool apartment on the Eastside. You'll come over, when we're back. I make a lot of pasta and fish. The secret to LA is that downtown has the best restaurants. They're few and far between, but they're sensational. And Chinatown has my heart."

I flash on my mother, dim sum splayed out before her, clapping happily as we all sing "Happy Birthday" to her. We haven't been in ages. Why did we stop going?

"I'll also never pass up In-N-Out." She clears her throat. "Shall we?"

We head down the stairs together, side by side. When we get to the landing, I stop and gaze back down over the sea. It's so much hotter than when we began, and my bottle of water is nearly empty.

"I'll see you at four?" my mother asks.

"Do you want to have breakfast at my hotel?" If she comes back with me, what will happen?

"I'd love to," she says. "But I have this project I'm working on." She looks sheepish when she says it, the first time I've seen the emotion on her since I encountered her here.

"What kind?" I ask.

I'm reminded of sitting on floors of showrooms as a young child with my mother. Watching her pick out rugs and fabrics for drapes and furniture for her clients. I'm reminded of playing on the floor of my father's flagship store, watching my mother arrange dresses on mannequins. I loved seeing her in her element.

"It's such a long shot," she says. She places her hands on her hips and shrugs.

"Tell me."

"I'm working on a design for the Sirenuse." She puts a hand on her face. "Remo told me they're remodeling the hotel, and I decided on a whim to submit a proposal. They have all these really famous people from Rome and Milan presenting. I don't know, it's silly . . ."

The Sirenuse is the nicest hotel in Positano, and it has the price tag to match. When my mother and I thought about going, it was seventeen hundred dollars a night.

She told me it was gorgeous, though.

"I didn't know that," I say.

"We just met! But no one does, really. Design is kind of a passion project of mine. I was an art history major, and I work in a gallery now, but it is—it's not really what I want to do. I want to design interiors. This hotel would be a dream."

She doesn't know yet, I think. She doesn't know that she'll do it.

I think about walking into my mother's office at home in Brentwood. The floor was soft white carpeting, and there were all sorts of movie posters framed on the walls—like she wasn't a decorator but instead a producer. They were films whose sets she loved. "Your home is your set" is a thing she'd often tell clients. I knew what she meant. That the homes in movies have to work—they have to show the audience who these characters are; they have to be revealing. She wanted people's homes to be reflections of them. She wanted you to be able to walk inside and say "No one else but Carol Silver could possibly live here."

"I've heard it's beautiful," I say.

She nods. "I stayed there when I came with my parents so many years ago. I never forgot that place."

"I can see why," I say.

She smiles. "So anyway, I should get going. But thank you for the major exercise. It completely cleared my head. I need to remember that!" She turns and walks off before I can stop her. "See you later!" she calls over her shoulder.

I watch her disappear down the steeply descending staircase. *I am watching her becoming*, I think. Here she is, at the start.

Chapter Twelve

I'm a sweaty mess and nearing dehydration when I get back to the lobby. Marco is gone, but Carlo is at the desk.

"Hot morning," he says. "Water?"

"Yes, please."

He hands me a bottle, and I down it in one long swig.

"Thanks, Carlo."

I turn to head upstairs, and he calls after me.

"You have a message, Ms. Silver," he says.

My first thought is my mother. Not Carol, not the woman I just left on the stairs, but my mom. That she's at home, arranging flowers and sending me a telegraph all the way to Italy: *How is the shopping? Buy me something for the house, I miss you. Xx.*

But of course there are no such things as telegraphs anymore, to start.

The second is Eric.

"Oh?" I say.

"Yes," he says. "A gentleman named Adam who is a guest here wanted to know if you were free for lunch."

I laugh. It comes out like a snort. Carlo notices.

"Thank you," I say. "I'll track him down."

I take the stairs up to the restaurant, where breakfast is in full swing. Nika is talking to a well-dressed couple in their sixties. They look French, impeccably matched up in white linen.

"Look who it is!"

Adam is bright and cheerful this morning, in striped swim trunks and a gray T-shirt. His hands are empty, and I glance over to see his room key perched on his usual table.

"Hey," I say. "I just got your message."

He looks me over. "You look worked."

"I am," I say. "I did the stairs this morning."

I feel my body, alive. The blood pumping through my veins, the sweat on the back of my neck, the heat from the exertion and sun. It feels good.

"Did you enjoy it?"

I smile, thinking of Carol, her head back, the ocean below us. "Yes. You can join me tomorrow if you think you can keep up."

A man in a Hawaiian shirt balancing a plate of eggs and sausage walks by, speaking fast Italian. "But now I'm going to eat all the watermelon on this table."

Adam cocks his head to the buffet. "Want company?"

He's squinting at me, his hand over his forehead like a visor, blocking the sun. "Sure," I say.

I ignore his recommendations. Today, I go for everything, the whole spread, like I'm on a cruise ship or in Vegas. I don't hold back. Two plates. One with fruit, pastries, and a yogurt parfait. The other with scrambled eggs, potatoes, and bacon. I sit them both down across from Adam, who is back at the table sipping coffee.

He looks up at me, impressed.

"Now we're talking," he says.

I plunk into the seat, down another glass of water, and then start on the fruit. I eat with a voraciousness I can't remember. The watermelon is sweet, the eggs are creamy, and the bacon is crisp and salty.

When my mother got sick, food immediately tasted like cardboard. One day I was coveting the salt and sweet of pad Thai from Luv2eat on Sunset, the next I was force-feeding myself a piece of toast after my stomach had gone unaccompanied for eight hours. Food had lost all sensation, all meaning.

Soon after, my mother lost her appetite as well. Before that she tried—she still cooked for us, putting on a brave face of enjoying roasted salmon and Broccolini or her famous linguine and clams. But treatment made her nauseous, and eating started to become painful. Hospitals, needles, and the pulse of medication do not pair well with an appetite. She got thinner and thinner, and so did I.

"You need to take care of yourself," Eric would warn me. He'd pick up pasta or pizza or a Caesar salad—things I liked, things I found palatable—and I'd nibble at them. I stopped opening our refrigerator. Pretzels became a meal.

The thing I never told Eric, because I didn't know how to say it without inviting in another conversation, because I didn't know how to tell anyone, is that I had no interest in doing anything that would sustain my life anymore. Food, water, sleep, and exercise are meant for those who are trying to stay alive, who want to thrive. I didn't.

"Coffee?" Adam asks me. I look across at him. His gray T-shirt is hiked up on his bicep, revealing a tan slice of muscle. How is it possible that just two weeks ago I was in a hospital somewhere, and now I'm sitting across from this man on the Amalfi Coast?

I nod.

He pours for me. The coffee is hot and thick and biting. Nearly deadly. Delicious.

"So what's on your agenda today?" Adam asks me.

I think about the folded papers upstairs. "I want to explore," I say. "My— A friend is taking me to this restaurant in the hills at four."

Adam squints at me. "I thought you were here alone."

"I am," I say. "She's— I met her yesterday. She's also from California, so we got to talking."

"That's great," he says. "It's wonderful making friends in foreign places. Am I invited?"

I swallow a mouthful of coffee. "No."

He cocks his head at me. "Okay then."

"But I was thinking about exploring a little bit today. Would you want to show me around?" I gesture to the life below our terrace. "Or do you need to spend it trying to con Marco out of his family's pride and joy?"

He sits back in his chair, threading his hands behind his neck. "Tough, Silver."

"No one has ever called me that."

"What, Silver?"

I shake my head. "No, tough."

"It wasn't a compliment," he says, but he's grinning at me. "So you want me to play tour guide for you?"

I lift my shoulders in deference. "You said you've been coming here forever."

Adam looks out over the ocean. I see a hint of something in his gaze I can't quite place, a passing thought that's gone before I can identify what it is. "Well then, let's go."

Chapter Thirteen

After two plates of breakfast, seconds of bacon, and a cinnamon roll to go, I head upstairs to shower and change. The French doors to my room are closed, beating out the morning sun. I take a cold shower—the water feels delicious on my hot skin—and get dressed.

I meet Adam in the lobby twenty minutes later. He's still in his gray T-shirt and board shorts, but now he's wearing tennis shoes and a baseball hat that says *Kauai* on it.

I point up. "Have you been?"

It takes him a second to understand what I'm talking about. "Oh. Kauai. Yes, of course. It would be weird to wear the hat if not, no?"

"I guess." I don't mention that Eric has a hat that says *Mozambique* on it. We've never even been to the African continent.

His eyes graze down my body. "You look nice," he says.

I've changed into denim shorts and a white lace top with a blue bikini underneath. Sun hat firmly on. My belly is full, and my legs feel pleasantly wobbly from the hike this morning.

"Thanks."

"Are you going to be able to walk in those shoes?"

He points down at my feet that are clad in pink plastic Birkenstocks. Besides my Nikes, they're the most comfortable shoes I brought on this trip.

"They're Birkenstocks!" I say.

"And that means . . . ?"

"It means let's go."

I have my straw cross-body around me, and I tuck a bottle of water from the front desk into it. I haven't stopped drinking since I got done with the walk. I want more and more and more water.

Adam holds his arm out for me to pass through the door, and I do. Outside, the day is bright and friendly. Tourists and locals alike are in the streets, finishing breakfast at outdoor restaurants and opening shops to begin the day's work.

"Where are we going?" I ask.

"Relax," he says. "We're going to walk. The best way to explore Positano is to simply wander."

We start walking down Viale Pasitea. I look at the red and orange buildings we pass. Shops and restaurants and little grocery stands. There are baskets of fresh produce, and mannequins wearing hand-painted dresses. I spot a blue one with silver stitching. There are racks of sewn dolls for children and wraps in every shade of blue the ocean and sky are capable of offering.

"It's all so beautiful," I say.

"The stuff to buy or the views?"

"Both. But the views really are incredible. Up high this morning . . . you could see the whole sweep. It was spectacular. I think Positano might be the most stunning place I've ever seen."

Adam nods. "You know where the real best view of Positano is?"

"I don't know how you could beat the view this morning," I say. "Today was pretty great."

"Be that as it may," he says, "the best view in Positano is actually from the ocean."

A bicyclist on the sidewalk almost knocks into me. I jump back out of the way, and a car honks. All the vehicles are tiny, like we're in a movie.

I'm reminded, when he says this, of something Eric used to say when we lived in New York. How the best view in New York was in Jersey City. *The best view in a place is actually a view of the place.*

Five years ago, my mother and I went for the weekend to the Bacara in Santa Barbara. It's a hotel on the coast, with grounds that have great views of the ocean. We got massages and then sat out in big Adirondack chairs and watched the sunset.

"Look at all the colors," she said. "It's like the sky is on fire. Burning up the whole day. Nature has so much power if we just pay attention."

"What's your favorite place you've ever been?" I ask Adam.

"Wherever I'm going next," he says.

We keep walking until we arrive at a bougainvillea-covered walkway. I remember it from yesterday. It leads down to the church square.

Couples stroll hand in hand as shops continue to open their doors. A few paces down, a young artist has set up a stand. Beside him are colorful landscapes of Positano and Rome and, for some reason, quite a few portraits of cats. Finally, we reach the square with the Church of Santa Maria Assunta standing in the middle, the golden dome high overhead.

"This is one of my favorite places," Adam says, surveying the structure. He tilts his head back and rests it in the palms of his hands.

"It's so grand."

"It was built when the Byzantine icon of the Virgin Mary was brought here on a ship. There's this legend that the icon was on a boat that was headed east when the ship stopped moving. The sailors heard a voice saying, 'Put me down! Put me down!' The captain thought it was a miracle that meant the Virgin statue wanted to be brought to Positano. As he changed course so he was headed for the shore, the boat began to sail again. It was a miracle. Incidentally, 'posa posa' means 'put me down' or 'stop there,' and that's how the town gets its name."

"Positano," I say.

"Indeed. Come here."

Adam motions me over to his side. He points upward, to the colorful dome. It looks gold from anywhere else, but here I see it's actually a pattern of yellow, green, and blue tiles.

"So the whole town was made around this one church, this one story," I say, still gazing at the sun-covered dome.

"Isn't that how all things begin?" Adam asks me.

I drop my head down, and see that he's staring at me. I let my eyes, protected now by sunglasses, gaze back at him. I notice the way his shirt clings to him. It outlines his torso, his sweat creating a kind of pointillism on the cotton canvas.

I was so young when I met Eric. I'd never even really had a boyfriend before him, just a series of dates and unanswered texts. He was exactly what I'd been looking for, which is to say, he was the answer to what I think was the broadest, most general question I could have been asking: *Who?*

At the time, I must have felt that this was right, that he was

The One, but looking back, it feels arbitrary, like I'm not sure what criteria I was using to evaluate him, the relationship, any of it. I wanted someone to think I belonged to them, the way I belonged to my family. That's how I figured I'd know. But now—

What if I got it all wrong? What if the point of marriage wasn't to belong but instead to feel transported? What if we never got to where we were trying to go because we were so comfortable where we were?

"Where to next?" I ask him. I want to keep moving.

Adam cocks his head to the left. "This way."

He takes me to the streets in and out of Marina Grande, the area by the water that is filled with shops. Gelaterias are next to small boutiques and stores that sell any number of overpriced Positano souvenirs. Everything seems to be printed with lemons. An irritable woman in her sixties sells all sorts of Positano merchandise. There are small glass bottles filled with sand, ceramic plates printed with tomatoes and vines, handmade gold sandals, and aprons printed with lemon trees. I pick up an apron, fingering it. It's lovely, bright, and fresh.

Instantly, I'm transported to my parents' kitchen, chopping onions next to my mother, who is dumping greens from the Brentwood Farmers Market into a wooden bowl. She's wearing a navy-and-white-striped button-down and jeans, cuffed at the ankles. And over it, her lemon apron.

As if I'd been burned, I stick the apron back. The store manager continues to glare at me.

"You okay?" Adam glances at me from where he's been leaning in the entryway.

"Fine," I say. "Yeah. We can go."

"You don't want that?" He gestures to the apron.

"No," I say. "I don't need it."

He follows me out the door. "Are you sure? I have cash."

"Do you want to get a drink?" I ask him.

"Now? It's barely eleven."

I take my sunglasses off and give him a pointed stare. "It's Italy."

"Hey, listen, I'm in. You're the one who wanted me to play tour guide. I was trying to get as much mileage in as possible."

"And you did a great job. Now I'd like some wine."

He grins at me. "As you wish. I know a great spot."

I follow him up the street onto Via Cristoforo Colombo. After a minute or two, we stop in front of a restaurant on the left-hand side. It's two stories, with a terrace on the second level overlooking the street and ocean.

Adam shakes hands with the maître d'. He points across the street to where there are two tables, right on the street, that look like they're literally hanging over the ocean. "Possible?" he asks.

The man nods. "Naturalmente."

We cross, and Adam pulls out my chair for me.

"We're in the middle of the street," I say to Adam.

"Pretty great, right?"

I look behind him, to where Positano's colored town rises out of the ocean.

"This must be spectacular at night."

Adam nods. "It is." He glances at me. There's a suggestion there, but I leave it dangling. A waiter appears with bread, water, and a carafe of white wine, snipping the moment. Adam pours for us.

"Very good," I say. I take a big gulp. "What is this?"

"Their house white," he says. "I order it every time I come here." He wipes some sweat from his forehead and lifts his glass to me. "To new friends," he says. He holds my gaze for just a beat longer.

I meet his glass with a clink.

"Do you ever wonder how people used to find this place? Before there were travel brochures or even word of mouth."

"I think there was always word of mouth."

"You know what I mean." I put my elbows on the table and lean forward. "So, okay, that ship. What must it have felt like to step onto this shore for the first time? I can't imagine that people built this place. It feels like it's always been, I don't know, undiscoverable. Like it's always just existed exactly as it is today."

Adam sits back, thoughtful. He takes a sip of wine.

"Sometimes, I guess," he says. "I feel that about Italy in general. All this living history. Different eras and experiences, joy and suffering stacked up on top of each other like sheets of paper."

"Sheets of paper. That's the perfect way to describe it."

I think of one of the final scenes in *The Thomas Crown Affair*, the remake with Rene Russo and Pierce Brosnan. Thomas Crown has stolen a painting from the Metropolitan Museum of Art, replacing it with a forgery. As the plot crescendos, the museum infiltrated and the sprinklers on, the forgery begins to disintegrate, revealing that the original painting has been there all along, just underneath it. The same canvas.

One thing on top of another on top of another.

"How often are you at home?" I ask Adam. "I have a vision of you in an apartment with gray walls and gray furniture. Maybe a red headboard."

He raises an eyebrow at me. "That's specific."

"Masculine and minimalist," I say.

Adam laughs. "I'm not a pack rat, you've got that right.

But I like Navajo pottery. Not sure where that fits into the equation."

"Really?"

"Really," he says. "I bought my first piece on a trip with my mom to Santa Fe, and I've been collecting ever since."

I imagine Adam in a room filled with colorful vases. It's hard to picture.

"But in answer to your question," he says, "I am not home that often." He rolls his neck from side to side. "What about you?" he asks. "What does your home look like?"

I think about the gingham wallpaper in the bathroom, the wicker furniture, the mid-century dresser.

"I don't know," I say. "It looks like me, I guess. It looks normal."

Adam clears his throat. "You don't look normal." He holds my gaze for a beat and then looks back down into the marina.

"Positano was really just a modest fishing village," he says. "Although, legend has it that the town was created by Poseidon himself, god of the sea."

"It seems like there are a lot of legends to this place."

Adam leans forward. He tips his wine to me. "Many people believe that Positano was and still is full of very real magic."

"Magic," I repeat. "Do you believe that?"

Adam's face hovers even closer. If he wanted to, he could lift his hand from where it rests on the table and cup my chin with it. It would take no more than a heartbeat, an instant, the space of a millisecond.

"How could I not right now."

Chapter Fourteen

Adam drops me off at half past two at the hotel. "You sure you don't want to have dinner tonight?"

"I told you I'm going to that restaurant."

"With your friend, right." He tilts his head to the side. His face is a little red at his cheeks and nose—the first hints of too much sun today.

We're standing in the lobby. The front desk is vacant. From upstairs, the sounds of guests at the pool trickle down.

"What?" I ask. "What's that look?"

Adam turns his palms up, then down like he's disregarding gathered sand. "Nothing," he says. He exhales out. "All right, enjoy your date. Call my room if you'd like a nightcap."

I put my hand up to wave goodbye, and then all at once Adam leans forward and kisses my cheek. His lips are soft and warm on my skin. I feel his body close to mine, right there, and something in me reaches out and hooks on. I lean into him.

"Thanks for a wonderful day," he says, and then he is moving away, his body now a separate entity, heading up the stairs.

I stand there, blinking after him.

My face is hot where his lips were. My whole body feels rooted to the marble floor beneath me.

"Buonasera!"

I jump and turn to the desk to see Marco behind it. He throws his arm up like he's tossing a hat into the center of the lobby.

"You look lost in the thoughts."

"Just wine!" I say a little too loudly.

"Perfetto," Marco says. "And where will you go tonight?"

"A restaurant out of town," I say.

"Alone?"

I shake my head.

"With Mr. Adam?"

"No," I say. "A new friend."

Marco beams. "Enjoy!" he calls.

I take the stairs slowly. For one, my legs are exhausted and my quads are starting to cramp from all the exercise this morning. The stairs, coupled with the miles around town, have left me feeling like Jell-O. I haven't used my physical being this much in years.

And for another, I feel swayed by something else entirely. The day, being with Adam. I am struck with the overwhelming clarity of how good it feels to exist, to be wanted and . . . not known. To have a man look at me who hasn't seen me wan and laid out with the stomach flu, or folded over on the first day of my period. And even better—how it feels to look at someone whose shape and mind and history are not familiar to me.

When I get inside, I lie down on the bed. I let my legs dangle, stretching out my back. I reach my arms up overhead and let them fall behind me.

In an hour and a half I will see Carol again. She will be

vibrant and real. We will spend an entire evening together. Eating and talking. It feels impossible, and yet—

I know she will show. I am no longer worried this is all an illusion. I no longer feel like I am having some kind of extended hallucination, if I ever did. She'll come. She'll be here. We will have tonight.

✦

It's just four o'clock when I head downstairs. I'm wearing a silk sundress with a puffed shoulder, in a purple-green-and-blue patchwork pattern. My still-wet hair is held back in a bun, and I have on earrings that my mother gave me for my twenty-first birthday—opals, surrounded by tiny pavé diamonds.

Disappointment floods my insides when I see Carlo alone at the desk.

"Buonasera," he says. "How are you, Ms. Silver?"

I glance around. "Good," I say. "Was there a woman here?"

"I don't know, signora."

"She comes here to mail things sometimes? Long brown hair?"

Carlo shrugs. "I don't think so, but look at you. You got sun," he says. He moves his finger in a circular motion around his face.

I touch my palm to my cheek. "Oh, yes, some."

I check my watch. It's now five minutes after four. *Italian time*, I remind myself. *She'll be here.*

"Can I help?" Carlo asks. "With the woman?"

I glance outside. "No, that's okay."

Just then Marco comes out from the back office. "Buonasera," he says to me. "You look lovely."

I smile. "Thank you, Marco."

"You need something? You need someone? Your American came in, he's upstairs."

I feel myself blush. "Oh, Adam. No, that's all right. Also he's not my American. Just an American."

Marco laughs. It's a deep belly laugh. "It's okay, signora. Positano is for the lovers."

I open my mouth to respond and then see a pink bus pull up across the street.

"What is that? It's adorable."

"For La Tagliata," he says. "And no one knows why it is pink. The whole restaurant is green!"

"The one in the hills?"

He nods. "Sì, certo. It comes for those with a reservation."

"Have a good night!" I run out of the hotel and across the street. There are a few people gathered at what seems to be the designated spot, and I catch my breath as I join their line. The door swings open, and we begin boarding the bus.

"La Tagliata?" I say.

"Sì, sì."

I don't know whether to get on or not. My heart rate is sky-high, I can feel my pulse in my ears. *Where is she?*

"You come or you go?" the man asks me. I look up into the bus, trying to see inside, but the windows are black. I arch around, and the man steps forward, blocking my gaze.

"I'm sorry," I say, craning my neck. "I'm just looking for my . . ."

"Sì o no?" the man asks.

I look across the street at the hotel. There's no sign of her. "Sì," I say, and then in an instant, I get on the bus.

Once I do, I see rickety seats, torn-up leather. There are no more than seven or eight people. And toward the back, lifting out of her seat, waving, is Carol.

Relief floods my veins.

"Katy, here!"

I make my way back to her. "Hi," I say. "I didn't see you at the hotel, and . . ."

She gets up and launches herself at me, her arms around my neck. I breathe her in. The smell of the ocean and just, *her*.

"Oh my god, hi. I'm so happy you're here. There was a whole thing with the pickup, I was late and they made a stop by me, so I got on, and then he wouldn't let me off the bus!" She pulls back and holds me at an arm's length. "Italians!" she says, and releases me. "See, Francesco, this is my friend!" She gestures to the man from the door, clearly the driver, and then rolls her eyes.

Francesco gives her a curt nod.

I think about my mother's color-coded calendar. Pink for errands, blue for my father, green for me, and gold for social obligations. I look at the bursting, bubbling mess of a woman before me. It's almost impossible that this is the same person.

She's so cool, I think as we take our seats. *Your mother is so fucking cool.*

She has on ripped jeans and a white lace top. Her hair is tucked behind her ears, and she has just a glint of lip gloss on.

"You look great," I say.

"Thanks!" she says, not a hint of modesty. "So do you."

The bus starts to move, and I lean back against the sticky leather seat.

"This place is amazing. I can't wait for you to see," she says. "What have I told you about it?"

"Just that it's high up," I say. I point outside. To where the town keeps ascending, even though, currently, we're headed downhill. There is only one road in Positano, and that road is a one-way street. One must go down before one goes up.

"La Tagliata," she says. "It's run by Don Luigi and his wife, Mama. All their food is from their own farm. They don't have a menu, so you just drink the chilled white wine and wait for whatever they're serving up tonight." Carol turns her head to me. "I really hope you're hungry."

I think about my marathon breakfast, and wine with Adam, which feels like days ago now. Hunger rolls through me. There's always room here.

"Definitely."

The bus makes a hard left by the Hotel Eden Roc, and we start climbing upward.

"How did you find this place?" I ask her.

"Remo took me a few nights into my trip," she says. Some hair sticks to her face, and she brushes it away. "He tells me it's hardly changed in twenty years. How many places can you say that about?"

"Definitely not anywhere in LA," I say. The Coffee Bean a few blocks over used to be a Walgreens.

"That's true."

"Where is Remo tonight?" I say.

"Working," she says. "But this place Bella Bar has a dance party at night. He'll meet us there after dinner. You must come. Honestly, I'm not giving you a choice!"

I think about my mother, dancing the night away in a club in Positano. She always loved music, loved to dance. But the only songs I can remember her moving to are Frank Sinatra at a wedding or Katy Perry at a cousin's bar mitzvah. This is something else entirely. "That sounds great," I say.

The trip up to the restaurant is a winding, fairly nauseating forty-five minutes. It gets so bad at one point that I have to stop talking.

"Just look to the front," Carol says. "The horizon—that'll help." She puts a cool palm on my mid-back and holds it there.

We pull up to the restaurant what feels like hours later. I walk out wobbly. By the side of the road there is a round sign that has *Fattoria La Tagliata* painted on it. We walk through an archway and then down a flight of stairs. We're surrounded by gardens, flowers, the sweet smell of the arriving summer.

The restaurant is no more than a tree house. But this tree house, like so much of Positano, has a sweeping view of the sea. Because we are so high up, you can see all the way to Capri, even. And it's early—the sun is still hours from setting.

"Wow," I say.

Carol smiles. "Right? Pretty special."

We're greeted by a boisterous man at the door. "Buonasera!" He kisses Carol first, then me, once on either cheek. "Welcome, welcome! You will dine with us! Let's go!"

We are shown to a table while he continues to greet the guests from our bus as they come down the path. There are maybe four diners, no more, already seated in the small room.

I learn from Carol that there are two dinner sittings—5 p.m. and 8 p.m. There are no menus, as she said, and the wine flows freely.

"This doesn't seem real," I say. "I've truly never seen anything like this."

Our table is situated in the corner of the room, right by what would be the window, but instead of a window, it's just open air, punctuated by a wooden guardrail that I can rest my elbow on from our chairs. White linen curtains sit pooled by two wood poles on either side of the room. Everything is light and open. Like we're having dinner in the sky—we are.

I look at her, my mother. She's thin, she always was, but there's a roundness to her, a fullness, that she lost in later years. That, or I'm incapable, now, of seeing her without illness. I close my eyes and open them again.

"Tell me more about California," I say to her.

My mother is from Boston, born and raised. I know she moved to California five years before she met my father. That she worked in a gallery in Silver Lake called the Silver Whale. She would speak about that era with a whimsical detachment. I was lucky. I didn't have a mother who longed for her youth. At least, I never thought I did. She embraced aging. I remember once noticing, on a particularly hot July day, that she never wore T-shirts anymore. When I asked, she told me she'd given them up years ago. She laughed when she said it—she didn't seem attached to a younger version of herself, a younger body. My mother never put herself in the center of my drama, either. Whether it was friends or Eric or the uncertainty of work. She seemed to love the stage of life she was in—somewhere past all the figuring out. Somewhere solid.

But here, now, so firmly planted in Before, I want to know what her life is like. I want to know about what has brought her here, and where she thinks she is going.

Carol blinks at me, like she's not sure what I've just asked. "California?"

"The gallery?"

Her face dawns in recognition. "Yes. Well, I'm just doing some assisting. It's nothing special, really. Did I tell you about the gallery?" she asks.

I nod quickly. "We were talking about the hotel redesign, and you said you work at a gallery back home."

All at once, her face lights up. "The Sirenuse. Yes! That would just be . . . I mean, it can't happen, I know that. It would be impossible. I think they only took the meeting because one of the managers is a friend of Remo's family. It was a favor. But I have this vision."

I love seeing her so animated, so engaged. "Tell me about it," I say.

The waiter comes over and plunks a bottle of red wine and a chilled bottle of white down on our table. Carol pours us both some of each.

"Have you been?" she asks.

"To the Sirenuse?"

She nods.

"No, never."

Her eyes get wide. "It's iconic Positano. Definitely the most famous hotel here, and probably on the whole coast, as well. Everyone must go once. Your trip wouldn't be complete without it."

I smile encouragement. This is the Carol I'm familiar with. My mother always had the answers, backed by strong personal preference, on what any one of us should love, on what constituted beauty, on what was valuable. She just knew.

The Beverly Hills Hotel was trash, but the Bel-Air was treasure. Bedding should be all white. Florals belonged indoors and outdoors. Birkenstocks were hiking shoes, not for the beach or lunch. Your closet should be color coordinated, and you could and should drink red wine all year long.

"The lobby is this beautiful, open-air place, but it's so stuffy. They have love seats that look like they were stolen from Versailles, and there's a wooden horse on the wall. A wooden horse!" Carol rolls her eyes. "I see this beautiful blue-and-white lobby that spills out onto the terrace. Mediterranean, clean, lots of tile and texture, white, yellow, and blue, complementing the colors of the sea."

Carol gazes out at the ocean, lost in thought.

"Are you going to propose that?"

Carol nods. "They're hearing pitches in a week. It's very old-school. You show up with sketches and you meet with the owners. It's a family business. Has been for decades. Most places here are. In Italy in general, I guess."

"I don't know anything about design, really," I tell her. "But that sounds beautiful."

I never had an eye for aesthetics the way my mother did. She picked out most of my clothes and furniture, designed my home. She had better taste than me, had seen more, been exposed to more, and had far more patience for the trial and error that comes with transforming a space. She knew how to eyeball a room; she understood spatial relation. She understood that however long a dresser was, you needed to factor in an additional six inches so the room wouldn't look crowded. She could tell what would look good on me and what wouldn't. She knew how to organize a kitchen so that all the appliances were exactly where you most needed them. The glasses were to the right of the sink, not the left, because everyone in our family was right-handed. The silverware was underneath the plates. The mugs were beside the coffee maker.

I think about the stories I've heard from my parents about their young marriage. My father started his clothing company, and my mother worked in the back office, keeping the books.

"She kept everyone in line," my father used to say. "She was the lifeblood of my business."

"*Our* business," my mother would remind him with a pointed smile.

"It is," Carol says. "The hotel, I mean. Beautiful."

"You said you once stayed there with your parents?"

She nods. "The place means something to me, you know?"

All at once I remember that my mother lost her own mother, my grandmother, when she was just twelve years old. I was always disappointed that I never met Belle. She was gone far before I ever arrived. What was it like for my mom to meet my father without her? To be married without her? To become a mother without her? Her father remarried, soon after. What did it feel like to have her replaced?

"I do," I say. "Very much so."

She smiles. "I'll take you there," she says. "You'll love it."

Our first course arrives. It's a plate with fresh-cut tomatoes, peppers marinated in olive oil, and the freshest farmer cheese I've ever seen. It oozes cream, like blood, onto the plate. Warm breads are set down in a basket next to our wine.

Carol rubs her hands together. "Yum," she says. "Here, give me your plate. Have you ever had burrata?"

I hand it over, and she serves me vegetables and cheese. As she's handing it back another bowl is set down with greens tossed in what looks to be a mustardy vinaigrette.

"This is amazing."

"Just wait," Carol says. "This isn't even the appetizer."

I spear a piece of tomato. It's perfect. Sweet and salty, and I don't even think it has a thing on it. The cheese is sublime.

"Ohmygod."

Carol nods. "So good," she says.

"You were right."

She winks at me, and it stops me, my wine suspended in my

hand in midair. It's something my mother has done for years, that wink. That acknowledgment that says without words: *I know I'm right, I'm glad you've come around.*

"My dad was big into food," Carol says. "He loved to cook and eat. He'd bake, too, which was unheard of for a man of his generation. He used to make the best hamantaschen. All my friends would come over and demand some." She laughs.

"You take after him," I say.

She smiles. "I guess I do."

Course after course is served to us. Pasta with ramp pesto, grilled whitefish, braised pork shoulder, lasagna with fresh ricotta and basil leaves that are the size of dinosaur kale. It's all sublime. By the time they bring out the second pasta course—butter and thyme—I feel like my stomach is going to burst right open.

"This meal is trying to kill me," I say to Carol.

"I know," she says. "But what a way to go." She pauses, refills our glasses. "I haven't even asked what you do for work."

"I'm a copywriter," I say. "Or I was."

People always asked me if I wanted to be a "real" writer, and the truth was, not really. It seemed like the kind of thing other people were. Novelists, poets, screenwriters. Even in a town full of them, it still was someone else's destiny.

I helped other people write. I took their businesses and blogs and spun them into narratives. I took their words and arranged them in a way that told a story. Their story.

"I enjoy it," I say. "There is something satisfying about helping someone distill their message."

Carol listens with patience and concern. "I can see that. It's sort of the same with design."

"To be frank, I'm not sure I really know what I want to be

in the long term. Seeing you talk about design, the way you feel about it, your vision . . . I'm not sure I have that."

"A passion?"

I nod.

Carol considers this. "Not everyone does. Not everyone needs one. What do you enjoy?"

I think about Saturday afternoons spent arranging flowers, picking tomatoes in her garden, long lunches. "Family," I say.

Carol smiles. "What a wonderful answer."

"I took a leave of absence about two months ago," I tell her. "From my job, I mean, I don't know whether to go back, or if I can, even."

"How come?" Carol asks. "Why did you leave?"

I study the wine in my glass. I can't begin to calculate how many times it's been refilled over the past two hours. My words are loose.

"I lost someone I love," I tell her. "And I couldn't really find my way to keeping my life like it was before she was gone." I lift my eyes up to meet hers.

Carol looks at me a long moment, and then she turns her head to gaze out over the water. The sky is fading—that familiar haze of golden, warm light bathing the city in a hue only Italy knows.

"I understand that," she says. "Life doesn't always turn out the way we think it's going to, does it? I understand that," she repeats.

"Your mother," I say. "What was she like?"

Carol looks back to me. "She was wonderful," she says. "A total firecracker. She had an opinion about everything and could drink any man under the table. That's what my father says. She's been gone so long sometimes it's hard to remember her. I was only twelve."

"I'm so very sorry."

"Thank you." She looks at me a long moment. Time seems to hover, and I want to ask her something else, something about what she did, how she got by, to offer up my own grief here, too, but instead what comes out is:

"I'm married."

Carol blinks hard.

"Or I was. Am? That's part of it. Eric, that's his name. I told him I was going to Italy, and I wasn't sure if I was coming back to him."

Carol's eyes get big. "Wow," she says, but that's it. She doesn't offer anything after, so I continue.

"We got married so young," I tell her. "He was my first and only serious boyfriend. And lately, I don't know. I'm starting to feel like he was there and it just happened and it wasn't based in anything. Like I didn't choose it. I loved him. I do, love him. I don't even know what I am saying, or what I am feeling, only that I got to a point where I just couldn't keep going as we had been, I had to—"

"—Katy." She exhales and then inhales, her warm hands on my shoulders, pressing down. "You have got to *breathe*."

My chest hovers, and then I follow her example. I exhale all the air I've been holding out of my lungs. It feels like relief. I breathe in the sweet and salty Italian sea air.

"Good," she says. She takes her hand back. "Sometimes you need time away to figure out how you feel about something. It's hard to know or to see what something is when it's right here, up close, all the bright and harsh details." She holds her palm millimeters from her face, then drops it. "And love," she says. "Who even knows about that one."

Eric would always tell me he looked up to my parents' marriage, that it was what he aspired to for us someday. "They love each other," he'd say. "It's obvious your mom gets on your dad's nerves, but also that he'd lay down his life for her. And he doesn't listen to half the things she says, but about the important stuff, they're always on the same page. At the end of the day, it's obvious it's them."

My mom was a better wife than I am. She was a better everything, but she was definitely a better wife.

"There is a saying, 'What got you here won't get you there.'"

I never heard Carol say that before. Not to me.

"What does it mean?" I ask.

"That the same set of circumstances, beliefs, actions that got you to a moment won't get you to what comes next. That if you want a different outcome, you have to behave differently. That you have to keep evolving."

Don Luigi rings a bell, startling me back to this moment, this restaurant, this place and time.

"Buonasera. I hope you enjoy La Tagliata. We welcome you, and long may we gather!"

Everyone lifts their wineglasses high in a happy and celebratory toast.

Carol tilts hers toward mine. We clink. "Long may we gather," she says.

Amen.

Chapter Fifteen

We arrive at Bella Bar a little after nine. The drive down from La Tagliata felt like it lasted a third of the time it had taken to get up there—that's how full on food and hazy from wine we were. The whole bus sang "That's Amore" as we made our way back down to the sea.

When the world seems to shine like you've had too much wine . . .

The place is small, across the street from where I believe Adam and I had wine . . . today? It feels like a month ago.

Carol grabs my hand and leads me over to the bar, where Remo is having a lively discussion with the bartender. They throw back bright orange cocktails, laughing.

"Sì, sì, certo," Remo says. He gestures to the bartender, then turns to greet us. "Buonasera, Carol, Katy." He kisses us both twice on each cheek. He smells like cigarettes and oranges.

"Hi," I say. "Ciao."

"Vuoi da bere?" Remo makes a drinking motion with his thumb, then claps his forehead. "Ah, would you like a drink?"

"Vodka on the rocks, two limes," Carol says. She shimmies

her torso a little. The top she is wearing falls off one shoulder. I see Remo notice.

"A glass of white wine," I say, and he turns back to the bartender.

Next to me, Carol starts moving to the music, free and loose. We are both filled to the brim with wine. She raises her hands up and throws her head back, shaking out her hair. I watch her, transfixed. So does Remo. He touches her shoulder, and I look away.

Part of me wants to take her home, to not let any man who is not my father even look at her, and part of me wants to pull her aside and explain to her what happens next. That she'll meet my dad. That she'll get married. That she'll have me. That she'll be a wonderful wife and mother, but that this time in her life is fleeting, almost gone. That this is her chance, while she is unencumbered, to be young and free and wild. To have a fling with a hot Italian because she is in one of the most romantic places in the whole world, and because shouldn't that be reason enough.

Eric and I weren't really partiers. Not in college, and not in New York, either. While friends were going to the Meatpacking District on Friday, we'd have people over for game nights, or wine tastings in our living/dining room. For a while we lived on Bleecker Street, right above a boutique that closed shortly after we moved in, and once we managed to get the keys to the space in between tenants. We threw a dinner party there—with folding tables and pizza from Rubirosa. People who walked by the window thought we were an art installation.

But I've done so little of this—this kind of fun, this kind of abandon. I feel the decade of playing grown-up clawing at me, all the years not spent getting drunk on dance floors presenting themselves here, tonight.

I lift my hair off my neck, taking the hair tie from my wrist and wrapping it back in a bun. I can feel beads of sweat down my back. There's no air-conditioning here, and the body count grows as the night wears on. The place is practically packed now.

Remo hands us our drinks. The glass of wine is sweating, too. It feels cool and damp in my hands, and I press it to my cheek, and then gulp it down.

"Is there water?" I ask Remo.

He points to the end of the bar where there is a jug set up with cups next to it. I make my way over and drink three glasses. The water is cold and satisfying. It tastes like taking a shower. I bring one full cup over to Carol.

"Ah!" she says. "Water, praise you." She downs it. "I was just telling Remo about dinner."

I point to my distended stomach. "So good."

Remo laughs. "Food is for eating," he says. "And music for dancing."

He takes Carol's hand and leads her away from the bar to the center of the room, through the gathered drinkers. A few couples are locked together. Two men who look to be no more than eighteen bob their shoulders to the music. Remo twirls Carol and then lets go, leaving her to spin.

The music kicks up, a remake of an eighties pop song. It gets louder. I watch Carol, eyes closed, moving to the rhythm.

I make my way to her. I take her hand. I begin to move to the beat, not letting go of her fingers. We sway and jump and dance together, like that. It feels like we're the only two people on the dance floor. It feels like we're the only two people in the world. Two young women having the time of their life on the Italian shore.

For the first time since she died—maybe long before that—I feel totally free. Not weighed down by any decisions I've already made and not constrained by what's to come. I am fully and completely here. Sweat drenched, wine drunk, present.

"Remo is so into you!" I call when he goes to get a refill on drinks. Carol crushes a bill into his hand before he departs.

"I insist," she says.

"No, he's not," she says. She brushes me off. "I told you. We're friends."

"Trust me," I say. "He is. Why wouldn't he be?"

Carol shakes her head. "You're drunk."

"Maybe," I say. "But why not? He's very cute." I look over to where Remo, head back, laughing, is at the bar. "You won't be here forever."

Carol looks at me, and there is a severity to her gaze that wasn't there a moment before. I suddenly feel myself struggle to be sober. "I can't do that," she says.

"Okay," I say. "It's just that he's hot and you're here."

And then she reaches into her bag and pulls out a pack of cigarettes. She fishes inside for one, lights it, and pulls. It all happens in the span of a second. So quickly I can barely compute it. Here is my mother, in Italy, *smoking*.

"Do you want?" she asks me, exhaling a cloud.

"No," I say.

She shrugs, pulls again, and then I see her watching Remo. "I think you should," she says.

"I don't smoke."

She rolls her eyes. "Sleep with Remo, I mean. If anyone should, it should be you."

"He's not my type," I say quickly.

Carol looks amused. "You're kidding."

"I'm not," I say.

"So who is?"

All at once, Adam's image flashes in my head. He's dressed like he was today. In a gray T-shirt and board shorts and then, nothing at all.

"You're blushing," Carol says.

"How can you tell? It's dark and it's a thousand degrees in here."

Carol smiles. "Fine," she says. "But then I'm allowed to have secrets, too."

Chapter Sixteen

I get back to the hotel after midnight. Carol drops me off at the entryway, clinging to me. We're both drunk, and I'm so sweaty I feel like I've just stepped out of a pool. The hike back up the hill from town coupled with some . . . vodka shots? tequila? both? . . . have made me feel like alcohol soup. It feels like I've been up for days, years.

"I'll see you tomorrow!" she calls. "Or today!"

She spins me around once, and then she's taking off up the road.

"Good night," I call after her.

I trip inside and up the stairs. No one is at the desk, and there are no bottles of water out. I'm dehydrating by the millisecond.

I stumble out to the dining terrace and then walk around to the pool. The bar window is open, but there's no one around. I peer close, and then I see cases of bottled water, right there under the sink.

The window isn't large, but it's wide enough to fit my torso through. I shimmy my body forward, and then lean down reaching, and then . . .

"What are you doing?"

I lift myself up and jump back to see Adam standing no more than three feet from me.

"Jesus, you scared me."

"Sorry," he says. "But the question stands."

"I need those water bottles," I say, gesturing inside the bar window.

Adam's face changes from curiosity to amusement. "Are you drunk?"

"No!" I say. I blow some air out of my lips. It tastes like vodka. "Kind of. Definitely yes."

"Ha," he says. "Stand back, I'll get you the water, Spider-Woman."

I expect him to do a running jump up onto the counter and then use his body as a seesaw, but instead he just walks through the sliding glass doors leading inside, and a moment later I see him in the window, under the sink, getting the bottles.

"I didn't think of that," I tell him.

"I'm aware," he says.

He returns with four in hand. I twist the top off one and down it in four large gulps.

"You may want to double it," he says.

"Wouldn't mind if I do." I chase it with another.

Afterward, I focus my attention on him. He's wearing a light blue linen shirt and jeans, like Jude Law in *The Talented Mr. Ripley*. He looks extremely handsome. I can admit that. Hot, even.

"You good there?" he asks, grinning. I have not stopped staring at him.

"Yes," I say. "I just need some air."

He opens his arms out wide. "We got a sky full of it. Come on."

He holds his hand out to me, and I take it. He walks us over to two side-by-side lounge chairs. I sit down in one, and then stretch out. I sink into the length of it—my body feels heavy, like I'm in a warm bathtub.

"Thank you," I say. Even here, away from the lights of inside, I can make him out surprisingly well. It's like the moon is always full here. There is no waning.

"You're making me think I have something on my face," he says. He glances at me and then looks up at the sky.

I realize my gaze is still stuck on him, but I'm not sure I can do anything about it. It feels like my body: weighted down, impossible to move.

"Hi," I say.

He turns his head to me. "Hi."

"I saw my mom tonight," I say.

His face doesn't change. "Oh yeah?"

"Yes. She's here. She's . . . here."

"Where?

"It's hard to explain."

"I see," Adam says. "Do you want to try?"

I shake my head. "The point is just that I've found her."

Adam nods. "I understand," he says. "You're processing."

"No, it's truly . . ." I tuck my hand under my head. "It doesn't matter, but it's making everything a little fuzzy. Like it's hard to remember."

"Remember what?"

"I don't know," I say. "What's true?"

"I see."

Adam reaches out and puts a hand on my shoulder. He runs his fingertips down to cup my elbow. I feel it. I feel it everywhere.

"Like that," I say. "That is also making things fuzzy."

He nods, considering. And then all at once he's close to me. Are our chairs this close? It's like he's separate, like I can see all of his details, all of his specific, individual parts, and then he's right here, indistinguishable. A blur of smell and skin and pulse.

"I'd like to kiss you," he says. I hear it in my rib cage. "But I'm not going to unless you tell me it's okay. I know you're in a weird spot. I also know we're here, and there is a very big full moon, and your lips look like watermelon. The good kind. The breakfast kind."

Wherever we are, my words aren't here. I just find the one.

"Okay."

I'm confused by the fact that there still seems to be space between us. It feels like he's everywhere already. I am caught in the impossibility of this, all of it. Of Carol and Remo and Adam here, millimeters from my lips.

Adam touches my chest, right below my collarbone. He moves his hand from my arm and just lays it flat there, right where my heart beats beneath. And then he kisses me. He kisses me like he's done it many, many times before. A professional kiss. Tender and gentle and with a simmering urgency just right there, right under the surface. I sit up, and in another moment I'm on his chair, in his lap, my hands everywhere.

He presses his palms into my back and kneads the muscles there underneath.

My blood thumps to the rhythm of *more more more.*

I feel his hands move up to cup the back of my neck, and I run my fingers, unthinking, through his hair. It feels like velvet. Impossibly soft.

His hands move farther up, to my face, and then he takes me and lifts me closer to him, so my chest is pressed against his and his lips are directly on my neck. I lob my head back; his hand catches it. He kisses behind my ear, down my neck, and then presses his lips into the dip in my collarbone. I gasp forward. And then, like a lightning bolt, Eric's face flashes in front of my closed eyes.

I scramble away.

"What?" Adam says, breathing hard. "Are you okay?"

I sit back. I rub my hands down my face. "I shouldn't be doing this."

"Yeah," he says. He blows some air out of his lips. "Right."

We sit there, not speaking, for as long as it takes our breath to calm.

"For what it's worth," Adam says, "that was a great kiss."

I touch my thumb to my bottom lip. "That wasn't me."

Adam moves so both his feet are on the ground. I'm sitting on the other chair, and we're facing each other now. "Yes," he says. "It was."

I focus on staying put with an intensity that feels almost cartoonish. I'm afraid of what will happen if I move.

Adam inhales next to me, and then he stands. "So listen," he says. "I'm going to see you at breakfast tomorrow. And there is no reason for this to be embarrassing or anything else. We're two adults. This is Italy. Shit happens."

I look at his face. His eyes look black in the moonlight. "Right."

"And hey, Katy?" he says.

"Hm?"

"He's a fucking idiot if he let you come here by yourself."

I stop. I put a hand to my forehead. "I didn't give him a choice," I say.

"Bullshit," Adam says. And then he's gone.

Chapter Seventeen

I sleep in phases, my REM cycles punctuated by the images of Adam's body close to mine, and the waning effects of all that alcohol. As the sun rises the next morning I call Eric from the room phone. I have a coffee next to me, and the robe from the room tucked around me. For the first time since I arrived in Positano, there's a slight chill in the air.

It's 6 a.m. in Positano, which means it's 9 p.m. in Los Angeles. As the phone rings I imagine Eric preparing for bed, taking a glass of water into the bathroom, spitting the Crest blue into the sink. Or is he downstairs, with a beer, watching a sport he doesn't follow on television?

The phone rings. Once, twice, three times, but no one answers. Our voicemail doesn't even pick up, which happens if the machine is full or the phone is off the hook. I swallow. Is he going to work, talking to his family, seeing my dad? Or has he decided in my absence that I was right? That in fact he's not waiting for me to come home, for me to decide. That he's finished, too.

Two weeks after we moved into the Culver City house, Eric

had to go on a business trip. Normally, I'd have spent the week at my parents' house, but I was finishing up a big commercial assignment for work that was on a tight deadline, and I decided to stay put.

"Are you sure you're going to be okay all by yourself there?" my mother asked.

"I'm twenty-seven," I said. "I should be able to spend the night in my own home alone."

"You don't have to, though," my mother said.

I must have been alone growing up—I was an only child, after all—but I never remember it. My mother was always there. She was my mother and my friend and my sibling, all at once.

That first night Eric was gone, I armed the alarm to the house and locked the bedroom door. But the next night I forgot. By the third, I was falling asleep on the couch to a movie, the windows wide open.

"You stayed here the whole week by yourself?" Eric said when he got back. His suitcase was dropped by the door. He was incredulous. I don't think he had believed me on the phone.

"Yes."

He kissed me, and then he angled me toward the couch, my makeshift bed.

We had sex downstairs there, on the floor of the living room, something we never did. I remember feeling sexy, independent. I had missed having that much time to myself, or rather, I'd never had it. And I liked it. When I looked back on that week, I remember thinking it was one of the happiest I'd had. I didn't know what that said about my marriage. Whether it was Eric's absence or return that made me feel that way.

Adam isn't there when I go down to breakfast, my hangover screaming, nor is he there when I finish (toast; fruit; black, black coffee) and wave to Marco and Nika, who seem to be in a heated discussion on the balcony. Today the itinerary upstairs says *Capri*, but what I really want to do is find Carol. Last I left her, she was in the street, dancing up to her pensione. I'm going to track her down this morning.

I climb the steps outside the hotel and try to follow the path to where she split off from me the other morning. I get to the landing. There is still a haze over town today. I'm comfortable in a T-shirt, but I've just been up fifty flights of stairs.

I look around me, trying to figure out where to start my search, when the stupidity of this plan hits me. I never knew the name of the street she lived on, just that she lived in a pensione near the Hotel Poseidon. The hotel was the marker. I have no idea where her room is, or where to begin looking.

There is a wraparound stone bench in this little square, and I take a seat. I watch an older couple drink coffee on the stoop. Two men pass by in bike shorts and tank tops.

I wait. I'm certain that if I just stay here, she'll emerge, present herself the way she has before. The way she did yesterday morning. That she'll spill out into the piazza and stumble into my life once again. But ten minutes pass by, then fifteen, then thirty, and I don't see her.

The boats on the water bob contentedly. I think about last night with Adam. The memory feels like it belongs to someone else. It could not possibly have been me, dancing in that club. It could not possibly have been me, straddling a stranger by an Italian pool. Was it?

Carol and Chuck Silver loved Halloween. I think my mother, more, and my father just went along. They'd go all out—decorated house; haunted pathway up to the front door;

spooky, voice-activated welcome mat; window decals, the whole thing. And their costumes were always over-the-top, too. My mom would go to Rhonda (a seamstress for my dad) in August and start planning. Their costumes were always classic, never topical. Carol Silver did not watch a lot of television. They dressed up as Count Dracula and Countess, *The Wizard of Oz* gone wrong, and Anne of Bloody Gables (my personal favorite). My mother loved passing out candy to all the neighborhood children.

Eric and I tried to do something similar at our house the past few years, but it always felt pointless. She was doing it better; we may as well go over there. So we did. She could transform her home and herself like no one else in the whole neighborhood.

After forty-five minutes, I concede she's not going to show and that it's time to head back. I go downstairs slowly, stopping a few times to take in the view from different vantage points.

The boats leave for Capri every hour. Maybe I'll go. I'm considering what I'd need to do to make that plan happen when I find Nika pacing outside of the hotel.

"Hey," I say. "Is everything okay?"

"Marco," she says. "Is an idiot."

"What happened?"

"He is so stubborn. Tutto questo è così frustrante."

"Here," I say. "Let's go upstairs."

I lead Nika inside, and we go up the steps of the lobby, taking a seat in a hidden bench in the great room.

"Now tell me what's going on," I say once we're sitting.

"He doesn't listen. Your friend Adam, yes?"

I feel my stomach drop. Last night. Adam's hands on my neck and back and . . .

"Yes," I say. "Adam?"

"He made an offer to Marco, and Marco will not accept."

"The hotel," I say. Of course. "He doesn't want to sell."

"He does not understand!" Nika throws her hands in the air. "We need the money. It has been a hard season, this last year, and the hotel needs money. I didn't think he was serious, but the offer is real. It's very real."

"Selling is a big deal," I say. "It's turning over a part of your history. I understand that your family doesn't want to do that."

Nika shakes her head. "What good is history if it cannot live?"

I don't say anything, and she continues. "We don't have the money to do the upkeep that is required, and if we let the hotel falter, our customers will not return. It doesn't matter if it is ours if we cannot keep our doors open. The history of this hotel is the people—the customers who come back every year and the staff that has been with us for decades. Katy, if we close, what does it matter who owns? If we are not open, what is history?"

"I didn't know it was that serious," I say. "The hotel's finances, I mean."

"Marco won't admit it. He thinks we will get the money by some sort of miracle. He does not understand that this is the miracle, this is what we've been hoping for. You know the story about God and the man on the roof?"

"No," I admit. We were not a particularly religious household, more traditional in our approach. I went to Jewish day school, and then secular after that. We went to temple on the High Holidays, but rarely others. My mother liked Shabbat, but we only lit candles probably half the time. "Religion is in the family," my father used to say.

Nika exhales. "A man is on his roof because there is a hurricane and his house is flooding. It's very serious, and the water level keeps rising. He is calling out and calling out for God to help him. *Please, God, do not let me drown! Please save me, God!*

"A man on a raft floats by and asks if the man needs help. *Let me help you*, he says. *I have a raft and it's big enough for two!* But the man on the roof says no thank you, he trusts God. *God is coming*, he tells the man on the raft. *And God alone will save me. I have faith.*

"Then a woman on a boat comes paddling by. She asks the same thing—*Signore, can I help you? Come get in my boat and we will row together to safety*. But again the man on the roof says no. *God is coming. I have faith.*

"Last a helicopter is overhead. The pilot calls down—*I will throw down a rope. Grab on, and we will bring you to safety*. The water is getting higher and higher. It is almost to the top of the house. But the man does not lose his faith. *No*, he says. *God is coming.*

"Finally, the water reaches the man, and he begins to drown. He calls out for God as the water floods his lungs. He dies, and arrives at God's door, and when he gets there, he asks God: *God, why did you forsake me? I trusted you! You abandoned me, your son!* And God looks at him and says: *My son, I never abandoned you. I sent a raft, a boat, and a helicopter. It was you who turned your back on me.*"

Finished with the story, Nika looks at me.

"Ah," I say. "So Adam is God in this situation?"

"He is at least a man with a raft," Nika says. She shakes her head and laughs. "It sounds ridiculous. I'm sorry for telling you all that."

"It doesn't," I say. "I understand. It's hard when someone you love won't see another perspective."

"Yes," she says. "I am afraid his stubbornness will cost us our business."

My mother and I didn't fight much, but when we did, it was usually about small things—clothes, food, the question of whether to take the freeway or side streets. On the big stuff, she was insistent; it wasn't worth going up against her, and I didn't want to. My mother had a very clear idea about the right way to do things, and most of the time, I was happy she had the answers. I listened to her; I trusted her. I didn't know the best way to live my life, so if she did, I figured following what she knew made sense. This was a problem for Eric. Not at the beginning of our relationship. In the beginning, I think we both liked it. We were so young, it was nice to have someone telling us which airline deal to take and which apartment to rent and what couch to buy and where to order chicken from. But as time went on, Eric would sometimes accuse me of heeding her advice to our own—Eric's and mine—detriment.

"You never stop to think about what you want," Eric once said to me. It was a night a year or so after we had purchased and moved into our new house. I didn't love that we were in Culver City—fifteen minutes still felt like a long time to drive when I was used to being able to walk to my parents' house—but the price had been right, and the house had a yard and was on a good block. We said we could start a family there, when the time was right.

We talked about having children casually, the way two people talk about how to spend their Sunday. We were aware we would, at some abstract point, and that until that point, time would unspool lazily. We weren't worried. At least, I wasn't.

On that particular night, Eric raised the question, abruptly, over takeout from Pizzicotto: Margherita pizza and a chopped salad.

"I think we should talk about having a baby" was what he said. We were talking about whether to drink beer or soda, and then we were talking about changing our whole lives.

I didn't answer for a moment. I blew on my pizza and then set it down. "Okay," I said. "What do you want to talk about?"

"I think we're ready."

I blinked at him. Ready? I was still working freelance, and he'd just switched careers. We could barely keep up with our modest mortgage; there was no way we could add a baby to the mix.

"How do you figure?" I asked.

"We have a house; I have a good job. Your parents are close by."

I imagined telling my mother that Eric and I were ready to start trying. I started laughing. I couldn't help it.

"What?" Eric asked.

"Nothing it's just, *we're* kids."

"We're not," Eric said. "My parents already had two kids by the time they were our age."

"We're not your parents."

"Are we yours?" he asked. "Because that isn't too far off, either."

"Three years!" I said to him. "That's plenty of time. That's loads of time. We have it; we should take it."

"But what if I'm ready now?"

It had never occurred to me that having a child before I was thirty was something Eric and I would entertain, let alone want. Let alone do.

"Eric," I said. "Are you serious?"

He speared a tomato from his salad. "I don't know," he said. "I just want to feel like we're doing something, making these decisions on our own. Like they're *our* decisions to make."

"We are," I said. "Who else's would they be?"

He didn't say anything, and I continued.

"I'll tell you what, I'll think about it. But I'm not going to start a family just to *do something*. Let's think about it, and we can talk about it in another week, okay?"

Eric smiled. He kissed me. "Thank you."

I talked to my mother about it. She said what I knew she would—that it was too soon, that we were too young. I told Eric.

"You said you were going to think about it," he said. "You didn't say you had to decide by committee. You never stop to think about what you want."

"That's not true."

"It is," he said. "She just decides what you think for you."

We got in a fight about it, one of our biggest, but I never wavered in the certainty that my mother—and I, by proximity—was right. Why would I make a choice this big without her? She knew what was right even when I didn't—why wouldn't I use that information, that help?

We shelved the baby discussion, another year went by, and then my mother got sick. Any questions of children were sent back where they came from.

I look at Nika now, seated next to me.

"Maybe Marco knows something you don't," I tell her. "If he believes that strongly, maybe he really does have some information he's not sharing."

Just then Adam appears in the lobby. He's wet from the

pool, and his chest is bare, revealing a very toned torso. A towel swings around his neck.

"Hello," he says.

"We were just talking about you," Nika says.

Adam raises his eyebrows and looks to me. "Really."

"The hotel," I say quickly. I can feel the heat creeping from my chest up my neck and into my face. "Your offer."

"Ah."

"I have to get back to the desk," Nika says. "Thank you, for listening. I appreciate the ear."

"Of course."

Nika waves to Adam on the way out. And then it's just the two of us. Last night might as well be playing on a movie screen in front of us. I know it's the only thing either one of us is seeing.

"Hi," he says. He's still dripping wet, the beads of pool water dangling like earrings from the ends of his hair.

"Hi," I say.

"Can I sit?"

I gesture to the empty space next to me. He does.

"How did you sleep?"

"Good," I say. I swallow. "Not great, honestly."

Adam smiles. "That doesn't surprise me," he says.

He holds my gaze, and I look away.

"I just mean," he continues, "tequila and red wine and limoncello will do that to you."

I nod. "Right."

"Can I ask you something?" Adam says.

"Sure."

"Last night," he starts.

"I thought we were not going to make this awkward. Italy and all."

Adam pauses. “Am I making this awkward?”

I look up at him. His face is relaxed, his body casual. “No?” I admit.

“No. So, last night.”

“Yeah, I’m sorry about that.”

“Which part?”

“I don’t know. Kissing you? I shouldn’t have done that.”

He nods. “I guess it occurred to me that I didn’t ask you what you want.”

“What do you mean?”

“Well, you’ve told me you’re married and that you’re maybe separating and that you’re heartbroken, because you’ve lost your mother.”

He says the last part delicately, tenderly, and I wince.

“I guess I just thought I should ask what you want. Whether you want your marriage to work out, rather. Whether you want to go home to him.”

This wasn’t what I expected him to say. I expected him to apologize for kissing me, maybe. Or to accuse me of bailing. Now I don’t know how to answer.

“Because, the thing is, yeah, we’re in Italy. Shit happens, like I said. This isn’t about me. I don’t even know you, and you don’t know me.”

“Right.” I feel a pang of something. Disappointment, maybe. Interesting.

“But you could,” he says.

“I could know you.”

He nods. “You could.”

I take an unsteady breath. “I don’t know.”

“Oh, I think you do.” Adam’s gaze sits heavy on mine. “Like

I said, it's not about me. But it would be a shame if you kept doing something only because you've done it before."

I think about the routine of my life back home. The coffeepot, the mail, the market. The same four shows on the DVR.

What got you here won't get you there.

"What are you doing tonight?" I ask Adam.

"Having dinner with you," he says.

Chapter Eighteen

Adam and I meet in the lobby at seven-thirty. It's still sunny out, but a bit cooler than the day. I chose a long Poupette silk slip dress in bright blue with an off-the-shoulder top. I put on a chunky rose quartz and topaz necklace, no earrings, then sweep my hair up into a topknot. Gold sandals and my Clare V. clutch—one of my mother's favorite local LA brands.

"You look beautiful," Adam says when he sees me.

He's wearing a white linen shirt, khaki shorts, and a beaded mala necklace.

"You too," I say. "I mean, you look nice."

"Hey," he tells me. "I'll take beautiful. Nothing wrong with beautiful."

We leave the hotel, and I'm starting to make a left, down into town, when Adam cocks his head across the street. There is a car waiting, with a driver standing by outside.

"For us?" I ask.

Adam nods. "We're going to broaden our horizons," he says. "After you."

The driver holds the door open, and I slip into the back of an old-time town car. Adam gets in the other side next to me.

"Where are we going?" I ask him.

"Il San Pietro," he says. "One of the most stunning places in the world."

I remember the name of this place. It was on our itinerary, day 6: *Drinks at San Pietro.*

"It's a famous hotel," Adam continues. "It's hard to explain, better to just see it."

We drive down past town and then back out, along the coast, and in no more than ten minutes, we are pulling off to the right side of the road.

"Here we are," the driver says.

"Grazie, Lorenzo," Adam says.

We walk down a small path, and then we are at the mouth of Il San Pietro, a sprawling estate built entirely into the rock of the seaside.

The lobby is open and white, and green ivy climbs the walls and saunters across swaths of the ceiling. Huge glass windows lead out to wraparound terraces that hang over the sea. Farther out, there is nothing but ocean.

"This is beyond," I say to Adam.

He smiles. "Come on."

Out on the veranda I see the tiers of the hotel—with what looks like millions of steps down to the ocean. Below us, hundreds of feet, there are tennis courts and a beach club—bright orange chairs sit perkily on the rocks of the shore. There is a 180-degree view of the Mediterranean Sea.

"This looks like a fairy tale," I tell Adam.

A waiter appears, handing us each a glass of ice-cold champagne. "Buonasera," he says. "Welcome."

"Thank you."

"Let's walk a bit before dinner," Adam says.

All around the main hub of the hotel are ivy-lined walkways. They weave in and out between rooms and levels, taking us down closer to the ocean and back up, toward the main restaurant and lobby.

"Have you ever stayed here?" I ask Adam.

"Once," he says. "It's extremely romantic"—he takes a sip of champagne and I look away, down at the water—"but I love the ease and convenience of the Poseidon. Here, you are really in another world."

"Yes," I say.

I don't see how you would ever leave. The magic of Italy seems to be in its ability to connect to some time out of time, some era that is unmarked by modernity. There is so much peacefulness in being present, right here.

I take a sip of the champagne. It's dry and crisp.

We walk on a stone pathway covered overhead by branches of lemon trees.

"This is heaven," I say.

"Every guest room is different," Adam says. "Totally unique. From the fixtures to the hardware to the decor. It's really special."

Down the path, a man and woman walk hand in hand in bathing suits. He has a towel slung over his shoulder.

"It's like being in a movie," I say. "Like *Only You* or *Under the Tuscan Sun*."

"I don't watch too many movies," he says. "But it is very cinematic, I agree."

"Who have you brought here?" I ask him.

Adam smiles at me. His dimples on full display. "Maybe someone brought me."

I shake my head. "No way."

"Why?"

"You strike me as someone who likes to be in the driver's seat."

"Well," he says. "I suppose that's true. But you can't know something without being introduced to it. Everyone has an entry point. An ex I dated brought me to Positano for the first time, actually. Granted, it was many years ago. We were barely more than kids. We stayed at a hotel called La Fenice. It was so high up and out of town we basically had to hike up to the path every day. We didn't have much money, but the view was stellar."

I look at him, a smile slowly spreading across his face.

"It was your favorite trip, wasn't it?"

Adam turns back to me. His gaze lingers on me. "It used to be."

Dinner is out on the terrace, bathed in the golden Italian light. There is a wood-fired pizza oven, decorated with beautiful blue and white and red enamel plates, and the meal is served on the same flatware.

We get pizzas—truffle with figs and roasted tomatoes—and the sweetest arugula, pear, and Parmesan salad and crisp calamari, fried to perfection. There is also a bottle of red wine that is so delicious I drink it like water.

"What happened to the girl?" I ask Adam. Our plates have cleared, and we are enjoying a second bottle of wine. The sun is setting on the sea—dimming the whole evening into blue hues. The ocean darkens from turquoise to indigo. All of a sudden, the terrace is lit by candlelight.

"Oh," Adam says. "It was a long time ago. We were young."

"How young?" I realize I don't know how old Adam is. Older. Thirty-five? Thirty-eight?

"Young enough," he says. He laughs. "We were traveling all over, and Positano was her nonnegotiable travel destination, so we came."

"And you fell in love."

"With the town, yes. I was already in love with her. She ended up breaking my heart six months later."

"What happened?"

"A drummer named Dave."

I nod. "I get it," I say, although I don't. I never let myself fall in and out of love. I never had other experiences.

I think about last night, Adam across from me.

"How about you?" Adam asks.

"Me?"

"Have you ever had your heart broken?"

I think about Eric, at college, his goofy charm, weekends driving the coast to Santa Cruz, Costco runs, pizza night at my parents'.

"No," I say.

Adam smiles. "You know what they say."

"What?"

"Never trust anyone who hasn't had their heart broken. It's a before and after. You never quite see the world the same way again."

All at once a cloud settles in over my heart. I see my mother, at the hospital, in her bed in Brentwood. The hum and beep of machines.

"I think I need to amend my answer, then," I say.

"You have?"

I nod.

From across the table, Adam takes my hand. He flips my palm open and grazes his fingers along the inside. I feel his touch up my spine—it gets stuck in my ears, vibrating sound, energy, electricity.

We order dessert. A pot of chocolate and cream I'd like to bathe in. There are delicate chocolate flakes and powdered sugar on top. It might be the best thing I've ever tasted.

"Before we leave," Adam says, "there's something we have to do."

We finish our wine, Adam pays the bill, and then he leads me over to the corner of the terrace. There's a green door, and inside is a glass elevator. It's nearly dark now, but the entirety of the hotel is lit up in light.

"After you," he says.

We get inside, and then we're going down—descending past the layers of gardens and rooms and terraces and dining areas, deeper into the rock. Past the gardens filled with fresh produce and the spa—down, down, down until we land in the middle of a rock cave.

Adam opens the door, and then I see the elevator has spit us out into a stone grotto. We emerge into the night three hundred feet below where we began. The hotel's tennis courts are to our right, and to our left is the hotel's lunch spot, followed by the beach club.

Adam takes my hand and we walk down, over to the chairs. The ocean plays just ten feet over, jumping, lapping at the rocks.

"Do you want to sit?" he asks me.

I take a seat on a lounge chair, and he sits down beside me, on the same one. I can feel Adam's shoulder against mine, and then the hint of his chest pressing into my back.

Down here, at the ocean, the evidence of nightfall is apparent. The moon slowly rises, the whole beach hovering in that space between things. I hug my arms to my chest.

"Are you cold?" Adam asks.

I shake my head. I am not cold. Not at all.

From next to me, gently, I feel him put a hand on the back of my neck and run it down my arm to cup my elbow. I breathe out into the night air.

"Adam," I say.

I turn to face him. Like last night, I have a powerful, nearly impossible-to-say-no-to urge to kiss him, to throw myself into his arms and feel his skin everywhere. But I don't. Because I have Eric, and whatever is happening here can't be enough to forget that.

"Hmm?"

"I can't," I say. I want to cut off my own tongue.

Adam removes his hands, slowly, from my body. "I understand," he says. "Do you want to go?"

I shake my head. I rearrange myself so my back is against the back of the chair. Adam sits up next to me. I feel his breathing beside me—in and out, in and out, like the tide.

We stay and watch the waves until the sky is near black. Until the stars look down on the boats at sea like steady, unblinking eyes.

Chapter Nineteen

Adam is gone the following day, traveling up to Naples for work, and I spend it looking everywhere for Carol. I go to Chez Black and wander down to the marina. I try the shuttered doors of Bella Bar: nothing. I wait by the entrance to the hotel for a solid two hours, but finally at 9 p.m., I have to concede defeat. She's not here.

I eat a bowl of pasta Carlo sends out to me on the patio. What if I've lost her again?

I should have made a plan. I should have said, *I'll meet you here at 10 a.m. tomorrow.* But I was drunk and happy and I forgot.

A few tables over, a group of thirtysomethings laughs over a bottle of wine. I have the impulse to pull up a chair, to talk to them, to express some of the wild and wonderful and complicated and confusing things that are happening in my life, in this foreign place, right now.

But I don't talk to strangers. My best friend is a woman named Andrea whom I met in college and who lives in

New York. She came out for the funeral, but we got no time together. The last time I remember us sitting down to dinner was at least a year ago. Eric and I never go to New York anymore, and Andrea is busy being a public relations manager. Watching these women now, though—laughing, drinking, talking—I feel a wave of regret that I haven't prioritized our relationship. That I've let so much drift so far.

I finish my food and go upstairs. I sleep fitfully and give up entirely before the sun comes up.

At six I go down to breakfast in search of coffee. I got maybe three hours, combined, of sleep last night. Breakfast isn't open yet, but Carlo is setting up the tables.

"Buongiorno, Ms. Silver," he says.

"Carlo, any chance you have some coffee?"

Carlo gestures to the kitchen. "I'll look. One moment."

I linger on the patio. There's a similar chill in the air to yesterday. But the whole town is still gray and blue.

Carlo returns two minutes later with a steaming Americano. It's almost black in color. Perfect.

"Grazie," I say. "Thank you a million."

"A million not necessary," he says. "But you are welcome. Shall I set the table?" He gestures to my usual spot, under the umbrella.

"No thank you," I tell him. "Maybe later."

I take my coffee and sit in a lounge chair by the pool. Without caffeine, everything feels as foggy as the day around me. I take a few sips.

Where is she?

When I was young, just a baby, really, my mother used to sing to me every night. I'd always request the song, the one that goes: *My mommy comes back, she always comes back, she always comes back to get me. My mommy comes back, she always comes back, she never will forget me.*

My mother used to sing it in a ridiculous Disney voice, making the whole thing just silly enough to almost eclipse the meaning. Almost. But it was her way of saying she'd always be there; she'd never leave.

I go back upstairs and put on my tennis shoes. I rub on some sunscreen, grab my sun hat, and then head up the Positano stairs. I get to the landing after ten heart-pumping minutes but keep pushing up. When I reach the Path of the Gods, I'm soaked. I take a swig of water and survey the day.

The haze is burning off, and the morning is breaking through. It looks to be another picture-perfect day. From up here, you can see all the way out into the ocean. It's not quite the panorama that Il San Pietro provided, but it's close. I can even make out the island of Capri.

There isn't another soul up here. I have the path entirely to myself. The coffee has kicked in, and the combination of caffeine, fresh air, and exertion has me feeling awake. I'm about to decide whether I want to walk the path, additionally, when I hear footsteps behind me.

I hold my breath, expecting to see Carol pop up, *please please please*, but instead it's Adam.

"Hey," he says. "Look who it is."

"Were you following me?"

Adam sticks his hands on his hips and leans backward, blowing some air out of his lips. "Whew," he says. "That's a workout."

I hold out my bottle of water to him, and he takes a long drink.

"Thanks."

I nod.

"And no, I wasn't following you," he says, handing it back to me. "I told you I like to hike. When you mentioned the stairs, it stuck with me."

"How was Naples?" I ask him.

"Good," he says. "It's a weird place, but I love it."

"Do you want to walk the path a little? I've never been any farther than this."

He picks up his T-shirt and wipes his forehead. I see the slice of skin of his abdomen. The taut muscle underneath. "Yeah," he says. "Let's do it."

We enter the path and continue on upward. The views are spectacular. After another ten minutes, I wonder if we're close to La Tagliata; we seem to be in the clouds at this point. We pause at an overlook. I hold on to a wooden rail, worn down to a smooth, satiny patina from all the travelers that have come and gone. Adam moves to stand beside me.

"I read that the path is where the gods used to come down to meet Poseidon at the sea," Adam tells me.

"It was Ulysses," I say.

"Right, Ulysses. I like that," he says. "I could see why they'd choose it here. To mingle with the earthlings. You'd want somewhere that felt like heaven on earth."

"I used to love Greek mythology. Roman? I can never remember."

"Roman," he says. "But I think they are quite similar. What about it did you love?"

"I think I liked that there was someone in charge of everything. A god for water, a god for wine, a goddess for spring, and a goddess for love. Everything had a ruler."

"That's interesting," Adam says. "They were still greedy,

though. They still wanted what the other one had. And they got all tangled in with the mortals. It wasn't a very orderly situation. Very human, actually."

I glance at Adam, who is looking out over the ocean. There is a breeze now, and the wind picks up the sticky hair on the back of my neck.

"Why do you want to buy the hotel?" I ask him. "Really. I know it's a good investment and all that."

"How is that not enough of a reason, especially for a company looking to grow?"

I shake my head. "You love Marco and Nika; you come here every year; you said yourself that this place is special to you. I just don't buy that someone sent you on this mission, and you want to take over a place you already think is perfect."

Adam doesn't immediately answer. He inhales, his eyes still on the ocean. "You know I didn't want to work in real estate? I love it now, but a long time ago I wanted to be a lawyer."

"Really?"

Adam nods. "My mother is one, and my father is, too. They met in law school. It felt like the thing to do. My parents are both so passionate about the law and they love their jobs. I figured I'd love it, too."

"So what happened?"

"I failed the bar," he says. "And then I failed it again. After the second time, I had to do some soul-searching."

"You discovered you didn't really want to be a lawyer?"

"It wasn't that. It was that I couldn't really *grasp* the law. I wasn't good at it. Even after all that time in law school, it felt like I was reading a foreign language." He pauses, wipes his forehead with the back of his hand. "In the end, I just didn't care enough. And I think it's hard to be good at something that you don't love." He clears his throat. "I know this hotel," he continues. "I love this hotel."

"I get it," I say. "I mean, I can see why. I love it, too."

"I'm not trying to change it," he says to me. His tone carries a charge. He really wants me to know. "I want to help; I want to make it even better. I want the Poseidon to be the best version of itself so it will be around for a very long time."

"Okay," I say.

"I'm an opportunist, but I'm not a bad person. They're stuck," he says. "They need help moving forward."

"And you?"

Adam puts both hands on the railing. I take another survey of the sea. "Am I stuck?"

I don't answer him.

"I think I'm really good at travel and less good at what happens when you stand still," he says. "I like to be a visitor. In places, in hotels, sometimes in other people's lives." He glances at me, and our eyes meet briefly. "I guess I'm not really sure where or if I'm meant to land yet, and the hotel feels like a good opportunity to dig in, where usually I'd just—"

"Keep renting?"

"Yeah, maybe."

We look out over the water for another moment. And then he taps me twice on the arm. It's sporty, maybe even friendly, but I feel it down in my stomach. "I'm impressed with your speed," he says.

"I'd say let's keep going, but I don't want us to die of dehydration."

"We can turn around," Adam says. "And we'll hit this lemonade stand on the way down. No water, but I do have cash."

"I feel like that might be your tagline."

"My tagline?"

"Like *The Real Housewives*? Tagline?" He looks at me blankly. "Never mind."

We walk in silence. It feels comfortable, familiar, even. Like we've known each other a lot longer than the few days since I arrived. We stop at a lemonade stand, and Adam buys us both one. It's sweet and syrupy and sticky and delicious. I down it and then pop an ice cube in my mouth, sucking on the cold until it melts. We wander back to the hotel through side steps. We stop at the landing and look down at the water. There is no rush. It is somehow, impossibly, still morning.

"I feel like there are more hours in the day here," I say to Adam.

"That's why I love it," he says.

Everything is longer in Positano. Even time.

Chapter Twenty

Over breakfast I ask Adam if he wants to go to Capri today. The weather is glorious—wide-open, bright blue skies. I look out over the water that looks like crystal. Spending the day going to an island paradise is a perfect plan.

"Sounds like fun, Silver," he says. "I think you'll like it there, and I'd be honored as ever to show you around."

"I asked you."

"Trust me," he says. "You want me in charge."

Adam has a connection for a day boat, and an hour later we're back at the Positano dock, loading into a small private yacht.

"This is Amelio," Adam says. He introduces me to the captain—a man who looks to be in his late thirties with a ponytail and a white cotton polo.

"Hi," I say. "Thank you for taking us."

"Watch your step," Amelio says. He speaks with an accent that sounds half-Italian and half-Australian.

He takes my hand and helps me onto the small yacht. The

entire front of the boat is padded, like a giant lounge chair. All browns and creams and whites. It's so old-school beautiful.

"Tornado, right?" I ask Amelio.

He smiles appreciatively and nods. The tiny yacht is a throwback to the sixties in its style. It looks brand-new, impeccably maintained.

"Some of the most stunning boats in the world," I say. "I love this one. Is it yours?"

Amelio nods. "Sì, è della mia famiglia."

I grab a beach towel. Adam raises his eyebrow at me.

"What?" I say. "My father loves boats."

When I was little, he used to take me down to the marina in Huntington Beach and show me the boats. Small catamaran yachts, like the one we're on, are his favorites. Mine too.

We settle down on neighboring beach towels as Amelio revs the engine. Then we're speeding away, toward Capri. The wind kicks up, and the air around us is salty and wet.

The trip to Capri is no more than forty-five minutes. The island emerges out of the sea like a giant perched rock—all jagged, dramatic cliffs. As we get closer I see a cove, then the rocks of a shore. There are about twenty swimmers bobbing their heads in the ocean.

The deep blue water gives way to a turquoise that seems fake, almost clear.

Amelio cuts the engine, and we drift. As we pull into the cove I turn to Adam.

"I want to swim," I say.

"Now?"

"Amelio," I call. "Can we hop in the water before we pull to shore? Can we swim?" I pantomime the breaststroke.

"Sì!" He gestures to the left side of the boat, where there is a step stool down into the water.

I pull my cover-up over my head and toss it down onto the mat. Underneath I'm wearing a white ribbed one-piece. I notice Adam noticing.

And then I make a single dive off the side. The water hits cold on my hot skin. It's nearly breathtaking. After a few seconds, the initial shock fades to a luxurious, refreshing sensation. Crisp and smooth, almost like velvet.

My head breaks the surface, and I shake the water out of my eyes and call up to Adam.

"Get in!"

He stands, looking over me.

"Is it cold?"

I blow some water off my lips. "It's actually quite warm," I lie.

I watch as he peels his T-shirt off. I dive underneath the water and when I emerge, he's half in, suspended on the step stool, bargaining.

"Christ," he says. "It's cold."

"C'mon, Adam," I say. "Take the plunge."

He dives off the step and emerges moments later, shaking out his hair. He's such an alpha male, but here in the water, his hair curling up with droplets, he's playful. He appears younger than he has since I met him.

Adam splashes some water toward me and then floats up onto his back. I do the same next to him. The sky is cloudless. One wide expanse of bright, impossible blue.

"I love it here," I say.

He laughs beside me. "We haven't even gotten to Capri yet."

"No," I say. "Here. All of it."

I flip back over so my feet are underneath me, and Adam

does the same. He treads water, and the current bounces him closer.

"Thanks for coming with me," I say.

He's so close I can see the water droplets on his eyelashes. They cling there like tears.

"Thanks for asking me."

His eyes scan my face. And then he ducks back under the water. When he emerges, he's back close to the boat.

"Come on, Silver," he says. "We've got a day to get underway."

We climb back on and towel off, and Amelio guides us between the rocks and into the cove, right up to the dock that bobs and weaves with the water.

Adam takes my hand and helps me onto the wooden plank.

"Thank you!" I call to Amelio.

"Come back maybe four or four-thirty."

Amelio nods. "No worry!"

He gestures out to sea, out to the blue water that surrounds us, miles of it in every direction.

Once we're on land, I take in our surroundings.

Blue-and-white-striped umbrellas dot the scenery like camera flashes. Underneath them beachgoers lounge in chairs. Some linger on the rocks; others swim. The beach club isn't crowded—more pleasantly populated. Beyond the rocks, there is a thatched building with the words *La Fontelina* on a wooden sign.

"I've heard of this place," I say, remembering. My mother and I had reservations at the neighboring beach club, Da Luigi.

"Welcome to heaven," Adam says. "Come on."

We check in at a stand and are handed two beach towels. A porter guides us over to two lounge chairs, a stone's throw away from the water. He sets up an umbrella overhead.

"This is spectacular," I say.

I haven't bothered to put my cover-up back on, and I toss my towel down, then plop onto the lounge chair.

"Just wait until lunch," Adam says. "They have one of my favorite restaurants in Amalfi."

I stretch out, feeling the sun on my legs.

Adam takes out a book. It's his copy of *A Moveable Feast*, the one he traded at the lending library by my room the day I met him.

"Is it good?" I ask.

"It's a classic."

"And?"

"Yes," he says. "It's very good. It reminds me of the best and worst of Paris. The romantic tragedy of that place."

"Does your mom go back often?" I ask.

"Yes, about once a year. Her sister still lives there, my aunt. They are close, and I think it's hard for my mother, being so far away from her." He pauses, looks down at my bag. "Did you bring anything to read?"

I shake my head. "No," I say. "I'm very content."

I say it, and I realize I mean it. I feel a strange calm take over my body. I close my eyes. There's a breeze off the water, and the umbrella overhead keeps me well shaded.

We sun for a little while. I doze in and out of sleep—lulled by the sounds of the ocean, the peace of this place.

"Are you interested in heading up to the restaurant?" Adam asks me after about an hour. "We can order some wine before lunch."

"Sounds great."

I toss my cover-up on, and we climb the steps into the breezy building.

We're seated out on the deck, overlooking the rocks, the whole ocean splayed out in front of us.

Adam orders us an ice-cold bottle of Sancerre. It's sweet and delicious. I gobble down a glass.

From our perched spot you can see all blue, clear water and the three rocks of Faraglioni. They rise out of the ocean like Viking warriors, stacks of the sea. A hundred meters high, like cliffs themselves. The middle rock is an archway, where you can pass through. It's impossible not to recognize them from thousands of photographs—on Instagram, or otherwise.

Adam follows my gaze. "You know the story about those, right?"

I nod.

If you kiss while entering through the archway of the middle rock, you will be happy in love for the next thirty years.

Thirty years. As old as I am. Thirty years. As old as my mother is here now.

"That's a long time," I say.

"Not here," he tells me.

My stomach rumbles. I feel like I'm always hungry. That something in me that has been shut off is waking up now. Ready to be fed.

We order. A plate of grilled vegetables, seared octopus, creamy burrata and vine tomatoes, and lobster pasta. A tossed green salad and light dinner bread round out the meal.

I eat. And eat and eat.

"I could constantly consume food here," I say. "I feel like I'm bottomless."

"I know," Adam tells me. "I told you. The food is amazing. Italian food has that effect. When the ingredients are high quality and simple, the meal is satisfying and doesn't sit on you."

I have a memory of Adam tapping his stomach, claiming to have gained ten pounds.

I take another sip of Sancerre. I'm pretty sure we're now on our second bottle. My limbs feel pleasantly loose. There is a happy buzzing in my chest.

"Do you always come to Italy for work now?" I ask him.

"Not always," he says. "We have a hotel in Rome, but Positano is a nice place to come in between when you have a little time off."

"It's pretty romantic," I say out of nowhere. It's the wine. I have the impulse to cover it with more words, but I don't.

Adam raises an eyebrow at me. "Yes, I agree. It is."

My stomach pulls, imagining Adam here with some other girl. Maybe he met her, like me, at the hotel. Maybe she was American, too. Or Swiss. Or French. Some fabulous brunette with legs a mile high and a tiny kerchief at her neck. Annabelle. No, Amelie.

"My most recent ex was more of a Rome person, truth be told," Adam says, reading me. "She was from Tuscany and had some prejudice against Amalfi."

"Is that a thing?"

Adam shrugs. "Some Italians think the coast is too overrun, too touristy, too expensive."

"It is all those things," I say.

"Yes," Adam says. "But I mean, look at this."

He gestures out to the ocean. To the rocks beyond. To the water and sky that look too technicolor to be real.

"What happened to her? Why did it end, I mean."

Adam picks up his water glass. "She wanted to live in Italy, and she didn't want me to travel. We fought about it all the time. She wanted a life she deserved to have, but it wasn't realistic for me. Last I heard, she got married in Florence. That was two years ago already. Crazy how time flies."

I can tell this still pains Adam. Or did, once. That there's something open or unhealed there.

"How long were you together?"

"Three years," he says. "Off and on." He looks at me. "It's hard for me to stay in one place. Sometimes I think it didn't work because it wasn't right, and sometimes I think it didn't work because I refused to let it."

I think about Eric, in our house, fifteen minutes from my parents. Our shared four restaurants, movie nights at the Grove. Concerts at the Hollywood Bowl. My whole life that has taken place in a ten-mile radius. I've been resistant to change, too. To letting someone change me.

Adam sets his water glass down with a clunk. "So what do you want to do now?" he asks me. "We could explore Capri. We can go shopping. We can go eat at the lemon tree."

The city center of Capri is up the hill from us. The problem is that the only way to get there is by foot, scaling the pathway up from the ocean. And after this morning's stair climb, I'm not sure I have the energy for ten thousand more steps.

"We could also go by boat to Marina Piccola and then walk," Adam offers.

I sit back. I see our beach chairs below us.

"You know what I really want to do?" I say to Adam.

"Tell me."

"Nothing," I say.

Adam smiles. "You sure?" he says. "We're already here. And Capri is pretty great. Great shopping, great bars."

"I've seen pictures," I say. "There's a Prada store."

"There are a lot of small boutiques. I thought that might be your thing. You dress well, different."

"Thanks," I say. Although, I'd never describe my style as different. Derivative with a twist, maybe. "I do like to shop, but today I just want to be here and not feel like there's anywhere I have to go or anything I have to do. Is that okay?"

Adam gives me a slow nod. "Yes," he says. "That is very much okay."

For the next four hours, all we do is nap and swim. It's heaven. I go from the ocean to the beach lounger to the rocks and back. That's it, that's all. Just the simplicity of water and rocks and stunning views. There is wine and water and icy lemonade. I reapply sunscreen, and Adam switches chairs with me once the umbrella can no longer cover us both. He reads. I close my eyes, and for the first time in months, there is a pleasant blankness there. I am not met with images of hospitals, or questions about my future, the uncertainty of what's to come. All I feel is this—this complete embrace of the present.

When four-thirty rolls around, we see Amelio bobbing on the water. Adam waves and we pack up, making our way to the dock as he slowly pulls in.

We board. My skin is full of salt water and sunscreen, and my cover-up is tucked in my bag. I haven't put it on once.

"Nice?" Amelio asks.

"The best," I say. "I think I might move here." I imagine a life full of endless beach days.

As we pull away from La Fontelina, I see the rocks of Faraglioni ahead. A few boats are passing under. A couple kisses in the archway.

"Would you like to go?" Amelio asks.

Adam looks to me. "Sure," he says. We're on the leather front of the boat. He sits up and slides his arms around his knees. "I feel I should give you the full Capri experience."

My heart starts pounding. I have no idea what he means by that. Does he want me to see the nature-made architectural wonder, up close? Or is he going to kiss me under those rocks? What's the *full* experience?

The thump of my pulse gets louder and louder like approaching horses. I feel the question hang there between us as we drive toward the rocks.

Once we're close, Amelio slows the engine. Adam stretches his legs out in front of him and leans back on his hands. He tilts his head to the side to look at me. But he doesn't move his body, not yet.

"Here go!" Amelio calls.

We begin to pull through the archway. There is a cool breeze off the water, and we're surrounded by rocks. I sense Adam close to me, closer than he was mere moments ago. I sense his skin—salty, warm—and the brush of his clothing.

We're fully encapsulated now. The moment hovers around us like an air bubble, threatening to pop.

"Katy," Adam says. His voice is barely above a whisper, and I turn to him. He's looking at me with so much intensity I think he's going to kiss me. He's really going to do it. The seconds crawl by like years. Time, doubled over, lapsed, like it is here, now, doesn't hold the same weight. It doesn't mean the same thing. We are young and we are old and we are coming and going, all at once.

We're almost out. I can see the sun begin to crest, straining to meet us. It's now or never.

And then Adam takes my hand. He takes my palm and presses his palm against it, interlacing his fingers with mine. He keeps it there as we pull back out, into the sunshine.

"Beautiful!" Amelio calls.

"Beautiful," Adam says, still looking at me.

Chapter Twenty-One

I don't see Carol the next day, either, and two days later, Adam takes me to Naples. One of his favorite places, he claims, in all of Italy.

"A lot of people don't love it," Adam tells me. "Tourists rarely visit. But I think Naples is one of the most beautiful places in the world. Plus, it's the best pizza you'll ever be lucky enough to eat."

"Better than Mozza? We shall see."

"How can you beat where it all started?" he says.

We get a car from the hotel after breakfast. A convertible that feels straight out of the 1950s. This time, Adam drives. The views out of town are just as stunning as the ones coming into it.

"I think I want to live here forever," I say.

Adam smiles. "It's why I keep coming back."

"I'm not sure that's a reality for me," I say.

"It is if you'd want it to be."

"That's really what you believe? Anyone could just live on the Amalfi Coast if they want to hard enough?"

"Hey," Adam says. "Settle. That's not what I mean. I just mean *you* could, if you wanted to. We're not talking about anyone. We're talking about you."

"You don't actually know that," I say.

Adam turns to look at me. "I guess I've got to get to know you better, then. Good thing we have all day."

When we pull off of the coastal part of the drive, and are about twenty minutes out from Naples, Adam gives me a brief history of the place.

"Naples is a strange city," he says. "It's in tatters in some places, absolutely run-down, but there's also this persevering Mediterranean beauty, almost Grecian. It was the most bombed Italian city in World War Two and has a largely tragic history—a huge cholera epidemic, poverty, crime—but there's this strength to this place and its people. I find that beauty next to decay is its own kind of stunning. You can really feel it when you're there."

"I also heard it's a town known for its pickpockets," I say. I remember reading it in a travel guide.

"That too," Adam says.

We arrive in Naples, and I see what he means—the outskirts look poverty-stricken. As we pull into the city center, things get noisier, busier—drivers peel around one another, ignoring any kind of road rules. It's so much more chaotic and stressful than where we've just come from.

We park near the Duomo, one of more than five hundred basilicas in Naples.

"It's probably the Italian city that has held on to its Catholic roots the tightest, and the longest," Adam tells me. "The people here are very religious. They are also very rowdy."

The streets are busy and gritty. There is more trash than I

have seen anywhere in Italy. My journey through Rome was brief, nearly nonexistent, but even so, I know the two cities are nothing alike. I'm struggling to determine what, exactly, Adam loves about the place.

"Come on," Adam says. "I want to walk a little with you."

He touches my elbow and turns me down a street. On the corner, a man and a woman are in a heated debate. She gestures with her hands in his face. He grabs them, and I think, for a sliver of time, he might shake her, but then she yanks his face down and they are making out, fast and furious.

"Italy," Adam says.

"Italy," I repeat.

"I just realized I don't even know what you do for work," Adam says.

"I'm a copywriter," I say. "I help companies and sometimes individuals say what they need to say. I give the language for their websites, and newsletters, and I've worked on a few books. I was in-house somewhere for a while, but I left when my mom got sick."

"I see," Adam says. "How long ago was that?"

"A few months. Caring for her was . . ." I look at two older women carrying plastic bags. The bags look too heavy for them. "My mother was my best friend," I say.

Adam tucks his hands into his pockets, but he doesn't say anything.

"She was the most vibrant woman. She just knew everything, you know? Everyone who knew her went to her for advice. She was so good at being human, she just had it all figured out, and I—"

"You come from her," he says.

"Yeah, but we're nothing alike."

Adam glances at me but doesn't break stride. "I have a hard time believing that's true. She taught you to be like her, no?"

I think about my mother in my home, bringing over a vintage kilim for our kitchen floor, new throw pillows for our couch, home-cooked meals for our fridge.

Something dawns on me, but I'm not sure how to identify it, what it will mean if I acknowledge it out loud, or even just to myself. And then I do.

"No," I say. "She didn't. I was just the recipient."

I don't cook; I don't decorate. I don't know the right place to order flowers from in the Valley, because I always just called her. And now she's gone and I can't help but think, in this moment, that she left me unprepared.

"I'm sorry," Adam says. "I know how hard this is for you." He clears his throat. "When I was very young, my sister died. She was playing on the jungle gym at the park. She fell the wrong way, and she just never woke up."

"Oh my god."

"My mom was there." Adam shakes his head. "Sometimes people ask me why I'm not married, and I think about Bianca, that was her name. That's my first thought. Is that strange? I don't even know why, exactly."

"Because you don't want to lose someone that close to you again."

Adam shakes his head. "I think it's more like . . ." He pauses, considering. "I don't want to see anyone suffer. When I think about Bianca, I don't think about me; I think about my mother. Watching her cry every year on the anniversary, on her birthday, at Christmas, every time anyone asked her how many children she had. It's the suffering that scares me. The way I might feel about someone else's losses."

"It's probably the worst thing," I say. "Losing a child."

Adam nods. "She never got over it. How could you?"

I think about how many times I've asked myself that. If I'll ever feel normal again. If I'll ever be okay. The answer has always been no, but being here now, I think that maybe there is space in that, too. That maybe the expanse of time without her isn't a battlefield, but an empty lot. With some dirt, even. Undeveloped land. That maybe, given time, I get to choose.

We keep wandering, this time in silence. We wind through street after street. We stop at a small café with what looks like two stray dogs out front and order espressos. We drink them and carry on.

As we wander, I'm struck by something so simple. In the heated couple on the corner, in the women carrying their shopping home, in the children playing and screaming in the streets. Naples is a place of connection. Of community.

There is beauty to the run-down buildings, the laundry strung high overhead, the rhythm and drawl of daily life here. There is beauty, too, in the old Mediterranean architecture, buildings left over from centuries ago, before Naples became what it is today. There is beauty in the discrepancy—two things that seem oppositional, coming together.

New and old, rich and ruined, history in its entirety, here at once. It's a place that was once glorious and carries the memory not as a chip, but a promise. Again, someday.

I take my camera out of my tote bag and hang it around my neck.

"That's quite an instrument," Adam says.

"Oh, thanks. It was a gift. There's something about photography I love. A whole memory, caught in a moment."

"That's very well put."

I snap a shot of a man in a full denim suit. He carries a wildflower and a plastic bag.

We wander for a few hours. The sun isn't as strong in Naples as it is in Positano, and the overhead canopies of roof terraces and balconies provide us protection.

It's after one by the time Adam suggests we go on a pizza crawl for lunch. "It's what Naples is known for," he says. "We should sample as much as we can. It's my favorite thing to do here."

I am once again reminded that my appetite has been reawakened in Italy. I'm almost never full now, and if I am, the hunger returns quickly.

"I'm in," I say.

We head to Pizzeria Oliva, a place Adam loves in the Sanità neighborhood—a very working-class area. They make all kinds of pizzas—lemon zest with ricotta, basil, and pepper, and a classic Neapolitan. We also order a fried concoction with smoked mozzarella that is divine.

"This shouldn't be legal," I say to Adam after the first bite.

"Good, right?"

Adam grins at me as he watches me eat.

"Certifiable."

From there we hit up another favorite of Adam's—a small shop that is no more than a window stand about ten minutes walking from Oliva. Unlike the last place, this one is all traditional. We get a classic Margherita pizza, and then Adam motions for me to follow him down to the sidewalk. He takes a few paper napkins and lays them out, gesturing for me to sit. I do.

In the street there is pleasant commotion. A few teenage boys talk in fast Italian, kicking a soccer ball back and forth.

Two women in their forties linger in front of an apartment entryway, gesturing with their hands. Bikers pass by. It's peaceful, a word that, a few short hours ago, I'd never think I'd use to describe Naples. The day has ebbed.

"What do you think?" Adam asks me.

I take a big bite. Absurdly good. "Oh," I say. "Heaven. How many more of these do we have?"

Adam shakes his head. "No, I mean about Naples. Are you glad we came?"

I look over at him. He's folded a slice in half and eats from the bottom. Some grease drips onto the sidewalk below us.

I see us as if I am above us. I see a man and a woman, out on a pizza crawl, on vacation in Italy. Honeymooners, maybe. Two people celebrating the middle of their relationship. You'd never know we were practically strangers.

How much of my life has been open, really? How much has ever lent itself to its own natural development?

I feel a sensation that is wholly unfamiliar begin to awaken down deep. It rustles, stirs, stretches, and then sits up here, right next to us.

I set my slice of pizza down. I wipe my fingertips, and then I reach over and take Adam's hand. His fingers are smooth and long—like each one is its own body, has its own organs, its own beating heart. A map of everything.

I squeeze once, as if in answer. *Yes.*

Chapter Twenty-Two

When we pull back into Positano, it's after six o'clock. Adam opens my door and offers his hand out of the car.

"Thank you," I say. "That was a really great day. The best I've had in a while."

"I'm glad you liked it," he says. "I haven't been in too long. Thank you for agreeing to come."

A moment hovers between us. The air feels thick with it. Possibility. Heat. The impending night.

"You're welcome."

"I have to run a quick errand," Adam says. "But I'll call your room when I'm back?"

I nod. "I might wander a bit."

Adam leans in close and in one swift movement kisses my cheek. "You're really special," he says. And then he leaves.

I walk back up to my room. I strip down and get in the shower. The hot water feels good on my salty, sweaty skin, and as I scrub I feel more and more refreshed. I step out, naked, and survey my body in the mirror. It feels like forever since I've looked at myself like this. I can't remember the last time.

My tan lines are visible, more pronounced than they've been since the summer I spent at Camp Ramah freshman year of high school. I'm bronzed and freckled, and my face looks just a little bit pink.

I towel off my hair and apply some moisturizer to my body. The room is now steamed up, and I go to the balcony doors and throw them open, inviting in the evening sunlight. Then I go and stand in front of my closet. Hanging there are the sundresses and tops I brought—bright colors, patterns, prints. I take out a long silk dress that's looped around the last hanger.

It's white with a spaghetti-strap top. I pull it on. It skims my body and pools at the bottom. A faint embroidery dances down the left side. It's yellowed at the hem and frayed under the armpits. It fits perfectly. It was my mother's.

I slip on a pair of canvas-and-gold espadrilles and head downstairs. When I reach the lobby, I see Marco beginning to set up dinner service.

"Bellissima!" he calls to me.

I smile. "Thank you." I glance around the empty restaurant. "Is Nika here?"

"No," Marco says. "She has gone tonight. She is crazy, that girl. She does not stop bothering me."

"Because of Adam and the hotel?" I ask.

"Sì, certo."

"I understand her point," I say. "If you need the help—"

"This hotel—" Marco starts. "It's my family's proudest moment. Our whole history, everything, is here." He moves his hands in an arc, making a circle. "Hotel Poseidon. Do you understand?"

My father retired three years ago. At the time of his retirement, he had five clothing stores, seventy-two employees, and a corporate office close to my house in Culver City.

He did not want to retire, but my mother wanted him to. Or rather, she wanted to.

"As long as your father works, I work," she said. "And I'm finished with that phase of my life. We don't live beyond our means. We can afford it. I want to do other things now."

My mother wanted to travel more, to read outside, to garden, to spend time with my father that didn't orient itself around cost models.

"But your father loves the business," Eric said to me. "Things are going well, and they're still young. I just don't understand what they're going to do."

I agreed with him. I didn't think it was a smart move for them, either. My father needed to be engaged, and my mother was used to a partner who had something outside their relationship. What would happen if that changed?

I confronted my mother about it, one Friday night after dinner. Eric and my father were in the family room, watching a game he had recorded. My mom was making us fresh mint tea in the kitchen. There was some strawberry cobbler. I remember because usually she made apple.

"I think it's a bad idea for Dad to stop working," I said. "He's going to drive you crazy if he's around all the time. He needs structure. What's he going to do all day long? I don't think it's smart. Eric agrees."

My mother stuffed the glass pot full of mint and let it steep for a full five minutes. She liked a strong brew.

"I don't agree," she said. "I think we both need a change."

"I don't think Dad does," I said. "He loves the business. He thrives on having a place to go and people who rely on him."

She set my cup down in front of me. I touched my fingertips to the ceramic edges. It was burning hot.

"He does," she said. "But he's also curious to see what could come next. We've talked about this for years now. This isn't a spur-of-the-moment decision. You act like we don't speak to one another. It's our relationship; not everything has to make sense to you. It's what we both want."

I never thought about my parents' marriage as being a separate entity from our family unit—we were one. This sentiment was new from my mother, or at least, it had gone unexpressed before.

"What are you going to do?" I asked.

"Something different," she said. "There is more to life than just continuing to do what we know."

I didn't understand it at the time, but I do now. They didn't get much time to travel, but in that one year they had, they did a lot—they went to Mexico and Nashville and the Bahamas. My dad learned how to play the guitar. My mother learned how to make pottery and pound cake and redecorated the family room, then my dad's home office. They were constantly in motion.

There is more to life than just continuing to do what we know.

What got you here won't get you there.

"Are you married, Marco?"

Marco's face erupts into emotion. "I am too old for you!"

"That's not what I mean."

Marco laughs. "Yes, yes, of course I am married."

"Where is your wife?"

"She does not love the life in Positano. She stays in Naples, quite often. I see her seldom in the summer."

"I went to Naples today!"

"You went?"

"Adam took me. I really loved it there."

Marco smiles. "It is a family place."

"You must miss her," I say.

"Of course, yes, but this is life, no? You miss. We miss. It is okay."

"Maybe if you had some more help here, you could see her more often."

Marco considers this. Then his face changes. "You agree!" he says. "You are one of them! You go away!"

But he is kidding, his hand waving me off with a playful flourish.

"Is there a restaurant you would recommend in town?" I ask him. We walk side by side down the stairs to the lobby. "Somewhere I can have a drink."

"Alone?"

I nod.

Marco looks pleased. "Terrazza Celè," he says. "Beautiful."

He gestures for me to follow him, and we cross out into the street. He points to the left. "You go down, down, and then up. On the right side. You take a map, but you do not need it. It's all blue."

"Thank you," I say.

Marco darts inside and returns with a map of Positano, the location of the restaurant circled.

"Have a wonderful evening!" he says. "Enjoy the magic of Positano!"

I turn left out of the hotel, and the moment I do, I hear my name being called. It's her.

"Katy! Katy, wait!"

There Carol is, dashing down the street toward me.

"You're here!" she says. She's out of breath, in a blue cotton dress, the straps falling over her shoulders, her hair tied down loosely at the nape of her neck. "I couldn't find you today!"

Emotion floods my body, but it's not relief, not exactly. It's happiness. At the sight of her. At the living, breathing incarnation in front of me. My friend.

"Carol," I say. "Hi. Where have you been?"

"Working, mostly," she says. "Where have *you* been?"

"I went to Capri! And then Naples today."

Her eyes get wide. "With who?"

"This guy. He's staying at my hotel."

"I wanted to invite you over for dinner," she says. "Are you free?"

"With Remo?" I ask.

She shakes her head. "Just the two of us."

"Now?"

"Why not?" she says. "Unless you have plans?"

"No," I say. "No, I actually have no plans."

"Great. Come with me. I just have to pick up a few things before we head back to mine."

"Of course," I say.

She smiles. She cocks her head to the right, for me to follow. "Wonderful."

We start walking. I have to hold my dress up, so I don't trip all over it.

"You look great, by the way," she says. "Very elegant. I love that dress."

It's yours, I want to tell her. *I took it from your closet. You once wore it to see Van Morrison play at the Hollywood Bowl. You were so beautiful.*

"Oh, thanks."

We keep winding up the hillside, and then Carol points to a little bodega up to the right. "Just here," she says.

We go inside. An older woman sits behind the register. Two young children play on the Formica floor.

"Buonasera," I say.

"Buonasera, sì," the woman says. She turns to Carol. "Ciao, Carol."

"Buonasera, signora. Hai i pomodori stasera?"

"Sì, certo." The woman leads Carol to a small produce section.

"Grazie mille."

Carol loads tomatoes and basil and some small shallots into her basket. I never knew she spoke Italian. A few words, maybe, but she always had to reach for them.

"I'm just trying to think," she says. She holds her fingers out and counts off them. It's something I've seen her do so many times over. On the hundreds of thousands, perhaps millions, of errands I ran with her over the course of her life. Trips to Rite Aid and Target and the Grove. Saturdays at the Beverly Center shopping for a new pair of flats and the Brentwood Farmers Market on Sundays counting the berry pints and the little pots of cashew cream cheese.

But standing here in this small Italian store, in this small Italian town, with my mother who very much is and is not at the same time, I realize how much of her life I was always missing. She knew me completely, but it didn't work both ways; it couldn't. Look how much life was lived before I ever even arrived. Look at who she was before she met me.

I think about her childhood in Boston, school in Chicago, moving to Los Angeles. I think about the death of her own mother—so young, far younger than me—and her warm but removed father. Who taught her how to love? Who taught her how to be the woman she became, the woman she is here today?

Carol pays, and we carry on with a small paper bag full of groceries.

"It's a steep climb," she says. "But quick. Are you okay in those shoes?"

I look down at my espadrilles. They're already rubbing. "Sure," I say. "No problem."

We take the stairs. After two flights, I have to rejigger my dress so it's looped over my arm.

"You're doing great," Carol says. "Almost there. You know I've been climbing the stairs almost daily since I saw you? It's actually a great way to start the morning once you get over the leg cramping and potential cardiac arrest."

I laugh. "I agree."

After another minute, we reach a split in the stairs. One set leads up and to the left, the other straight ahead, and to the right there is a small turquoise door.

"We're here," Carol says. She hands me the paper bag, a sign of casualness and warmth that fills me with a particular kind of ease, and takes out her key.

Inside is immediately warm and bright and cozy. Carol's taste is not my mother's, not even close, and this is a temporary living space, of course, but there is a familiarity here that I would recognize anywhere. A small kitchen that spills into a living room. To the right is a bedroom and beyond the living room, a balcony. The view is not the same as at Hotel Poseidon, but it looks out over town, and you can see the ocean beyond. A sarong covers the couch. There is a brightly colored rug on the wood floor. A map of Greece is taped to the wall. The whole place feels a little like an English cottage in the middle of the Mediterranean.

"This is lovely," I say.

"Oh, thanks. If you want, you can take your shoes off." She gestures to a rack by the door. "But fair warning, the floors might be a bit dusty."

Dusty floors? Carol? I kick off my shoes, intrigued by the possibility of dirt in a Silver house.

It feels good to release my feet. I set my espadrilles down by her tennis sneakers and a pair of flip-flops.

"Red or white?" Carol asks. "Or I could make negronis."

"Whatever you prefer," I say. "I'm easy."

Carol sticks her hands on her hips and surveys me. "But what do you want?"

I consider the question. "Red."

Carol nods. "Me too."

She disappears into the kitchen, and I make my way around the living room. I want to take it all in. This place Carol resided—resides—in, even briefly.

There are small remnants of her everywhere—a pile of *New Yorkers* on the coffee table, a vase of half-dead flowers, a sweater tossed over the chair by the dining nook. Intentioned clutter.

I pick up the sweater and hold it to my nose, breathing her in.

"I opened a bottle of Montepulciano," she says. She comes around the corner and catches me with the sweater.

"Soft," I say.

"Oh, thanks. I'm newly obsessed with stitching and fabric. I can't tell if it makes me look like my grandmother, but I like the feel of the materials. Here." She hands me a glass. I take it.

"Have you been crocheting?"

"Knitting," she says. "A bit. It's enjoyable to do something just because."

"I know what you mean. I brought a camera here, and I've been taking some photos." I take a sip of the wine. "Maybe that's my vocation."

Carol laughs. "Well, I'll tell you, knitting definitely isn't mine."

My mother knew fabric—textures and textiles and materials. She could hold a sweater in her hands and tell you what she thought it should cost. *You won't knit*, I think. *But you'll use this, all of it.*

"I'm going to start dinner. You can take your wine out onto the patio?" She gestures toward the French doors that lead outside.

I look down into the kitchen. "Could I help you?"

She smiles. It feels warm, so very safe and familiar. "I'd like that."

One side of the kitchen is wide open, leading into the living room, and I perch on a stool opposite Carol as she takes ingredients out of the bag, refrigerator, cabinets. Olive oil and flaky salt and tomatoes and fresh lemons. Ricotta and pancetta.

"Do you cook?" she asks me.

"No," I say. "Not really, I'm not very good."

She shakes her head. "You're too self-deprecating."

"I swear," I say. "I'm very bad at it."

"The difference between being good and bad at something is just interest," Carol says. "Would you like to learn?"

"Yes," I tell her.

"Lemon ricotta pasta and tomato salad."

It's a meal I've had many times before, at a very different

kitchen table, thousands of miles away. I never learned how to make it, though. Not until now. Did she ever offer? Or did I just never sit down, listen, and watch?

I take a sip of wine.

Carol puts on music, some old Frank Sinatra, and I am immediately transported to my parents' house in Brentwood. Tony Bennett on the stereo, my father pouring wine, and my mother cooking. The smells of garlic and basil and lavender.

A peace washes over me that's so heavy I feel like I can see it.

"Are you a good chopper?" Carol asks me.

"I'm decent."

She smiles and shakes her head. "I'll do the onion if you slice the tomato." She hands me a cutting board, a small, serrated knife, and a bowl full of freshly rinsed vine-ripened tomatoes. "The key is a serrated knife and to tuck your knuckles in." She demonstrates.

"I love this music," I say.

Carol closes her eyes briefly and hums. "Moon River" is playing.

"Me too. When I was younger, my father only listened to Frank."

"Pop liked Frank Sinatra?" I say without thinking. I remember him as a stoic guy. The idea of him listening to anything romantic feels impossible.

Carol looks at me curiously.

"I mean my pop did, so it makes sense yours likes him, too."

She nods. "I think he used music as a way for the house to feel full, to give it life after she was gone."

"I understand that," I say.

She continues looking at me, and I see something familiar in her eyes. It's sorrow, the pain of being a motherless daughter.

She never let me see it before, but here, I am not her daughter. I am just her friend.

"Tell me more about her," I say.

I never asked about her mother. I never asked her to tell me stories about what kind of parent she had been, what she had meant to her. It seems impossible, now, that I never did. And I recognize how selfish it was. How much she probably wanted to talk about it. How I could have offered her a space to share.

Carol takes out an onion and begins peeling. "She was very funny." She laughs, recalling something. "She loved playing pranks on people. She'd hide cream cheese in my dad's medicine cabinet and make him think it was toothpaste or shaving cream."

"Was she strict?"

"No!" Carol says, practically yelling. "No, she was the opposite. She never raised her voice, never got angry, even though she was spunky. She'd let me have chocolate chips in the morning. She believed in play. She was fun."

Carol Silver would never serve chocolate in the morning, and yet—

I remember homemade banana frosties on birthdays with a tray full of toppings. Chocolate chips were always an option.

"It must have been hard to lose her," I say. "You were so young."

She looks up from the onion, thoughtful. "It was," she says. "I still miss her every day."

"I understand."

We chop for a moment, in silence. And then it's there, right in front of me. And I have to share it, I have to tell her.

"My mother died," I say. "Recently. Very recently, actually. A few weeks ago."

Carol keeps chopping with perfect precision. "I'm really very sorry to hear that," she says. "You told me you lost someone close to you. I didn't realize you meant your mother."

I nod.

"Is that why you're here?"

"We were supposed to come together."

Carol swipes the chopped onion off the knife, wipes the side of one eye with her sleeve, and places the entirety in a saucepan with olive oil.

"She was the best," I say. "She was my everything. She was good at whatever she did. Just a real, true mother. She was a decorator, too."

Carol begins grating a lemon, collecting the zest in a small wooden bowl.

"What did she like?"

"Cooking," I say, "to start."

Carol laughs. She takes a sip of her wine.

"She could do anything. Roast a chicken to perfection, make a lemon meringue pie. She rarely used a recipe. She loved a good white button-down and a solid brimmed hat and a well-planned trip."

"She sounds wonderful."

"She was."

Carol fills a pot with water, turns over a palmful of salt, and sets it to boil. She turns back to me. "What did she think about your marriage?"

She keeps looking at me. I drop my gaze down to the uncut tomatoes. "I don't know," I say. "I made the mistake of never asking. Maybe because I knew what she'd say."

Carol sets her elbows down on the counter. She leans forward toward me. "I think you still know."

I think about Eric in my parents' living room all those years ago, asking for my hand.

"I think she thought I wasn't ready," I say. "She thought it was too big of a commitment for someone to make at twenty-five."

"To get married?"

I nod.

"But what did she think about your husband?"

I look at Carol now. She looks so much like her. Her concerned expression, her eyebrows knit together in a show of solidarity, support.

"What would you tell me?" I ask her.

Carol doesn't blink. Her expression doesn't change a molecule. "I'd tell you that no one knows your marriage or your heart better than you."

She turns back to the stove. The water is humming now, dancing. Behind us from somewhere, Sinatra sings.

I did it my way.

Chapter Twenty-Three

The pasta is creamy and tangy. The pancetta is salty and fatty. And the tomatoes are plump and sweet. There is wine, and then there is chocolate cake, decorated with powdered sugar and cut fresh strawberries. It's a dessert I know well, one she has made for me many times before, and there is a supreme comfort in that here tonight. It was a special occasion cake. Carol Silver did not believe in dessert every day. As time went on, my parents assumed a largely vegetarian diet but remained familiar in their habits nonetheless. Special nights were still for chocolate.

We settle on the floor by the sofa, our wineglasses and plates on the coffee table.

"Tell me about the plans for the hotel," I say.

"The Sirenuse?"

I nod.

"Yes," she says. "Actually, I already had a preliminary meeting and it went well." She looks a little sheepish. "They'd like me to come in again."

"Wow," I say. "That's great." Something pulls in my stomach, but I ignore it. "Do you want to show me? I mean, I'd love to see what you're thinking."

Carol smiles. "Only if you promise not to judge me."

The idea of my mother being insecure is laughable, so I laugh. "Are you kidding?" I say. "You're the most confident person I know. I'm sure whatever you're doing is great."

"That's kind."

She disappears into the bedroom and then returns with a box. It's wooden, long, and flat, almost like a drawer. She lifts off the top and takes out papers—there are sketches inside, tons of them. Loose-leaf paper with pencil markings.

"So the first thing you need to know is that the Sirenuse is iconic. Classic old-world Italy. Really just the staple of luxury in Positano. I still have to bring you."

"That guy at my hotel took me to Il San Pietro," I say. "A few nights ago. Have you been?"

Carol smiles. "It's beautiful there, but it's like another world."

"True."

"The Sirenuse *is* Positano. Two entirely different experiences."

"I know you said you wanted to make it more Mediterranean," I say.

Carol squints at her papers. "Well, yes, sort of. Here, I'll show you."

She places a map onto the table. It's of the hotel.

"So here is the entryway." She sets her wineglass down and points, reorienting the paper. "And if you walk through these doors, there's this lobby that's pretty stuffy."

"The horse decor."

"Right! Yes, the unfortunate horse decor. And then you

keep going, and their terrace is—their terrace is probably the most beautiful place in all of Positano. Not just to have a drink, but to be at all. It's connected to a restaurant called the Oyster Bar."

"Sounds fancy."

Carol nods. "It is. Very fancy. Expensive champagne, the whole thing. I have this mental image of myself as a five-year-old standing out there. Anyway, I think it would be interesting to bring some of the sunlight from outside into the lobby. If you just got rid of this one wall"—she circles with her pointer finger—"you could really make the whole entryway feel like one big terrace. And your welcome would be the ocean instead of some stuffy ottomans."

I think about our own home. The way the kitchen spilled out onto a deck behind. The big glass windows. The sense of welcome, and nature, and light. Everyone who came to visit fell in love with our house. It's where my mother hosted birthday parties and anniversary dinners. It's where she made Shabbat on Fridays, for whoever wanted to come. On the open lawn is where I had both my bat mitzvah and my engagement party—in a tent lined with silk and stars, roses and candlelight.

"It sounds incredible," I say.

"They're hearing pitches tomorrow and Thursday," she says. "I know it's stupid, I really do. I'm not even Italian or professionally trained. But I feel like I could pull this off. I feel like I have a shot. That sounds ridiculous, right? I sound ridiculous."

I shake my head. "Not at all."

She looks down into her wineglass. "Refill?"

"Yes, please."

"And would you like some tea?"

"Sure," I say. "I can make it."

"Okay, so you're not great in the kitchen, but boiling water is your strong suit."

"My one and only."

Carol smiles. She touches my arm. "Well, that's certainly not true."

I leave her in the living room and go into the kitchen. I put on the kettle. I open the cupboards. I see three different teas—green, English breakfast, and peppermint.

I take out three tea bags. I pop two into hers, the way I know she likes, and then I take out another and add two to mine, too. When the water boils, I fill the mugs three-quarters of the way up.

"Here you go," I say. I set the hot cup down on the coffee table.

Carol peers inside the mug. "Two peppermint," she says. "How did you know?"

I shrug. "It's how I like it, too."

We blow on the tea silently.

"Now tell me, who is this hotel guy?" Carol asks.

I take a small, scalding sip. It does taste better with two; she's right. "He's American."

Carol cocks her head to the side. "And? What's going on there? You've spent a lot of time with him recently. You just said he took you to the San Pietro. That place is romantic."

"Nothing," I say. But that isn't true, of course. And here my mother is, alive, present. If I can't be honest now, I'll never be able to be. "I mean, we kissed."

Carol's eyes go wide. "Now we're getting somewhere."

I set the mug down and rub a hot hand back and forth across my forehead.

"I'm not divorced. I'm not even really separated, I don't think. I just told Eric I needed some space on this trip."

"Does it matter?"

Mom, I want to say. But instead I say, "Carol."

"I'm sorry, but I have to ask. You've told me you don't know if you're happy. Isn't seeing if you can be happy somewhere else a good way to figure that out?"

"I'm not sure that's how it works."

"Maybe it should."

"Eric is a good person," I say. "He doesn't deserve this. Honestly, I don't know what came over me."

I think about Adam's hands on my back by the pool. I think of his eyes looking at me down by the water's edge. The trip to Capri, the afternoon in Naples.

"It's possible actions only have the weight we give them," she says. "We can decide what something means."

I look into my cup. The tea is so heavy it's nearly opaque. "I don't think that's true."

Carol nods. "I guess it doesn't matter, because it's clear you think that cheating is unforgivable."

"Isn't it?"

Carol lifts her shoulders, slowly, to her ears. "I don't know, is it?"

"We made vows, we made promises. I don't think I'd ever be able to forgive him if he did this to me."

"Maybe Eric doesn't exist right now."

"What do you mean?"

"I mean maybe this trip isn't about him. Maybe it's not about whether or not you love him or whether or not he's a good person and a good husband or does or does not deserve this. Maybe this is just about you."

I look at my mother, at Carol, impossibly, solidly, here.

"Do you think that's true?"

Carol blinks once, slowly. "You know good people make bad choices." She looks down into her cup. "Good people do bad things all the time. Does it make them bad, too?"

Carol is still staring at her tea. I see her swallow.

"Are you okay?" I ask her.

She nods. "Yes, yes, of course. That's just my opinion, for whatever it's worth. I don't think bad action makes you a bad person. I think life is far more complicated than that, and it's reductive to think otherwise."

There's the Carol I know, opinionated about everything.

She stretches. "I'm going to clean up these plates."

Carol gets up to her feet and begins stacking the dinner plates from the coffee table.

"Here," I say. "I'll help you."

I lift one and then it spills over. The remaining contents of oil and garlic go straight down my dress, soaking into the silk.

"Shit."

"Oh!" Carol says. "Not your gorgeous dress!"

"I'll blot it," I say. "Do you have baby powder?

"Blot?" Carol asks me.

I stand up. "You can dab it with powder and then let it sit. It should get most of it out."

"How do you know that?"

The question startles me. *You taught me.* But she didn't. Carol didn't. In fact, the reality is that right now, I'm teaching her.

"My mom," I tell her.

Carol hooks a wineglass between her chest and thumb. "Of course," she says. "The woman who knew everything." She smiles.

"Where is your bathroom?" I ask.

She points with her free hand. "Just through the bedroom on the right-hand side. Powder should be in the cabinet. I'll lay out something for you to put on."

"Thanks."

Carol heads to the kitchen, and I hear the clattering of plates and the turn of the faucet. I go into the bathroom.

I take off the dress and loop it over my arms in the sink. I dab it with a hand towel to rid the fabric of the excess grease, and then locate the baby powder and sprinkle a generous helping over the material. As I'm washing my hands I notice all Carol's products on the sink. Some tried-and-true—Aveeno, she used that right up until the end. Others will be discarded later. I pick up a bottle of golden perfume and inhale the scent. Honeysuckle.

I open the door and can hear Carol back in the kitchen, the water on. I've found myself in her bedroom. I see the clothes she just laid out for me on the bed—a button-down shirt and a pair of drawstring shorts. I fold the towel I'm wearing and put them on. They smell like her. I smell like her. I think about all her clothes lying in her closet in Brentwood, waiting for her return.

There's a double bed with a white linen bedspread. To the left of the room, curtains billow in the breeze. There is a small closet where a few dresses hang. Colorful, floral prints. One blue linen. I recognize a pair of purple sandals that lace at the ankles.

I move around the room and touch everything softly, gingerly. I don't want to disturb the air molecules. It feels like being in a museum—that she just stepped out for coffee, tomatoes, to mail a letter thirty years ago and never came back. Perhaps that's what this is. A snapshot.

A big gust of wind blows the window back up against the

wall. It makes a snapping sound, and I go over, making sure it's not broken. It isn't. Outside it appears like a storm is brewing. The evening is overcast, now, and the wind riled.

I close the window, snap the safety guard in place. And just as I'm turning to head back into the kitchen, I spot a framed photograph. It's on the nightstand, propped up on top of a book. I recognize the frame. It's small, silver. It has sat in my parents' house, on my mother's nightstand, for thirty years.

I take it in my hands now. My heart beats wildly. It's not possible, it couldn't be . . .

The baby looks back at me. She wears a bright yellow dress and a bonnet stitched with lace. She's laughing.

"Everything all right in there?" Carol calls.

But I do not answer. I can't. Underneath the photograph, the frame is engraved. I run my pointer finger over the words, the ones I know so well, because they are my own.

Katy Silver.

The woman in the kitchen is already my mother. She is already my mother, and she has left me.

Chapter Twenty-Four

My hands feel numb, my throat itches like it's on fire. Vaguely I hear Carol at the door.

"Hey," she says. "I think it might rain. We can . . ."

I turn around and shove the photograph forward. Carol's face changes. Her eyes dart down at my hands and back up again.

"What is this?" I ask her.

She exhales, crosses her arms. "I haven't told you everything about my life."

"Like that you have a fucking baby?"

She is taken aback. "Yes," she says. "I have a baby. She has your name. Katy. She's six months old." She smiles, then a warm, familiar tenderness spreads over her face. I think I might be sick.

"You're here," I say.

Carol nods. "There are some things I have to figure out. I don't . . ."

"You left?" I say. I'm practically screaming. "You left me?"

I feel hysterical now. My mother. My mother who tended

every scrape and bruise and put cool compresses on my head when I was sick and made tea from lavender root and took photographs of absolutely everything. Who knew the right Band-Aids to buy that would stay on even elbows and ankles, and who always made toast with garlic and butter on it when I had a cold. Who gave me my first haircut in the backyard, and who bought me ballet shoes on my third birthday. Who knew exactly how to touch to make me feel loved and protected. Whose warmth I miss daily, acutely. The same woman who is standing here. The same woman who left me.

"You? Look, Katy, this really isn't any of your business."

"How can you say that?" I ask her. "Don't you see me?"

I run to her. I toss the photo down on the bed and grab her by the shoulders. Her eyes go wide, but I don't let go. "It's *me*. Katy. I'm her. I came here to Italy because we were supposed to come together and then you died, you just died, and I'm so lost without you. I don't even know who I am anymore. And then miraculously you showed up. You were just here! You always told me about this summer you spent in Italy, but it was supposed to be before I was born. Before you were married. You were supposed to . . ."

But I'm crying too hard now; my body convulses in sobs.

Carol wriggles out of my touch. "I don't know what you're saying, but I think you need to go."

"How could you leave?" I ask. "She's just a baby. She needs you. How could you come here and party and *Remo*?"

"I told you, we're not together."

I push past her into the living room. I find my bag on the small sofa.

Carol follows me. "You can't judge someone's life until you

have lived it," Carol says. "I love my baby and I love my husband. I'm not the one who's cheating."

I feel her words like a sucker punch to the soul. I turn around to look at her.

"I'm sorry," Carol says. "I shouldn't have said that."

I look at her. My mother. My friend. I've been betrayed by them both.

"How could you do this?" I say. "Only a monster leaves her infant."

I see the hurt flash through her eyes, like a gunshot. But I don't care. She's a stranger to me now, someone I do not know. The woman I thought I had recovered is gone.

Carol just stands there, stunned, as I leave. I close the door behind me, and then I'm running. Down flights of stairs. I feel something bite at my heel, a rock, the trickle of blood. I let it run.

I fall and right myself. My knee bleeds. Somewhere, behind, someone calls. *Signora! Signora!* I keep running.

And then the sky opens up and it begins to rain. Not a light mist, but a heavy downpour. Buckets and buckets of water. I keep moving.

I get back to the hotel and dart inside. I want to be somewhere she cannot find me. I want to be where I do not have to face this treacherous, impossible reality that has, in a single instant, proven the entirety of my life to be a lie. I cannot contend with what is now true: that my mother lied to me, that she left me. That she danced and drank and laughed and that all the while, her baby was a continent away. That this woman who was supposed to be my friend lied about the biggest thing in her life. That I do not know either one of them.

I'm soaking wet, my top—her top—and shorts cling to my body like Saran Wrap.

Carlo is at the desk, but I ignore him and head up the stairs. The elevator is on a different level, and I continue to climb—out of breath, dripping. I bolt down the hallway and am almost to my room when I feel an arm reach for me and then there Adam is, right next to me.

He considers my panting, soaking form. "Are you all right? You didn't answer when I called your room. I thought maybe you wanted to have dinner and . . ."

But he doesn't finish his sentence, because in an instant, my lips are on his, and I'm kissing him.

I feel his initial confusion, and then he locks in on me. His lips pull mine and his hands wrap around my waist. He kisses me with an intensity that is foreign to me, different, new. I feel lost in the landscape of this moment. I do not want to find my way home.

He pulls back gently, keeping his hands firmly on my sides.

"Hey," he says. "Hey, are you sure you're okay?" His eyes search mine.

"No," I say. I'm out of breath—from the run, the rain, his kisses. I take my key out and open the door. "I want you to come inside."

He nods. "Okay."

Inside I hear the rain battering the patio. The doors are drawn, but the curtains are open. Behind me, the door closes.

"Come here," Adam says, but it's not a question; it's a directive. I do.

I go to him and wrap my arms around his neck. I thread my hands through his hair, tug down on his soft curls. He drinks in my bottom lip, pressing my body closer and closer to his.

"Take these off," I tell him, pulling at Carol's button-down. I want them gone. I want to be out of these things that are hers.

"Don't move," he says. He kisses my neck, and my head falls back into his cupped palm. He starts unbuttoning my shirt—slowly, torturously. With each loop that comes undone, he bends and kisses the skin beneath it until the shirt is off, crumpled to the floor.

Then he crouches down at my feet, undoes the drawstring of the shorts, and lets them fall. He kisses the skin inside my left thigh. My eyes close.

"You are so fucking sexy," he says. "Open your eyes."

I do. "Say that again."

Adam stands. He moves his mouth to my neck and whispers in my ear, "You are. So. Fucking. Sexy."

I reach up and pull his lips down to mine. Our tongues battle.

"What do you want?" he says into my mouth.

"More," I say.

Adam puts his hands on my arms. And then he removes them, places them down by my side, presses his thumb into the dip of my hip bone. I exhale out. I grab for his fingers but he leans back, bringing his hands up to my chest and stroking them back and forth below my collarbone.

I take his hand and place it flat down against my stomach. I can feel my heartbeat everywhere.

His hand is warm on my cold skin. I inhale. He doesn't move, not a muscle. And then he replaces his hand with his lips. He kisses down my stomach and then loops an arm under my low back and lifts me onto the bed.

I reach up and grab for him. I unbutton his shirt, and it falls away. The rest of our clothes, gone.

And then he's on top of me, naked.

I must have felt this before, I must have inhabited my body like this, but I can't remember.

I drop my lips to his shoulder. I trail the flesh there, biting down. He moves on top of me and then I feel his hand underneath us, flat up against my back.

I arch against him and then it's like something else, someone else, takes over.

"Kiss my neck," I tell him.

He brushes his lips along my collarbone and then presses them into the skin right below my ear.

I clutch at his back. He moves his hand underneath us down, cups the flesh below my back.

I lift my legs and wrap them around his torso. I feel like I'm on fire, like I'm going to be returned to ash.

"Turn me over," I tell him.

He looks up at me, kisses me, and then rolls us. I pin his hands up, over his head, and then I start moving my hips in circles. I see him looking at me, a mix of curiosity and intensity. Everything is foreign. Everything feels different.

I close my eyes. His hands escape mine and find my hips. He pulls me down, hard. He does it again and again and again. I tear at his shoulders, then the sheets around us.

I've never had sex like this. It feels like I've never had sex. Like I've been living right under the surface, watching the reflections above, no idea that the boats and people and birds weren't shimmery images but in fact real, tangible things. Everything has been a mirror; everything I've seen has been skewed and reflected. None of it has been real.

I fall apart on top of him; my eyes squeeze shut, my pulse lighting through us like a laser beam.

"Holy shit," he says when it's over.

I don't say anything. All I can feel is this rapidly contracting moment. Everything that once was, evaporating.

Chapter Twenty-Five

Adam falls asleep—I hear his restful snoring next to me. But the more we descend from the high of sex, the more I feel the reality of what has just occurred—what I just saw—landing.

My mother left. Carol left. She lied to me. Not just here, on this trip, but throughout my life, in everything she did. She told me she had all the answers, that she knew. She made my life into a reflection of her own. But she didn't know. She didn't have all the answers. Here she is in Italy—singing and drinking and forgetting. She made me in her image, but she forgot the most important part. She forgot that one day she'd leave, that she already had, and then I'd be left with nothing. When you're just a reflection, what happens when the image vanishes?

I pull a robe around me and head out onto the balcony. The storm has broken: it's not raining anymore, and the air is light and new. I think about that night, the last one, the one I swore I would lock away forever.

I knew the end was close; they had warned me. The hospice nurses who came and went knew what it looked like when there was no more time left. It could be days, hours, they said. Stay close.

We had already moved home. Moved up to her bedroom. She hadn't left the retractable bed in days. There was nowhere to go.

My father spent his days in a chair next to her. He changed her straws after every sip and kept fresh ice in a bowl, even when all it did was melt. At night he'd sleep in the family room, falling asleep to old episodes of *Full House*, *Friends*, whatever was on.

I'd wander the house, sometimes falling asleep in my old room, sometimes on the bath mat by the tub. Eric came and went, the only prisoner allowed outdoors.

I'm embarrassed to say that in those last weeks, I didn't want to be around her. I was, all the time, but I hated it. I was embarrassed by what the disease had done to her, how it had shrunken her down to a fragment of her former self. How she could not lift her head to drink water, and grew fitful and irritated at the suggestion of medication. The disease made her hostile, and I felt that hostility, I felt it down into my bones.

For months I had felt a quiet rage inside me. It bubbled, it had been bubbling, and that night, her last, an ember jumped and caught fire. It felt like I could burn the whole house down.

Her breathing was haggard; she was struggling for air. I looked at her and felt wild, maybe even evil. I wanted to lie down next to her and cut my veins open. I wanted to slam a pillow over her head. I wanted to do anything except exist there, in that room, with her.

"Katy," she whispered. I bent down close to her, but that was all, that was the whole ask and answer: Katy.

Those were her last words to me. The reminder of my own singularity, the impossibility of my name without hers.

How could she do this to me? How could she tell me year over year that it was okay, that I didn't need to know, that I didn't need to have all the answers, because I had her? How could she make herself so indispensable, so much a part of my life, my very heart—so woven into the fabric of who I am—only to leave? Didn't she know? Didn't she know that one day I'd be left without her?

I kept my face close to hers, I held her hand, and all the while, as I walked her to the other side, I kept thinking: *How will I get there without you? How did you not tell me while you still could?*

Standing on the balcony in Positano now, the world freshly washed, I feel the emotion rise up in me again. The fire, the anger. But now it is mixed with grief. It is mixed with all the things I did not see, because I couldn't, all the things I believed because she told me they were true.

Mom, I think. *Carol. How could you? She's just a little girl.*

Chapter Twenty-Six

When I wake up after a fitful sleep, I'm hit with a certain numbness—the sun is shining and the French doors are open, revealing an already-awakened morning. And then the events of last night smack me in the sternum. I put my hands to my chest and press, like I'm trying to arrest the flow of blood out of my body. So this is what it feels like to see the world as it is. This is what it feels like to reach out and find nothing but your own hand.

Next to me, Adam sleeps. He's naked, and I see fingernail scratches—mine—along his back.

He stirs next to me. One eye opens. "Hey."

I sit up, gathering some sheet with me. "Hi."

He stretches, slings an arm over toward me, and rubs my knee. "What time is it?"

I glance at the clock on my nightstand. "Eight-forty-five."

"Shit."

"Are you late somewhere?"

Adam starts searching for his clothing. He gets dressed hastily. "Yes, sorry, shit. I need to shower. I'm supposed to be at the Sirenuse in a half hour."

"For what?"

Adam looks at me, stops what he's doing. He puts a knee on the bed and leans forward. "It's just a meeting."

"Adam," I say slowly. "Are you thinking about buying that hotel?"

"It's not even on the market," he says. He picks up his shirt and pulls it over his head.

"That's not an answer."

"I'm just having a meeting." He slides a shoe on. "It's for a friend; I said I'd help them out with some plans."

"And what about Poseidon?" I say. "They're in trouble here, Nika told me. Is that over?"

"Marco is stubborn; what am I supposed to do? Steal it from him?"

"Talk to him."

"I have. Look, I need to go home with a win. I want to. I need an excuse to keep coming back." He winks at me. It feels hollow, though. Like a gimmick. Like he's done it many times before.

"What about knowing the hotel and loving it and all of those things you said about this place feeling like home?"

Adam sighs. He sits back down. "All of that is true, all of it. I love it here. And also, money is real; his will is real. If they don't want to sell, they don't want to sell."

He finds his other shoe, slides it on. "I have to run, but can we please have lunch later? I'll meet you at Chez Black in the marina. We can talk about everything." He gestures to the bed. To what has transpired here.

I nod. "Okay."

Adam leans over me. He touches his lips down to mine and then plants a kiss on my cheek. "I'll see you soon."

"What time?"

"Let's say two?"

"Yeah, sure." He gives me another kiss on the cheek, and then leaves.

When the door shuts behind him, I feel a strange calm. There is no cacophony of thoughts. I do not think about Eric, although I should. I do not even think about my mother. What I think about is Carol. I think about the thirty-year-old lady standing in her flat in Italy, a world away from her baby.

I need to find her. There is one thing I know for certain, the only true thing I can place right now, the only thing that's real: Carol needs to go home.

I toss on jean shorts and a T-shirt and my pink Birkenstocks. I grab a bottle of water from the lobby and wave goodbye to Carlos. And then I take what is now the familiar path upward, toward the stairs.

I know where she lives now. I was just there, just last night, before the entire world changed. I've never been able to find her—the whole time we've been here it's just been her finding me—but I have to now. Now it's different.

I get to the landing, where the stairs split off, and I see the turquoise door. It looks faded, more worn blue, in the daylight. For a moment the practicality of our realities gives way in my abdomen. The questions mount. *Is this possible? What reality is she in? Am I finding her here now? Or is she back lost to her time? Is she even inside?*

I knock. Once, twice. There is no answer. I try the doorknob, but it is locked. I sit outside. I try again. Nothing.

I think about my options: stay and wait or head back to the hotel. And then a third dawns on me. And it's the right one, the true one. I know where she is. I know where I can find her.

I start climbing. My sandals slip, and I grip on with my toes. I should have worn sneakers, but it doesn't matter now. Up, up, up.

As I walk, I feel her. Each step I take I know she has taken before, I'm certain of it. Thirty years or fifteen minutes she has just been here. She has just cleared the way. Somewhere in time she is walking, and somewhere in time I am walking, too, and we will find each other on this path. We will be here together.

And sure enough, just as I am cresting the final staircase, right in view of the Path of the Gods, I see her.

She's wearing a sundress and sneakers, with a sun hat on, a linen shirt tied at her waist. I spot her first, the back of her head, the curve of her waist. Her long hair looped in a knot down her neck. She flings an arm up and rests it on top of her head, surveying the ocean below. What is she staring at? What is she thinking about? Is she looking for me, too?

And then once I've asked it, as if in answer, she turns downward and sees me. Neither of us says anything; we let the recognition pass between us like bathwater—it moves, changes direction. It flows both ways now. It always has.

"Hi," she says. She's cautious but not angry, not exactly.

"I thought I'd find you here," I say.

We are both sweaty and sun-beaten. I feel the exertion of the stairs now that I'm no longer in motion. I drop my hands to my knees and exhale.

"Are you all right?" she asks me. "You look a little white."

"Just out of breath," I say.

She nods. She folds her arms across her chest. "We can sit." It's not a question, and we do.

Carol plops herself down on a step. I sit on the one below her. Here, high up, there is no one around. We're totally and completely alone. It occurs to me that, with the exception of Adam, I've never seen another soul on this hike the entire time I've been here.

We sit in silence for a moment. I take a long drink from my bottle of water. Finally, when my breathing slows, I start.

"I'm angry," I tell her. I try and keep my voice level.

"I know."

"No," I say. "I don't think you do. Why didn't you tell me?"

"I don't know," she says. "I wanted to. But we'd just met, and all you knew was this fun summer girl. I wanted to be that fun summer girl. I thought you'd judge me, but maybe not as much as you did. I just didn't know how to bring it up."

"That you have a baby?" I look down at my feet. They're covered in dirt. "I don't think you know what you're doing to her. I don't think you have any idea what this means."

"I didn't leave," she says.

I look up at her, but her eyes are down at the marina, the ocean. Somewhere else.

"Not exactly, anyway. I always wanted to come back to Italy, it was my dream for so long, and . . . I got pregnant so quickly after meeting my husband. Three months, we barely knew each other. I don't have a career, I'm still an assistant at a gallery—"

My stomach squeezes—*she only knew my dad for three months? I thought they were together for over a year. She wants to redesign the hotel—will she stay? Does she want to stay?* But I say nothing, I let her talk.

"We got married because we love each other, but sometimes I wonder if we would have if I hadn't gotten pregnant."

"But you did get pregnant," I say. "You have a daughter."

"And I love her, too. More than anything. But when she

came, I felt like I lost . . . like I didn't know who I was anymore. It's like my old life was gone. I was gone. I used to be the woman you knew before you found that photo, and I'm still her, it's just that no one sees that anymore. Maybe I don't see it anymore. I just wanted to recapture a little bit of that. A little bit of who I was, or who I thought I'd be."

"That's why you came here?"

A long beat passes between us. The wind picks up and lifts the sweaty hair up and off the back of my neck.

"At home," Carol says slowly, methodically, like she's placing every word down, arranging them in one of her famous floral bouquets, "I'm defined by this role. I have a feeding schedule and a shopping schedule, and on Saturdays I clean the house. My work . . ." Her voice trails off. "He doesn't mean to, but I know he doesn't think it's as important as his. And I don't blame him. I barely make any money at all."

I think about my mom, in the kitchen three years ago, talking about how she wanted my dad to retire. I think about the way his work became hers, how I never knew it wasn't what she wanted, how I never even asked. How too often my father and I treated her design work like a hobby. Why?

"Listen," I say. "I know this won't make sense to you, and I'm sorry about last night, I really am, but you have to believe me. You need to go home. You'll work it out, you'll figure it out, and you'll get good at it. You'll be good at it."

She looks at me. Her eyes are wide. I see the water there, threatening to run. "I'm not a monster," she says.

And then, for only the third time in my life, I watch Carol cry.

She drops her head down into her hands. Her shoulders shake in small, staccato bursts.

I put an arm around her. I lean my head down on her shoulder. I hold her like she's held me so many times before.

"You're going to be a good mom," I say. "A great one, even. You already are."

"That's not true," she says.

"It is," I say.

Carol straightens up. She wipes her eyes. "How could you possibly know that?" she asks me.

And then she meets my gaze, and when she does, it's like she knows. For just a beat, a breath, a millisecond. She sees. I'm certain of it. There our life is, caught between us. All the love and pain and connection. All the impossibility of her loss and what remains. Everything, in the space between us. Then:

"I'm sorry. I'm a mess. And I'm going to be late for the Sirenuse pitch if I don't get going. They were really clear that they have a tight schedule today, and I've been going over it for days. I can't miss it."

"That's today?"

Something twists in my stomach.

"Yes," she says. "I was just trying to clear my head a little before and then—"

"Who are you meeting with?" I ask her.

She stands up. She brushes some dirt off the skirt of her dress. Her eyes squint into the sun.

"A developer this time," she says. "I think his name is Adam."

Chapter Twenty-Seven

I leave Carol and dash down the stairs to the hotel. Nika is at the desk, and I go up to her, gulping air. "Have you seen Adam?" I ask her.

"He just left," she says. "Is everything all right, Ms. Silver?"

"Nika," I start. I want to know, but I also don't. I'm terrified, and yet I need an answer. I need one *now.* "What year is it?"

"What do you mean?"

"What is the year? Right now?"

She laughs. I feel her casual, befuddled amusement. "Nineteen ninety-two," she says. "Last time I looked."

I feel a rush of cold air across my skin. *This whole time.*

I'm not finding my mother's world when she finds me; I've dropped into hers. Adam, Nika, Marco. They all belong to the past.

I dissolve into a chair by the desk. I sink my head down into my hands.

"Ms. Silver," Nika says. "What is wrong? What is happening?"

I do not know. I do not know where to begin. My mother died, and she left me with no instructions. Nothing on how to live or who to be in her absence. Now she's here, and she wants to stay. Oh, and last night I slept with a guy who isn't my husband, thirty years ago. What isn't wrong?

"Nothing," I say. "Nothing. Everything is fine."

"Okay . . ." Then Nika holds up her hand like she's just remembered something. She disappears in the back and returns a moment later holding a letter. "This was returned," she says. "Your friend Carol mailed it a few weeks ago, but it came back."

I see the stamp, the Los Angeles address.

"Will you give to her?"

Nika hands it to me, and I tuck it into my shirt. "Yes, absolutely. Thank you, Nika."

I turn and walk up the stairs, take the elevator, and arrive at room 33. I put the letter down on the bed. I take a shower. I go through the motions of this day. The utter incomprehensibility of everything that has happened, is happening.

I put on a dress; I brush out my wet hair. I think about Carol, right now, getting ready for this meeting. I don't know if she heard me on the path. I don't know if I got through to her.

I take out some sandals. The ones I bought at the Century City mall with my mother two Augusts ago during an end-of-summer sale. I didn't like them. I still don't. Why did we buy them then? Why did I bring them? They're my shoes. They're my feet.

So I don't put them on. Instead, I put on a pair of white flats. I take a look at myself in the mirror. I'm tanned, freckled—rosy, even. There is no other way to put it: I look healthy. It's startling after so many months of sunken, hollow skin.

I take my room key and then head back downstairs. I have to go intercept that meeting. I have to make sure Carol understands. She cannot stay here. This is not the life she is meant for. She cannot take this job, and they cannot offer it to her.

I have realized, between the time I left Carol at her door and right now, walking the stairs back down to the lobby, something important. Something obvious. The truth of why I have come and why I have found her here. My mission—to send her home.

"Listen," I say to Nika when I'm back at the desk. "I need you to do something for me. It's really important."

"Of course, Ms. Silver. Anything you need."

"I need you to tell me how to get to the Sirenuse. And then I need you to please call them and ask if they can find Adam. Tell him I'm on my way and not to meet with anyone until I get there. Not a single person. Can you do that?"

Nika looks at me curiously. "Katy," she says. The first time she has used my first name. "Are you all right?"

"I will be," I say. "Everything is fine. I just have to hurry."

She nods. "Okay," she says. "You follow the same road down, and then by the church, you turn up. It is a big red building—you cannot miss it. If you get lost, you can just ask. Everyone knows the Sirenuse."

"Thank you," I say.

I do as she instructed. I take the path down to the ocean, and when I almost get down to the marina, I follow the road up. On the right-hand side, right on Via Cristoforo Colombo, is the Sirenuse. It is set back from the road with a small driveway, the outside of the building a deep and striking red.

It's a beautiful hotel. Immediately upon entering I feel swept away. I consider her suggested renovations. The scope of the place. In my opinion, it is perfect. I wonder why we try and change anything. We should do it less. Some things do not need to be tampered with.

"Excuse me," I say to the girl at the front desk. "Do you know where Adam Westbrooke is?"

Her face folds into a frown.

"The meeting about the hotel?" I say. "I'm here to present my designs."

She brightens. "Yes," she says. "They are downstairs, in the restaurant."

I follow the stairs, and then I'm in a mint-green dining room, the ocean behind me, and I see Adam and two older gentlemen seated inside.

"Katy," Adam says. His face is befuddled. "I thought we were meeting in the marina at two? Is everything all right?"

"Is she here yet?" I ask.

"Who?"

I shake my head. "I need to talk to you," I say.

The men exchange a glance. Adam shoots them a placating smile.

"Can it wait until lunch? We're kind of in the middle of something here."

"No," I say. "No, I'm sorry, it can't. She'll be here any minute now."

"Who? Who are you talking about?"

"Carol."

"Who is Carol?" Adam asks.

"The designer."

"The designer?"

One of the men says something I can't make out in Italian, and Adam holds up his hand to them. "I'm so sorry, one minute."

He walks out of the room toward me. We step into the hallway together.

"Did they give you my message?" I whisper.

"No," he says. "What message? What's going on?" Adam's face is expectant, concerned, even a little annoyed. And it's at this moment that Carol comes walking down the stairs.

She looks first at me, then at Adam.

"Hi," she says. "Katy . . . what are you doing here?"

"Are you Carol?" Adam asks.

She nods. "Yes, hi." She tucks her portfolio folder under her arm and extends her hand. They shake.

Carol drops her hand, and then she's looking from me to Adam and back again. The question still hovers: *What are you doing here?*

I'm saving you. I'm making sure you don't make a mistake. I'm making sure that everything will turn out exactly as it has. I'm doing what you always did to me: protecting me from a different life.

And then something hits. Recognition. Like a lightning bolt. I look at Carol now, a crisp white linen dress on, her sandals tied, ready to have the meeting of her dreams—and I don't see my mother. I see a woman. A woman fresh into a new decade who wants a life of her own. Who has interests and desires and passions beyond my father and me. Who is very real, exactly as she is right here and now.

Who am I to rob her of them? Who am I to tell her who she is and isn't? I do not have the answers. I do not have the answers for her life any more than she has the answers now for mine.

My eyes well with tears. I swallow them back down.

"I'm sorry," I say. "I had to tell Adam something, and I forgot we had lunch plans and . . ."

"You two know each other?"

"We're staying at the same hotel," Adam says.

Recognition dawns on Carol's face. She does a terrible job of hiding it; maybe she doesn't want to. She looks at me with a small smirk. *This guy?*

"I'll see you at lunch, okay?" Adam asks. "We really do need to get this underway—now."

I nod. "Yeah," I say. "Okay."

Adam squeezes my forearm, and then he turns and opens the door. He holds it for Carol, and then the two go inside. I stand in the hallway for another thirty seconds. And then I head back up the stairs. In the lobby a harpist plays something light and melodic. I wander out onto the terrace. There are sweeping views of Positano. It's beautiful up here, magical. I understand why she'd want to have a hand in it. I understand why she'd want to stay. Why they both do. There is no denying that Positano is something incredibly special.

I sit down on the terrace. A waiter comes over. "Buongiorno, signora."

"Buongiorno."

"Would you like a drink?"

He sets down a glass of water.

"No thank you," I say.

I drink the water. It's cool, refreshing.

Right now, downstairs, my mother is having a meeting to determine her future, and therefore mine. If she gets it, she may very well stay. She will design this hotel and I won't know her, not like I did, not like I do. What will that mean for my life? What will that mean for who I turn out to be? It's all too mind-bending to think about. I let the thought pass out to sea. *Posa posa*. Stop here.

I sit on the terrace for another twenty minutes. And then I walk back up to the Hotel Poseidon. I go upstairs; I lie down. And then I go to the safe in the closet. I turn the dial and wait for it to unlock. There inside on a black wooden panel are my wedding and engagement rings, just as I've left them. And tucked beneath them is my cell phone. I take it out. I dial Eric.

The phone rings—once, twice, three times, four times. It continues on until there is a staccato sound, like a nail on concrete, and then the phone disconnects. He is not there; that is not his number.

I hold my engagement ring between my fingers. I remember that day in my parents' kitchen. The memory comes back strong, almost like I can smell it. How Eric got down on one knee right there, right by the sink. He had bought me my favorite cupcakes—ones from this tiny Pasadena bakery that used to make my birthday cakes as a child—and they were sitting on the counter. "Check the frosting," he said.

He had to lick the ring before he put it on my finger.

I check my watch: 1:30.

I put the rings and phone back, and I tuck the letter Nika had given me from Carol with them. I lock the safe and take one last look in the mirror. Once again, I'm met with a woman

I do not entirely recognize but who feels more familiar to me than any version I've previously known.

This is who I am, I think. This healthy and strong and alive. And for just a moment, I understand. I understand what she saw when she looked at herself here, too.

Chapter Twenty-Eight

Adam is seated at a front table at Chez Black when I get there, feet in the sand. I see him before he sees me—his broad shoulders and hair that looks blond in the midday sun. He's dazzling. He's staring ahead at the horizon. He seems distracted, though. He adjusts his shirt, pulling at the collar.

"Hi," I say.

He stands to greet me, placing a kiss on either cheek. "Hi," he says. "Are you all right?"

I think about my earlier outburst. "Yes," I say. "I'm sorry about that. I should not have just shown up there. How did the meeting go?"

We sit down, and Adam fills my water glass. "Well," he said. "She's talented. She has some really innovative ideas. I think she'd be a great pick."

Inside, my stomach tightens. "Did they hire her?"

"I don't think they know yet. There's a lot that has to be sorted out." He peers at me as he hands me the glass. "Why?"

"I know Carol," I say. "We met here. The friend I was telling you about, the one who took me to dinner. She's important to me."

Adam nods. "I liked her vision. She would bring the hotel right into the current moment."

The waiter comes with a bottle of uncorked wine. Adam pours.

"So," Adam says. "About last night."

I think about his mouth on my neck. My naked body under his.

"Yes," I say. "Right. I'm sorry if I just . . ."

Adam wears an amused expression. He's flirting, now. There's a part of me that wants to climb into his lap, right here. "If you just?"

"Attacked you?" I feel my cheeks flush pink.

"Trust me," Adam says. "I welcomed the attack. I wanted last night."

I feel his words lace through me. "Me too."

I look at this man I barely know. Who has helped bring me back to life here. Whose passion and insight and intelligence I find incredibly sexy. And for a moment, I think about what it would be like to fold myself into the past and everyone who remains in it. To continue to have dinners with Carol and afternoons on the boat with Remo. To travel with Adam. To make my world here, to stay.

"Adam, listen," I say.

He laughs, but it's quiet, maybe even a little sad. "Uh-oh," he says. "Nothing good ever comes after *listen*."

"We're not . . ."

How do you tell someone that you're thirty years apart? How do you tell someone you're not in the same time?

I start over. "Last night was really great, but there's so much I need to figure out about my life right now. There's so much I haven't told you."

"I know," he says.

"I haven't done that work before," I say. "I let other people do it for me. And I want to now. I think it's time. Can I ask you something?"

"Of course."

I pick up my water glass. I look at him. "What do you want?" I ask. "We've spent so much time talking about me, I've never asked. And I'd really like to know."

Adam looks thoughtful. He doesn't speak for a few moments. Long enough for me to take a drink and set my glass down again. "Maybe I don't know, either. I travel so much. I love it, but it's like I don't know how to not be in motion. I think there are real things I want, too."

"Like what?"

He looks out past me into the restaurant. "A home, maybe, if I found someone who made me want to stop moving. A garden."

I think about my mom, dad, Eric. I think about nights in front of the television with CPK, weekends playing board games and eating Mike and Ikes out of glass bowls. Birthday parties in the backyard. The rose fence. Window decals for every holiday. Family.

"It's nice," I say. "It's worth it."

Adam nods. "Do you know what you'll do?"

I shake my head. "No," I say. "Not yet."

"But you're starting to know what you want." It's not a question.

I nod. "I think so."

"I'm glad," he says. "And I can't believe we are here at the same time. Life is really a trip."

Capri, Naples, the watermelon at breakfast. "It's been a magical time," I tell him.

We finish lunch and walk back up to the hotel.

"I'm going to go find Marco," Adam says. "I need to be up front with him."

"Hey," I say. I touch his elbow lightly. "Hang on."

"Mm-hm?"

"You don't have to listen to me. I mean, I don't know why you would, but don't buy either hotel. Keep this a place you love. Don't make it about work. Let it be pure and good, so you can bring someone you care about back here someday."

Adam gives me a small smile. "That's good advice."

"Will you follow it?"

He shrugs. "I guess time will tell."

He gives me a little wave, and then he's gone. Nika comes through the office doors to reception.

"You found Adam?" she asks.

"Yes. Listen, Nika, I don't know what's going to happen with Adam and Marco and the hotel, but can you do me a favor?"

She nods.

"Do you invest? Does the hotel? The stock market, I mean."

Nika's eyebrows knit together. "We have a man who manages the finances. Marco usually speaks to him, but I do, too. That's how I know we need Adam."

"This is going to sound crazy," I tell her. "But just trust me, all right? Can you do that?"

She nods.

"Invest in Apple. Starbucks, too. But next year, around the summertime."

"Starbucks?"

"I'm going to write it down, okay?"

I take out a pen and paper. I make the notes.

"Promise me."

She nods. "I will."

Just then Carol appears in the doorway. "Hi," she says. "I was hoping I'd find you here."

She has a package tucked under her arm. She sets it on the desk.

"Carol, do you know Nika? Nika, you know Carol."

"Of course," Carol says. "Hi, Nika. Would you mind? It's all paid for."

"Yes, naturally," Nika says. "Did you . . ." she starts, and I know she is going to ask about the letter. I quickly jump in.

"Would you like to have a drink?" I ask Carol.

Carol looks from Nika to me. "Sure," she says. She hands off the package. "There's a little spot up the way," she says. "It's a good place to sit. I'll show you if you haven't been."

"Great," I say.

We wave goodbye to Nika, and I follow Carol out of the hotel. No more than forty paces up, we come to an outside restaurant on the left-hand side of the road. It's strung up with ivy and flowers and has a spectacular view of the water. There are only four tables: it's like sitting in your own private gazebo overlooking the sea.

We sit.

Carol orders an Aperol and soda.

"Can I have a coffee?" I ask the server.

"Long night?" Carol asks.

"You could say that."

She takes out a pack of cigarettes, shakes one into her hand.

"You really shouldn't smoke," I say. "That stuff kills."

"You're probably right."

"I know I am."

Carol tucks the pack back into her bag. "You know, for someone who considers herself to be a wallflower, you can be quite bossy."

I smile. "Working on it."

Carol grins back at me. "So Adam," she says. "That's the guy, right?"

I nod.

"He's handsome," she says. She looks off behind my shoulder, like she wants to say something else.

"What?"

"I don't think I'm going to get the job. Adam said something about how they want to keep the aesthetic the same. I just didn't feel like they were sold, if they even know what they want to do." She pauses, and I feel the air in my chest hover. "I'd really like to design something someday, you know?"

I think about Addy Eisenberg's Malibu home, the Monteros' ranch in Montecito. Our Brentwood house. All remarkable achievements. All we should have celebrated more, with her, when we had the chance.

"You will," I say. "I promise you will. I think you are enormously talented."

"Thank you." She shakes her head. "Adam isn't who I would picture for you," she says.

I laugh. "Oh?"

"No way."

"Okay," I say. "What would you imagine for me?"

Carol grins. She likes the question. "Someone kind," she says, "of course. Someone who can let you shine. Someone who is cozy and warm. Someone who will look after you. He'd have brown hair, be a little dorky, but in that handsome way, you know. Clark Kent and all that. Maybe glasses." She pauses. "Someone who thinks he won the lottery, because he did."

I feel my eyes grow heavy. In a moment they are filled with tears.

"Carol," I say. It comes out in a whisper. "I need to apologize to you."

"For what?" she asks. She is unconcerned, unconvinced.

"For telling you to go home," I say. "I've realized something, and it's important that I say this to you. It's important that you know."

"Okay," she says. "I'm listening."

"It's not my choice whether you stay or go. I can't make you do that. It's no one's actually. Not Da—er, your husband's, and not even your little girl's."

I close my eyes, willing them to dry. If even a single tear falls, I know the dam will break. *Not now.* "You did your best. You're doing your best. Whatever happens now . . ." I exhale; I clear my throat. "I realized no one can tell you to go home, because no one can tell me to go home, either. It's your choice, just like it's mine."

Carol's eyes find mine. She looks at me for a long beat. And in that gaze I see it all—birthdays and dinners and shopping trips. Mornings spent watching soap operas in her bed. Nights on the phone. Care packages mailed to New York City. Scraped elbows and fevers and her voice, always her voice. *Everything is going to be all right. You're okay. I've got you.*

Carol nods. It's almost imperceptible.

"There is a great life waiting for you at home. It's beautiful and hard and joyful and real. It will be messy and you'll get it wrong sometimes. You should be more honest when you do—it will help her, your daughter. She doesn't need you to be perfect;

she just needs you to be you. That life is good, Carol, but it may not be the one you want."

I rub the back of my hand over my eyes.

"Katy," Carol says. She leans forward, all the way. "That thing you said last night to me. About it being you."

I nod.

"Is it true?" she asks. "Did I leave you?"

I see her here, seated across from me. I see her in the marina, in the water, on the Path of the Gods. I see her in her bed in Brentwood. I see her everywhere.

"No," I say. "No, you never did."

Chapter Twenty-Nine

When I get back to the hotel, it is evening. I feel exhausted, wrung out. I go upstairs. The doors are drawn. I open them. The evening is turning over—day to night. Shops are closing, and restaurants are reemerging from their afternoon downtime. There is a quiet hum to the town.

So much history, so many stories. So many love stories, too.

I suddenly realize that tomorrow is my last day here. After tomorrow, I am meant to go home. Back to Los Angeles, back to a life that is changing—that has already changed.

I lie down in my clothes. I do not want to fall asleep, but I feel like I haven't rested for years.

✦

I wake up to the brightest morning. Sunlight streams in through the open doors. I squint into the sunlight. I brush my teeth, change, and head down to breakfast. A sundress and sun hat. I stop by the lending library outside my door and pull out *Big Summer* by Jennifer Weiner. Maybe I'll do some reading at breakfast.

The red chair covers are back. The buffet breakfast has been moved down, closer to the kitchen. The pool . . .

And then I hear his voice, the same one I've heard nearly every day for the past eight years. Calling me.

"Katy," he says.

He's standing in the open lobby, at the top of the stairs. Eric. My husband. Here on the other side of the world.

"Eric?"

Is it possible he's found me in this other time? Is he here now, too?

But as he walks closer to me—his face threaded with relief and intention and a little bit of joy—the world around me reveals itself to be exactly what it is. Present. There is a book in my hand that was published two years ago. Of course, I am here, I am back now. Which means she is gone.

Eric reaches me. He's carrying a small duffel bag—a J.Crew tote I got him for his twenty-eighth birthday. It has *EB* monogrammed on it. He's wearing jeans and a light blue T-shirt. He has a hoodie draped over his arm. He's fresh off the trip.

"Hi," he says.

I search his face. "You're here?"

"I kept calling you," he says. "I left you all these messages, but your cell phone wouldn't even connect."

I think about my phone, locked up in the safe.

"I turned it off," I say.

"I called the hotel; they could never seem to find you. There was a mix-up with your room, maybe?" He shakes his head. "It doesn't matter. I realized about thirty seconds after you left that I shouldn't have let you go."

"That wasn't . . ."

"That's not what I mean," he says. "Can we . . ." He looks around. "I really need to set this down."

I nod. I gesture out to the patio. There is a couple sitting at my regular outdoor table. But the small tables by the pool are empty. I lead Eric over. There are stacks of bottled water by the open window. I think about Adam—days—years?—ago getting me one from inside. I hand Eric the bottle. Some water falls onto his T-shirt, dotting the light material dark. I know when he puts the cap back on, he'll twist twice, to make sure it's really secure. I know he'll take a little bit of water at the end and run it over his face, which I can tell is hot. He does.

I choose a table in the shade. We sit.

"Sorry," he says. He twists and sets the bottle down. "I didn't mean I shouldn't have let you go. I meant I shouldn't have let you go without asking if you wanted me to go with you, without telling you I wanted to."

"Eric . . ."

"No, listen, I know. I'm so glad you came here. You look great, by the way." His eyes graze over my face. I feel a familiar tenderness. It tugs at me, like a small child at the hem of a dress. *Look. Look at me.*

The first time I brought Eric home to meet my parents, it was a hot October day. We drove down from Santa Barbara blasting Destiny's Child and Green Day. We took the long route, by the water, winding in and out of towns, the ocean always on our right.

When we got to my parents' place, it was well after the hour we said we'd arrive. I figured my parents wouldn't mind, but they'd want a reason. My mother wouldn't want the time to go unremarked.

Eric opened my door for me, took our luggage, and then took some sunflowers out of the backseat. I hadn't even noticed them there.

"You told me she likes yellow, right?"

I remember thinking it was so thoughtful. I remember thinking it was proof of what I already knew, what I had already uncovered: I loved him.

I loved him far before she ever met him. It might have mattered, had she not loved him. But it wouldn't have changed things.

"Thank you," I say.

"I love you, Katy," Eric says here, now. "Always have, always will. I didn't come here to tell you that I want you back. I don't. I want you . . ." He winces. "Forward."

"You want me forward?"

He nods. "I want whatever is next for us."

I think about the house in Culver City, the garden we never made. What is our life, alone? What does it look like when it's just us?

"How do we know it will be different?" I ask him.

He thinks about this. He wipes his hand across his forehead. "It's up to us. We have to make it different," he says. "You have to want to find out."

"I can't believe you're here," I tell him.

"Me neither."

He looks out over the town. He sees the ocean, takes it in for the first time. "This place is incredible," he says.

I nod. "It really is."

"We should have come here," he says. "On our honeymoon, we should have come here."

I think about our four days in Hawaii. The mai tais on

the beach, the tiki torches, the luau filled with tourists and cameras.

I look at him. His brown hair, fogged glasses. The freckles on his face. All the tiny, microscopic familiarity.

"We're here now," I say.

He smiles. There is beauty in his smile, the beauty of the familiar.

"Yes," he says. "We are."

✦

As we finish up breakfast, Monica emerges onto the balcony. She has on loose linen pants and a white T-shirt, her hair slicked back into a low ponytail.

"I'll be right back," I tell Eric. He is tucked into eggs and potatoes, downing coffee. He waves me off.

I stand up and make my way over to her.

"Katy!" she says. "How are you?"

"I'm good," I say. "How was Rome?"

"Wonderful," she tells me. "Always too hot, too crowded, but somehow just right. I like to leave and I like to return."

"Not a bad way to live," I say.

She smiles. "I see you've had someone join you?"

She gestures to Eric, who in the thirty seconds since I've been gone has struck up a conversation with a man and woman at a neighboring table. But it does not make me annoyed today. It makes me feel affection, warmth—it makes me feel touched by the soft hand of grace. He laughs at something one of them says. I see his easy joy, his easy smile. The way in which he is comfortable in the company of anyone. All at once, he reminds me of her.

Eric notices Monica and me looking at him. He waves at us,

and we wave back. He smiles his goofy grin at me, readjusts his glasses on his face.

"My husband," I say. Yes. My husband.

Monica raises her eyebrows at me. "He came here?"

"He did."

"That's a long way," Monica says.

I look to her. She's smiling a knowing smile at me. A familiar one. And then I notice her necklace. An iron chain hangs around her neck, supporting a turquoise pendant. All at once, the hairs on the back of my neck stand up. I have goose bumps everywhere.

"Nika?" I ask her.

Monica startles. "No one has called me that in a long time," she says. She squints further. "How did you know?"

My heart beats wildly. I can barely believe it. "Do you remember a man named Adam Westbrooke?" I ask her.

She laughs. "Of course," she says. "He was always a friend to the Poseidon. He used to come every year, first alone, and then many years later with his wife."

"What happened to him?"

"They live in Chicago, I believe. He never had children; he didn't meet Samantha until he was well into his fifties, lovely woman. He still emails sometimes. Life gets busy."

"So he never bought the hotel?"

"Oh my goodness," she says. "Do you know him? That was a long time ago. No. He never did. We got by on a few lucky investments and never needed a partner."

Monica eyes me. "Why are you asking me this?"

"Do you remember a woman named Carol Silver?"

Monica gives me a soft smile. "Your mother?"

My pulse stops. I nod.

"Yes," she says. "I knew her. We met in the summer of

1992. She used to come here to mail packages back to . . ." Monica looks to me. "To you," she says. "To her daughter."

I see Carol in the lobby that first morning.

"She used to send photos, for a while, after she went back home. When you two decided to take your trip this summer, she got back in touch with me. I knew she was sick; I just didn't know how ill."

Monica touches my arm. I think about Nika's sweetness, the powerful woman before me she's grown to be. How was it just yesterday that she was twenty-five years old?

"I'm very sorry for your loss," she says.

"Thank you."

"You know," Monica says, "when I first saw you, I knew there was something so familiar about you. It was almost like I'd known you before." She pauses. She touches my cheek. "You really must take after her."

Chapter Thirty

I take Eric upstairs to room 33. When we get inside, I notice it has been made up. There's a new quilt on the bed, fresh towels in the entryway.

"I feel pretty gross from the plane," Eric says. "Is it all right if I shower?"

"All yours."

I gesture to the bathroom. "I'll be on the balcony," I say.

He sets his bag down, unzips it. I see him take out all the familiar toiletries. His Old Spice deodorant. Electric toothbrush. The Burt's Bees face cream I buy him at Whole Foods.

He gives me a little wave and heads into the bathroom.

I go to the safe and take out my cell phone. And then I walk onto the balcony and dial the most familiar number in the world to me.

He picks up after the third ring.

"Hello?"

"Hi, Dad," I say.

"Katy!" His voice, lately devoid of warmth, immediately lifts. I hear the familiar rumble in it, the energy of his personality behind every syllable.

"Hi," I say. "How are you?"

"Oh, you know, getting by." I hear a clattering of something—plates?

"It's late. Are you in the kitchen?"

"Indeed I am."

"Dad," I say slowly. "Are you *cooking*?"

"There's this corn salad she used to make that I miss," he says. "How hard could it be?"

I look out over the late morning. Everything bathed in a bright yellow light. Blue. Green. Brilliant.

"Dad," I say. "Why did no one ever tell me that mom left? When I was a baby, why did no one ever say she came here?"

There is silence on the other end of the phone, and then I hear him inhale. "Who told you that?"

"Someone here at the hotel," I say. "They remembered her."

I hear my father clear his throat, then: "She loved you so much. Immediately. I'd never seen a bond like the two of you shared. But we . . . It happened fast, Katy. And I think she got lost in the shuffle. It was all too much for her, and she needed some time."

"What did you say when she wanted to leave?"

My father pauses. "I told her to go," he says.

The wind picks up. From somewhere in the marina, I hear music begin to play. I think about my mother here, mere hours ago. I think about the sacrifice of my father. I think about Eric in the shower.

"How did you know she'd come back?"

"I didn't," he says. "That's how I knew I really loved her. I knew already, but that changed our marriage for me. Ultimately I think it let her come home."

"What do you mean?"

"Because she knew it, too. She felt that freedom. It felt like love. The best thing I ever did was letting your mother go. No one is perfect, Katy. Perfect doesn't exist. What we had was pretty fucking good, though."

I've never heard my dad swear. Never, not once. And for some reason, this makes me laugh. I feel the bubbling in my belly, and then my shoulders are shaking, right on the balcony.

"Eric is here," I tell my dad, gulping in breath.

"I know," he says. I hear the lightness in his tone, too. "He called me. I told him to go." He pauses. "Did I do the wrong thing?"

I hear Eric, out of the shower. I see him in the doorway, a towel wrapped around his waist. "No," I say. "You didn't."

"Katy," he tells me. "History is an asset, not a detriment. It's nice to be with someone who knows you, who knows your history. It will get even more important the longer you live. Learning how to find your way back can be harder than starting over. But, damn, if you can, it's worth it."

Eric begins walking toward me. I see him backlit by the sun.

"I'm sorry," my father continues.

"For what?"

"That you never got to take this trip together. I think the reason she wanted to go back there with you is she wanted to tell you herself. I think she wanted to show you this place that was so transformative for her." He pauses. When he returns, his voice wobbles. "I'm sorry you never got to experience that together."

I think about Carol at the docks, Carol at lunch, Carol at La Tagliata in the hills, Carol in the kitchen at the apartment with the bright blue door.

"I get it, though," I say. "I got it here."

We hang up as Eric reaches me. "My dad," I say. I hold the phone up like evidence.

Eric takes it out of my hand. He sets it down on the outdoor table. He's still wearing only the towel. His body looks good—different, somehow, fuller. Or maybe it's just been this long since I've really looked at him.

He puts both his hands on my arms and runs them down so his fingers interlace with mine. I feel heat spark through me, like an engine starting, sputtering to life.

He moves his hands to my lower back. The familiarity of him—of his smell, his warmth, his touch—makes me want to fold into him.

"Katy," he says. "I—"

"Eric, listen."

"Tell me. If it's too soon, if you don't want to—I understand. I just want you to know that I'm here for you, whenever you are. Italy or home or—"

"I love you," I say, and I watch Eric's face dissolve into a smile so wide it changes his entire profile. I realize I haven't seen him smile like that in a long time—too long. "It's been a really hard year, but it's true, I love you. And I want to make the choice to be with you."

"You do?"

I nod. "Yes," I answer. "You know me."

And then we're kissing. His towel falls. I feel the cool shower droplets on my skin. They evaporate in a moment. We kiss each other inside, and once we are, I lift my dress up and over my head.

Any remaining clothing, off. There is an urgency to this I don't remember ever experiencing with Eric before. But of course I'm wrong about that, too. There were hungry nights—afternoons spent in a dorm-room bed. Crashing into apartments after dinner, subway makeouts. They were lost to the soft beating of time, too, but now here they are, with us. Everything that was old, born new again.

I sit back on the bed. We lock eyes. I feel this pull, this electricity between us. The air is charged. I feel my body. This return to myself. The same one that was barren and starved with her passing, now brought back to life. Adam, the stairs, the food and wine. It has all made the blood pump faster and my skin feel softer, weightier. The blessing of this life, this one, brilliant, beautiful life. All the loss and anguish. All the joy that makes it possible. The tender connections, the fragility, the impossible odds of being here, now, together. The choice of continuing to make it so.

He hovers over me. And then we're kissing again. I feel his warm hands on my sides, my back; they drift over my stomach. I feel his legs, intertwined with mine. I feel his chest—labored, heavy.

I thread my arms around his neck, stretch my body underneath his, and breathe with him—this man, this moment, this return.

I never felt like I belonged to Eric. I used to think it was because I belonged to her, but I know, now, that that wasn't the whole truth. I did not belong to Eric because I do not belong to anyone. Not in that way, not any longer.

I am my own, just as she was hers.

✦

Afterward we get ready to go into town. Eric changes into a new T-shirt and then puts on floral board shorts my mom had bought him. I eye him.

"What?" he says. "They fit. I like them."

He grabs my arm and swings me into him. I feel the warmth of his body, the low hum of his heart.

"You're beautiful," he tells me. "Really, honestly stunning. I think about it every time I look at you."

"Can I ask you something?" I say.

"Of course."

"Did you know when you met me? Did you think, I don't know, I was the one?"

Eric considers this. He's thoughtful when he speaks. He never takes his arms away from me.

"I don't think so," he says. "We were so young, I'm not sure I was thinking like that back then."

"So when did you know?"

Eric wraps his arms even tighter around me. He brings his face close to mine. "I know now," he says.

History, memory is by definition fiction. Once an event is no longer present, but remembered, it is narrative. And we can choose the narratives we tell—about our own lives, our own stories, our own relationships. We can choose the chapters we give meaning.

Carol was an incredible mother. She was also flawed and complicated and a woman, just like me. One summer does not make that untrue. One summer is one summer. It can be a watercolor of beach days. It can change your life.

"Let's go home," I tell Eric. "I want to call Andrea. I even think I might miss La Scala."

He smiles. He kisses my cheek. "There's just one thing I think you may want to do first."

Chapter Thirty-One

It's barely sunrise when we take the boat out. It's just me and an older gentleman named Antonio. "He's the best; we've been working with him forever," Monica told me when she arranged it.

I had to fight the urge to tell her I knew.

Eric is asleep in bed. We decided to stay, to spend an extra few days together in Italy. It's been wonderful.

I toss on a pair of shorts, a T-shirt, and a sweatshirt; grab my bag; and pad down to the dock. The boat is waiting.

We pull away from the marina, Positano behind us, still shadowed in the time between days.

The day is warm, but the combination of the water and the speed makes me pull my sweatshirt tighter around me. The wind whips by; the sea caps dance strangely in the darkness.

When we get close to the rocks, Antonio cuts the engine. We bob in our little vessel; the three rocks like monuments before us rise out of the sea. Testaments to the resilience of the past, nature, perhaps the gods themselves. How many people have gazed upon these rocks? How many people have kissed underneath their archway?

Thirty years of happiness.

I nod to Antonio. I remove the small tin container from where it sits secured between my legs. I screw off the top.

"I brought her ashes," Eric had said. "I thought you might want to do something with them here."

As we near the rocks, the sun begins to crest, break. The dawn awakens around us; the smallest crack of sunlight gives way to more and more and more light. Every day the world is born again. Every day the sun rises. It is a miracle, I think. A simple, everyday miracle. Life.

We move forward, bobbing on the ocean. And it's then that I take out the letter. The one that has sat in the vault for days, for thirty years.

I thread my finger along the edge, breaking the long-held seal. And then I open it, uncurl the paper, and read what is scrolled there in her own calligraphy.

My darling Katy, my baby girl—

Italy is so beautiful. It reminds me of you. How happy everyone is in the morning, how the stars come out at night. I know I am not there, and I hope someday to explain to you why. I hope so many things for you, baby girl. I hope you walk through the world knowing your value. I hope you find a passion—something you love, something that lights you up inside. I hope you find the peace and confidence it takes to trust where your path leads. Remember, it is only yours. Others can wave and cheer, but no one can give you directions. They have not been where you are going. I hope you'll understand someday that just because you become a mother doesn't mean you stop being a woman. And above all else, I hope you know that even if you can't see me, I am always with you.

Forever,

Your Mama

I fold the note in my hand, now dotted with water, and tuck it back inside its envelope. But then I feel it is not the only thing in there. There is a slim photograph. I pull it out. It's of Carol, laughing in the marina. Her face is turned slightly from the camera, and the sun is setting behind her. She is bathed in light. *A whole memory*, I think.

And then the archway is upon us. I bring the tin to my lips. I kiss the top of it. And then as we move through, shadowed by rock, I empty it out the side of the boat. I watch as the dust descends into the water, scattered on the breeze.

She is everywhere, I think. She is all around us.

And then just like that, we are through the archway and the tin is empty. I feel a sinking hollow in my stomach, the recognition of completion. The understanding that she is gone now. She will not be waiting for me at the hotel, and she will not be home in Brentwood. She will not arrive through the front door of my home, unannounced, with produce from the farmers market. She will not leave fifteen second voicemails on my machine. She will not call. She will not hold me anymore, her arms enveloping me in her certainty, her presence. There is so much life ahead to lead without her, and she is gone.

Antonio circles the boat around. He looks to me.

"Yes?" he asks. As if to say *Are you done? Is that enough?*

"Antonio," I say. "Where does the thirty-year legend come from?"

Antonio squints at me. "No thirty years," he says. "Per sempre."

"For always," I say.

"Sì," Antonio says. "For always."

The motor turns back on. We pull away from the rocks,

back to Positano. In a few days, Eric and I will go home. To an old life that is new now. To a future that we do not yet know how to live.

You will learn, I hear her say. Her voice echoes on the wind, the water. I hear it in the quiet corners of me.

I see Positano before us. The sun is fully up now. I can make out every building—the Sirenuse, the Poseidon, Chez Black. This foreign landscape, so familiar to me now.

"You will come back?" Antonio asks me. He interrupts my thoughts. I arch back to look at him.

"Yes," I say.

He nods.

"They always come back," he tells me. "It is too beautiful for one and only."

We are caught up in docking then. Gathering bags, stepping over ropes. The present is relentless. It forces us over and over again to pay attention. It requires all of us. As well it should.

"I see you," Antonio says, and then he is gone.

I climb the stairs back up to the hotel. I am barely winded when I arrive. My lungs have gotten stronger here. My legs, too.

I smell the smells of breakfast, the sea, coffee. The sounds of bicycles and children.

It is enough.

It is more than enough.

It is everything.

RS

Rebecca Serle <rebecca@xxx.com>
Thu, Apr 16, 2020, 5:34 PM
To: Hotel Poseidon <prmanager@xxx.it via>
Subject: Your Beautiful Hotel

Hi Liliana,

I'm not sure if you remember me but I was at your hotel in late July/early August of last year. My name is Rebecca Serle and I came with a friend. We ended up eating at the hotel more nights than we planned, and you and I got to chat a bit. I am in my early thirties and have brown hair. I had so hoped to return to your hotel this summer—particularly because I am setting a book in Positano and wanted to do further research. The book will take place in large part, in fact, at the Hotel Poseidon. But the book takes place in the early '90s—was your father the manager at the time? Did the hotel look much the same? Any information you could provide would be so helpful.

How are you doing? I'm thinking of Italy, and your slice of paradise in particular. Sending warmest wishes and love.

Rebecca

HP

Hotel Poseidon Positano—PR Manager

<prmanager@xxx.it via>

Wed, Apr 22, 2020, 9:55 AM

To: Rebecca Serle <rebecca@xxx.com>

Subject: RE: Your Beautiful Hotel

Ciao Rebecca,

It's very nice to hear from you!

I hope you are doing well in these difficult times. We are all doing good here in Positano, although we're looking forward to getting back to "normal" again.

It's wonderful to hear you're writing a book set in Positano and here at the Hotel Poseidon!!!

Here's a short "background" history that may help:

The Hotel officially opened in 1955 (*65 years ago!*), although it had been my grandparents' Liliana and Bruno's private villa for a couple of years prior to that.

Their villa (and the hotel at the beginning) included the big living room, which is where the breakfast buffet is set these days, and the rooms below (room n°1, 2, 3, 4, and 5).

Since the opening, they have been working to buy more

land all around the existing property and slowly they were able to add more and more pieces around it. The last addition was the pool area (the pool and the terrace where the sunbeds are spread out), and it happened in the 1970s.

The looks of the hotel haven't changed much ever since. It has been run by my grandmother Liliana and then passed onto her children, Marco and Monica (my uncle and my mother, who are the current owners!).

In short—in the 1990s the hotel was run by Liliana, Marco, and Monica, and yes, it looked pretty much the same as it does now. My father is a photographer and he's never worked for or at the hotel.

I hope this helps so far! Let me know if you need further information or explaining—I'd be happy to share more.

Hope you're staying safe and well. I look forward to hearing back from you and of course to read this book when it's out! 😊

Kind regards,

Liliana

Public Relations

HOTEL POSEIDON, in the Heart of Positano

Via Pasitea, 148—84017 POSITANO, Amalfi Coast (SA)

Rebecca Serle <rebecca@xxx.com>

Tue, Jun 29, 2021, 5:24 PM

To: Hotel Poseidon <prmanager@xxx.it via>

Subject: RE: Your Beautiful Hotel

Hi Liliana,

I wanted to say that we just announced my new book. It will be out next March and takes place in large part at your stunning hotel. Thank you for making the trip so memorable I simply had to write about it. More soon. It's called *One Italian Summer*, btw 😊

I cannot wait to return. Summer 2022 is coming! We will get there.

Love,

Rebecca

Acknowledgments

First:

To Melissa, Jennifer, and Leah Seligmann—and Sue who made them. Thank you for letting me in this close.

To Jessica Rothenberg, for sharing with me all the boundless love and impossible grief that comes with having her for a soul mate. I told you once I would never forget—now it's in writing.

And to Estefania Marchan, who over a decade ago said she missed her mother at eighteen, and twenty-six, and five—all the ages and women she had never known.

This is for you, and for them.

Now:

To my agent, Erin Malone, for being everything I'm not: meticulous, flexible, professional. I am prone to hyperbole, but you're #1, it's just the truth. I could not possibly ask for a better or more fruitful partnership. You are never getting rid of me.

To my editor, Lindsay Sagnette, for being the greatest champion and cheerleader. Thank you for your trust in me, and for opening your doors so wide and offering me absolutely everything inside.

To my publisher, Libby McGuire, who has made Atria my dream home. Thank you, thank you.

To my publicist, Ariele Fredman, who is part wizard and part witch. I don't know how you do what you do, but I sure am lucky you do it for me.

To Isabel DaSilva—I'm sorry I suck at the Internet. I'm trying (I should try harder). Thank you for making my books soar.

To Jon Karp and the late and brilliant Carolyn Reidy for helping *In Five Years* achieve so many career highs. I'll be grateful forever.

To my manager, David Stone, for the long history and the new beginning.

To my agents Chelsea Radler and Hilary Michael for thinking (almost) everything I write is worth people reading and watching.

To Sabrina Taitz for being the best substitute teacher in the biz. We'll always have Maui.

To the entire sales team at Simon & Schuster: you do the impossible for me.

To Camille Morgan, Fiora Elbers-Tibbitts, Erica Nori, Gwen Beal, and Anna Ravenelle for holding all the details together.

To Caitlin Mahony and Matilda Forbes Watson for making sure Dannie and Bella and Katy and Carol and Sabrina and Tobias are well looked after abroad.

To Lexa Hillyer for being the most wonderful friend and

the most wonderful mother. Our mornings are my favorite time of day. And to Minna, my angel girl.

To Leila Sales for thinking I'm nuts, but voting for me anyway.

To Hannah Brown Gordon for forgiving me countless indiscretions, and for making it ever easier to fill an ever-expanding list.

To Danielle Kasirer for being my pod, my family, for making my coffee with just the right amount of creamer and for always having the peanut M&M'S.

To Niki Koss for being my big/little and the black T-shirt to my Ross.

To Jodi Guber Brufsky, whose home and heart is my happy place.

To Raquel Johnson for the love and the years and the glue, baby.

To Morgan Matson and Jen Smith for walking the path so close by.

To Laurel Sakai—because I would never be here without you, and it's time I said it in print.

To my dad, who is a wonderful man and a wonderful husband and a wonderful father. And who takes great pride and joy in my mother's and my union, however many bagels or however much pasta it might not allow him to consume.

To the wonderful people at the Hotel Poseidon Positano, most especially Liliana.

And finally to you, this time around: one of life's most important challenges is determining what to hold on to and what to let go of. Do not be fooled into believing that you do not know which is which. Follow the feeling, follow it all the way home.

BONUS CONTENT

Silver Girls
Positano Itinerary

Note: Summer in Amalfi is usually hot, but let's be advised that we could have some cool nights. I've noted **outfit suggestions**. Donna from Amex has gone ahead and confirmed all restaurant reservations, but we do have SOME flexibility with the days. I am so excited to show you around this place that has always meant so much to me, my darling Katy. To Italy we go!

DAY ONE

FLIGHT 363 arrives in Roma at 11:00 a.m. local time. From there we will take a taxi to the Termini Train Station where we will take the 12:42 train to Naples, arriving 2:56 p.m.

The Hotel Poseidon has arranged a car service from Napoli Centrale to Hotel Poseidon. There will be a chauffer with a name card "Silver" waiting.

The ride from Naples to Positano is just under an hour and a half, traffic depending. It is a lovely ride. I remember renting a car when I went and being utterly terrified I was going to drive right off the side of the road. The scenery is beautiful. We will inquire about making a stop for photographs before we descend into town.

Check in: Hotel Poseidon Positano. Viale Pasitea, 148, 84017

**I never stayed there, but Monica runs the hotel. I met her as a very young woman in Positano. My flat was just up the way, and I came to the hotel often to mail packages. Monica will be expecting us—oh, I can't wait to see her!!

5:30 p.m.: Cocktails by the pool. They serve Aperol spritzes with an array of snacks—olives and potato chips. We will linger.

7 p.m.: Dinner at the Hotel Poseidon restaurant, Il Tridente.

The restaurant at the hotel is world-class. All meals are served out on the terrace. I remember they had a tomato salad that was to die for! You know how much we love the caprese at Cecconi's? It's a hundred times better.

CLOTHING SUGGESTIONS: A lovely dress with a wrap. I suggest the black lace Kooples dress we purchased with the turquoise buttons.

We will be tired that night but should stay up until 9 p.m. in order to avoid jet lag.

DAY TWO

7–9 a.m.: Breakfast on the terrace.

Every morning, the hotel lays out a big, gourmet breakfast. Breakfast is included in our room rate, and we should take full advantage.

Depending on when we get up, we may opt to have breakfast in soft clothes—leggings, workout attire, tracksuit. If we go down any time after 9 a.m., we should be dressed for the day.

12–3 p.m.: Da Adolfo. Via Laurito, 40, 84017

12:30–1:30 p.m.: Marina. The boat to go to the beach club leaves around* 1 p.m. from the marina. We should plan to be there a little after 12:30.

*Always delayed in Italy

Da Adolfo is a beach club that serves lunch along the coast. The boat ride will be our favorite part. I recall the food being subpar, but this was thirty years ago! So who knows how it's changed.

CLOTHING SUGGESTIONS: Please wear a swimsuit under your clothing. I suggest a one-piece and shorts and a cover-up to keep your shoulders out of the sun. But I'll leave it to you!

7 p.m.: Dinner at Hotel Poseidon, Il Tridente.

Da Adolfo is a day event, so we will see how we feel. We will either dine again at Il Tridente or we can wander down into town and try one of the smaller restaurants.

DAY THREE

7 a.m.: Hike the Path of the Gods.

Everywhere in Positano there are stairs. We will take the ones closest to the hotel up to the path and then walk for as long as we are comfortable. The Path of the Gods is a special hiking trail that connects all the towns on the Amalfi Coast. It gets its name from a legend. It is the place where the gods would come down to the sea and meet the Sirens that enticed Ulysses with their singing. How exciting!

CLOTHING SUGGESTIONS: Under no circumstance are you to wear Birkenstocks. I know you believe they are "comfort shoes," but this is a serious hike that requires proper footwear. Let me know if we should make a trip to the Beverly Center prior to departure.

9 a.m.: Breakfast on the terrace. Please note that this will be our only meal before dinner (early).

4–8 p.m.: La Tagliata. Via Tagliata, 32B, 84017

4 p.m.: Bus picks us up in front of the Hotel Poseidon.

Oh, this place is so very special!!

It is a run by a couple who have a farm up in the hills. The reason the reservation is so early is that there are only two sittings, and we must catch the early one in order to appreciate the view.

Everything is family style per table and there are no menus. We simply choose red or white wine and the food comes! Pastas and salads and vegetables and cheese and meats, oh my! Daddy would love it . . . there is so much to eat it's beyond. Even he wouldn't leave hungry.

CLOTHING SUGGESTIONS: Please wear a dress or a cute skirt, as there are some great photo opportunities at the top and we will need to take a fabulous picture. I had a dress I got in Positano (well, it was sort of gifted to me) that I'd love for you to bring. You know the cream silk? Would be great for this night.

I had so hoped to take you to Bella Bar to dance, but I cannot find it online and I believe it has since sadly closed. I remember a particularly wild night there with a new friend. We danced the night away!

DAY FOUR

Capri Day!*

Note for DONNA: Ferry reservations are not taken in advance, but I simply do not think being on that big of a boat will be enjoyable. Might we price out taking a smaller catamaran or the like over? How costly will this be?

8 a.m.: Breakfast on the terrace. Depending on what time our boat leaves, let's go down fully dressed.

CLOTHING SUGGESTIONS: Pack a big tote. We will wear: bathing suit, cover-up. We will pack: a dress, shorts, sweater, and tennis shoes.

The boat will drop us off right at the dock for La Fontelina Beach Club.

11 a.m.: Check-in at La Fontelina Beach Club. Via dei Faraglioni, 2, 80073 Capri

*We will call ahead and reserve two loungers and an umbrella.

1 p.m.: Lunch at La Fontelina.

We will have lunch at the beach club and then change into our tennis shoes (see prior note re: footwear) and walk up the drag into town. This is a LARGE WALK. We will need to be prepared. Otherwise, we can take a boat around the island and then a taxi, but it is more of a schlep.

3–5 p.m.: Shopping.

Capri has a lot of designer stores that we do not need, but there are some beautiful shops off the main drag. In particular, I'd love to get two glass vases, one for your house and one for mine.

6 p.m.: Dinner at Da Paolino, or the Lemon Tree. Via Palazzo a Mare, 11, 80076 Capri

The most marvelous restaurant. The setting is breathtaking.

A boat will take us home. Arrangements TK.

DAY FIVE

8–10 a.m.: Breakfast on the terrace. We will have an easygoing day, as we may be tired from all the Capri action.

12–1 (?) p.m.: Lunch at Chez Black. Via del Brigantino, 19, 84017

Chez Black is in the marina and was one of my favorite places to hang out. It's fabulous people-watching and great food. I remember the restaurant was turquoise. I wonder if it still is.

1–4 p.m.: Shopping in the marina OR hanging by the pool.

Positano has better shopping than Capri, by far. We will need to get a few hand-painted dresses and some dish towels for the kitchen. We should absolutely take advantage of the gorgeous pool at our hotel, as well.

7:30 p.m.: Dinner at the Sirenuse. Via Cristoforo Colombo, 30, 84017

I never told you this but when I was in Positano, I wanted to decorate that hotel. I even had a meeting if memory serves. Can you imagine? It's stunning as it is. I looked up photos, and I think I appreciate the old-world glamour now more than I did back then. We will have dinner and drinks on their terrace—one of the most magical spots in all of Positano! Grandma loved it there. So many generations on this trip, Katy, I just can't wait.

CLOTHING SUGGESTIONS: Sirenuse is dressy, but beach-dressy. I know I said we shouldn't bring heels, but perhaps for this night? Although we will walk to dinner, so unlikely. A lovely dress and sandals would be appropriate. Although you could wear the gold lamé we bought in

Vegas? I know you will roll your eyes at me, so I will keep quiet now.

DAY SIX

8–10 a.m.: Breakfast on the terrace.

11 a.m.: I have arranged for us to have in-room massages. After that, we will hang by the pool, read, and relax!

6:00–8:30 p.m.: Drinks at San Pietro. Via Laurito, 2, 84017

6 p.m.: A car will come and take us to Il San Pietro out of town. The most magnificent hotel!

We will have drinks there, followed by dinner and watch the sunset—magical! There is an elevator built into the rocks there that we can take down to the ocean. You've never seen anything more beautiful in your life.

CLOTHING SUGGESTIONS: I think a chic pant and a cotton top might be ideal. I'm thinking of the set we ordered from Aura (sp?), in beige? What do you think?

DAY SEVEN

7 a.m.: Breakfast on the terrace.

8:30 a.m.: Boat to rocks of Faraglioni.

The rocks are situated near Capri. There are three of them, and the middle one has an archway you can pass through by boat. There is a legend that if you kiss under the rocks, you will be happy in love for thirty years! Which brings me to . . .

Before we confirm return details, might I suggest Eric come and meet you for a few days at the end? I think you two would love it there, and it would be special to share it with him. You never went for your honeymoon, after all.

Just think about it.

I love you. Our adventure awaits.

Forever,

Your Mama

BOOK CLUB FAVORITES
READER'S GUIDE

One Italian Summer

Rebecca Serle

This reading group guide for One Italian Summer *includes an introduction, discussion questions, ideas for enhancing your book club, and a Q&A with author Rebecca Serle. The suggested questions are intended to help your reading group find new and interesting angles and topics for your discussion. We hope that these ideas will enrich your conversation and increase your enjoyment of the book.*

Introduction

When her mother dies, Katy Silver is left reeling. Carol wasn't just Katy's mom but her best friend and first phone call. Even Katy's husband can't seem to get through to her—she is lost without her anchor. Her mother was her true north.

To make matters worse, the planned mother-daughter trip of a lifetime looms: going to Positano, following the very same route Carol did as a young woman. Katy has been waiting years for Carol to take her, and now suddenly she is faced with embarking on the adventure alone. But as soon as she steps foot on the beautiful Amalfi Coast, buoyed by the stunning cliffsides, delectable food, and charming hotel staff, Katy begins to feel her mother's spirit.

And then Carol appears for real—in the flesh, healthy and suntanned . . . and thirty years old. Katy doesn't understand what is happening, or how. But over the course of her time in Italy, Katy gets to know Carol in this new form, and soon she must reconcile the mother who knew everything with the young woman who does not yet have a clue.

One Italian Summer is Rebecca Serle's next great love story, a transcendent novel about how we move on after loss, and how the people we love never truly leave us.

Topics & Questions for Discussion

1. The novel begins with "Carol's rules to live by." How does this set up the story and both Carol's and Katy's characters?

2. Katy describes her mother as "the great love of [her] life." How does their relationship change over the course of the novel?

3. When Katy married young, Carol told her, "You have so much time. Sometimes I wish you'd take it." How does this sentiment recur throughout the story?

4. Katy finds herself in something of a time slip, as if she has "stumbled into some kind of magic reality where we get to be together . . . Time here does not only move slower but in fact doubles back on itself." How does time operate in this novel? Why do you think the author made the choices she did to allow Katy

and her mother to take their trip to Positano in the end?

5. Observing Carol, Katy understands that she is "watching her becoming." How does the Carol in Positano differ from the one Katy presented as her mother at the beginning of the book? Do you see glimpses of a younger Carol in the one the reader only hears about?

6. Positano itself acts as a character in the novel, "full of very real magic." What makes Positano distinctive? What is its draw for each of the characters, both locals and tourists?

7. A large subplot focuses on the struggles of Hotel Positano and Italy itself, a place out of "some era that is unmarked by modernity." What did you think of Adam's plan to purchase the hotel? How do the local characters interact with Adam, Carol, and Katy?

8. Adam admits that he's "really good at travel and less good at what happens when you stand still." How do each of the characters grapple with their own restlessness?

9. Reflect on how mythmaking—in reference to Capri's rocks of Faraglioni and the Amalfi Coast's Path of the Gods—plays a role in this novel, especially in Katy's relationship with her mother.

10. In Katy's final interaction with Carol as a young woman, Carol asks, "Did I leave you?" and Katy responds, "No, you never did." What was your reaction to that scene?

11. Much of this novel is about belonging—where and if we belong to whom. Katy notes at the end of the novel that "I do not belong to anyone." Does that ring true to you?

12. What did you think about the two major twists toward the end of the novel—one about Katy's mother and one about time? Did either of those surprise you?

Enhance Your Book Club

1. Celebrate *One Italian Summer* with an Italian-inspired feast. Bring pasta and pesto, calamari, and don't forget the Aperol spritz!

2. Bring in a photo of a mother figure in your life. Share any stories you have of her as a young woman with your group.

3. Visit rebeccaserle.com to learn more about the author and the inspiration behind this book.

A Conversation with Rebecca Serle

Q: This novel is dedicated to your own mother. What made you want to tackle a mother-daughter story?

A: My mother is truly the great love of my life, and my greatest fear is her dying. This book is part love letter to her and part love letter to my future self—the one who will have to live in this world without her. To me mother-daughter stories are extremely intimate, rich, heartbreaking, and challenging. Our mothers are our first blueprint of love, but they are also people. So many of my readers have lost their mothers or have challenging or nonexistent relationships with them. I want to pay tribute to how we honor this very deep connection, and then also how we break away. Because we must.

Q: Some early copies of *In Five Years* and *One Italian Summer* arrived with a pack of tissues. How do you create these

emotional, wrenching moments that speak to a wide swath of readers?

A: I try to write the truth, as I feel it. If my books touch people and I can say to them: "Yes, that thing you feel? I'm going to name it. I feel it, too"—that's a beautiful connection. Tears are not bad, you know? They don't always convey sadness. They are just an expression of emotion.

Q: **All of your novels start with a compelling question: *Which five people, dead or alive, would you invite to dinner? Where do you see yourself in five years? What if you knew your mother as a young woman?* Where does your inspiration come from?**

A: If you're asking where the conceits of my books come from, they come from a theme I want to explore—usually that's the dialogue between fate and free will. How much is in our control, really, in life? I'm not sure if I come to the same answer every time or if the answers vary. Sabrina (*The Dinner List*), Dannie (*In Five Years*), and Katy (*One Italian Summer*) are all very different people with very different lessons to learn. But they are all, probably, facets of me. I see writing as a kind of communion—with the universe, my intuition, whatever you'd like to call it. It's a magical process by which I get to tap into something beyond me and come back with the words to show other people what's there.

Q: A lot of this novel is about grief, and how Katy is able to move forward after her mother's death. Grief is a theme that shows up in a number of your novels. What draws you to that subject matter?

A: Andrew Garfield recently said about the death of his mother, "Grief is unexpressed love," and I think that's it. I write love stories. There is grief in love stories, because of course there is. I'm also interested in probing the seam of the human experience—the very edge. I write about things I'm afraid of, maybe.

Q: Why did you decide to set this book in Positano? Given that the setting is so vivid, what kind of research did you do?

A: In the summer of 2019 I took a trip to Italy with my mother. She and I spent a week in Rome, and we got to meet her ex-love from when she was twenty years old! She always talked about how special Positano was to her and how much she loved it. When I went back, I understood why. I had no plans to write a novel set in Italy, but on my last day in Positano I took photographs of every street sign. That's how I knew eventually I would want to tell this story.

Q: This novel is coming out at a very different time than your last (the week the pandemic began to shut down the US), and this book features a time slip. Did the events

of the past couple of years have anything to do with that choice?

A: Honestly, no. I didn't even know that I was writing this book in a different time until Katy realizes it. We literally uncovered that at the exact same time! It worked out, I guess, but it was not intentional.

I started *One Italian Summer* in April of 2020. I wanted to travel somewhere and live in a world filled with salt air and hugs and lots of fresh tomatoes. It is my sincerest hope that this book will bring that same sense of escape to my readers.

Q: **You've spoken before about the question of fate or free will in your novels. At the end of the book, Katy realizes that her mother has to make her own choices. How has this theme continued to resonate in your work?**

A: It is the central question of the human experience I am most interested in. I am probably tormented by trying to determine what I can control in life. I have this sense I can stop bad things from happening if I just do it "right." I think a lot of people can relate to that. But it's not, of course, a fair way to go through life. Life is going to happen. I think what I keep coming back to is that how we react to what happens is what really matters.

Q: What was your favorite scene to write and why?

A: I loved writing this entire book. I really mean that. I enjoy writing in general, and this book was particularly special, given the time in which it was written. But the final scene of Katy and Carol is probably my favorite.

Q: The process from first draft to publication is a long one. Were there any major changes or revisions you didn't foresee?

A: I am twelve years into this career and I am lucky to now have a team that trusts my process. They push me when I need to be pushed but they always read my books on their own terms. For now, in where I'm at in my professional journey, my first draft really has to sing for the book to work. I've never had a book published where the first draft really didn't work. Because of this, my editorial process is about broadening the scope, adding details, rounding it out. The plot does not often change in a meaningful way.

Q: What are you working on next?

A: A love story. Would you expect anything else?

About the Author

Rebecca Serle is the *New York Times* bestselling author of *Expiration Dates*, *In Five Years*, *The Dinner List*, and the young adult novels *The Edge of Falling* and *When You Were Mine.* Serle also developed the hit TV adaptation *Famous in Love,* based on her YA series of the same name. She is a graduate of USC and the New School and lives in Los Angeles with her husband and daughter. Find out more at RebeccaSerle.com.